A LODGE
WILDEI

JOHN BUCHAN

ZINCREAD

Published by
1st Floor H49-A4 Mohan Garden 110059

Design and setting By Zinc Read
Email- zincread@gmail.com
ISBN-978-93-5839-221-0

CONTENTS

THE CHARACTERS

Mr. Francis Carey: An intelligent millionaire *Lord Appin*: A Conservative; sometime Prime Minister of England *Lord Launceston*: An Ex-Viceroy; attached to no political party *Mr. Ebenezer Wakefield*: A Canadian Statesman *Mr. Eric Lowentstein*: A Jewish financier

Sir Edward Considine: An Explorer and famous Big-game Hunter *Colonel Alistair Graham*: A Soldier and Traveler; now of the Intelligence Department *Mr. Lewis Astbury:* A Journalist

Sir Hugh Somerville

The Duchess of Maxton: Wife of George, 14th Duke of Maxton and Champfleury, at one time a Liberal Secretary of State; Sister of Lord Appin *Lady Amysfort*: A Tory; Wife of a well-known member of the Jockey Club *Mrs. Wilbraham*: Wife qf Colonel Wilbraham, C.B., on service in South Africa *Lady Warcliff*: Wife of Sir Arthur Warcliff, K.C.B., K.C.S.I., a General Officer commanding in India *Lady Lucy Gardner*: Wife of Sir Hamilton Gardner, G.C.M.G., High Commissioner of East Africa *Mrs. Yorke*: An American; Wife of the Rt. Hon. Henry Yorke, a Liberal Secretary of State *Mrs. Deloraine*: Of Deloraine Manor, Shropshire *Lady Flora Brune*: Niece of the Duchess of Maxton Miss Marjory Haystoun

PROLOGUE

MR FRANCIS CAREY has been long a familiar name to the world—to some people as the most patriotic of millionaires, to others as the richest of patriots. Exiled in early youth to the Colonies for his health's sake, he made a profession of a necessity, and secured in a short space of time bodily well-being and an immense fortune. Few could trace in the square muscular figure of forty-five the pallid and consumptive boy of twenty. By a singular turn of fate he had stood by the cradle of great industries. He was the pioneer of the richest gold-mining area in the world, and scarcely less famous were his shipping lines, his railways, his newspapers, his teak-forests, and his vast tobacco-farms. Money made by enterprise was invested with wisdom, and his fortune was already almost out of bounds when it was doubled by the success of a copper venture which bade fair to rival Montana. And yet in the prime of life, in spite of the wiles of many women, he remained a bachelor. Some attributed the fact to an early and melancholy love affair; others, with better judgment, ascribed it to his preoccupation with the fortunes of his country. In Bacon's phrase he had "espoused the State," and found in her a mistress fairer and more exacting than any mortal Amaryllis.

In London he had modest chambers on a second floor in Half-Moon Street, but no man owned more lordly country-houses. The feudal manors of impoverished English squires, the castles of impecunious Highland chiefs held for him no charms. It was his business, he said, to show the world a more excellent way. At the head of a long glen in the Selkirks, where snow-peaks rose out of pine-forests, he built himself a hunting-box. In a scented Kashmir valley, among thickets of rhododendron, he had another, where lamas and Turcoman merchants, passing on their way from Leh to Srinagur, brought all the news of Central Asia. A bungalow in a Pacific isle, a fishing-lodge in New Zealand, and a superb farm of the old Dutch style in the Blaauwberg, were other of his dwellings. But his true home, if a nomad can be said to have one, was his house of Musuru, on the scarp of the Mau plateau, looking over the great trough of Equatoria. Here, in the midst of a park of many thousand acres, he lived as Prester John may have lived in his Abyssinian palace. He might lounge through the world of fashion in an old tweed coat, but his heart was on the side of magnificence. He sought for romance in life, and found it by the device of importing the fine flower of civilisation into the stronghold of savagery. It pleased him to shuffle unregarded in a London crowd, knowing that over seas half a continent waited upon his will. His amazing energy annihilated space, and he found time in a crowded life to live in his many houses more regularly than the modest citizen who owns a mansion in Bayswater and a villa at Cannes.

To the world Carey remained a mystery. Every halfpenny paper placarded his achievements, his arrivals and departures were chronicled like those of Royalty, his speeches in the City and his rare appearances on public platforms drew crowds which were denied to eminent statesmen. But the man himself was obscure. He was rarely seen in society, and country-houses knew him not. Nevertheless he contrived in some way to obtain the friendship of most men and women who were worth knowing. His influence was so well recognised, and yet so inexplicable, that many good people were heard to call it sinister. And yet few had any complaint to make of his doings. He spent his great income generously and prudently on public needs. A vast scheme of education, inaugurated by him, tied the schools of the Colonies to the older institutions of England. One ancient university owed the renewal of her fortunes to his gifts. In the slums his dwellings for workmen had made his name a household word, and at his own cost he yearly relieved the congestion of great cities by planting settlements in new lands. His activity, indeed, was so boundless that, had he figured more in the public eye, enemies would have sprung up out of sheer dullness of understanding. Knowing this, he kept wisely to his humble retirement, that his usefulness might be marred by no private grudges. He was accepted as a kind of national providence, scarcely more to be criticised than the Monarchy. If some called his faith Imperialism, others pointed out how little resemblance it bore to the article cried in the market-place. It was a creed beyond parties, a consuming and passionate interest in the destiny of his people.

On one point alone he found critics. It was his habit to take every year a party of his friends to some one or other of his remote homes. Now it would be a band of sportsmen whom he would carry off to the Selkirks or Kashmir for some weeks of unforgettable hunting. Now he would take a group of his less active acquaintances to his house at the Cape, where in the midst of vineyards and heathy mountains they could find good talk and a complete seclusion from the world. Once in a while he would have a gathering at his East African dwelling, and these were the choicest of his entertainments. The guests who were fortunate enough to share his hospitality came to form a set by themselves, bound together by the tie of delectable memories. Their enemies christened them "Careyites," and said hard things about the power of the purse; but the coterie was too large, too distinguished, and too representative to be sneered at with impunity. The Radical journalist found nothing to cavil at in the man who, so far as he saw, lived simply and wrought effectively for the poor. The Tory member could not speak ill of one who was so noted a sportsman and so generous a host. The plain man could only admire a figure of such vitality, who was original even in his pleasures.

It will be remembered that some little while ago the creed which is commonly called Imperialism was tossed down into the arena of politics to be wrangled over by parties and grossly mauled in the quarrel. With the fall of the Government which had sanctioned such tactics there came one of those waves of reaction which now and then break in upon our national steadfastness. The name of "Empire" stank in the nostrils of the electorate. Those who used it fell like ninepins; in the huge majority which the new Ministry acquired there were many who openly blasphemed it; and the few who still cherished the faith thought it wise to don temporarily the garb of indifference. Carey viewed the change with philosophic calm. He trusted the instincts of his race, and was not sorry that the dross should be purged and the spirit purified by misfortune. It occurred to him, however, that a little quiet conversation among some friends of his own way of thinking might be useful by way of clarifying their minds. It is well after defeat to make a short sojourn in the wilderness. That year, accordingly, he selected his party with especial care, and fixed Musuru as the place of entertainment. The months of August, September, and October were chosen as the best time, partly because it was the cool season in East Africa, partly because it was the Bar and Parliamentary vacation—though, indeed, as he reflected, none of his guests had for the present much to do with Parliament. His old friend the Duchess of Maxton, and Mr Hugh Somerville, a young man of thirty, who, after some years of foreign travel, was now endeavouring to make a fortune, were called in to assist in his selection. One rule only he laid down as inviolable—"I will have no husbands and wives, remember, Susan. If a man is married he must come without his wife, and the same for the women. We must all be unattached, for domesticity, as I have often told you, is the foe of friendship."

With this guidance, and after long consideration, a list was prepared. Lord Appin, the Duchess's brother, was the first to be selected. Once the leader of the Conservatives, he had found the trammels of politics too hard to be borne, and had given up to mankind what the virtuous declared was due to his party. In German metaphysics, French furniture, and the Turf he found his nominal interests; but his friends, of whom Carey was the most intimate, were well aware that beneath his insouciance he cherished political dreams which, though unacceptable to the hustings, were none the less broad-based on prescience and understanding. Lord Launceston, Hugh's former chief, came next; and Mr Eric Lowenstein, a Jewish financier, who had been Carey's partner in many schemes. Mr Ebenezer Wakefield, that eminent Colonial publicist, was added by Carey; and Hugh stipulated for Lewis Astbury, a young journalist who had won fame first as a war correspondent and then as a military critic. With Sir Edward Considine, the traveller, and Colonel Alastair Graham, of the Intelligence Department, the masculine side of the party was complete. The women were more difficult, and the Duchess spent many anxious hours. It was easy enough, she said, to get men without their wives, but it looked so odd for women to go travelling without their husbands; and Hugh's suggestion of a party of girls was refused on the ground of the appalling duties of chaperonage. In the end Lady Lucy Gardner, the wife of a Colonial governor, and Mrs Wilbraham and Lady Warcliff, whose respective husbands were on duty in Africa and India, were selected as the nucleus. Hugh begged for Mrs Yorke, the American wife of an English statesman, the Duchess insisted on Mrs Deloraine, and Carey added Lady Amysfort, the Egeria of her party, who, like her votaries, was out of power since the elections. "I will bring two charming girls," the Duchess said, "Marjory Haystoun and my niece Flora—it will do them all the good in the world. And Marjory is as serious as you, Francis, and nearly as clever. There! I think our list is complete. We have the sexes in equal numbers, which is more than you will find in any English country-house."

These details being settled, it only remained to arrange for the voyage. Following a rule of his own invention, Carey always decreed that his guests should come within the pale of his hospitality at Southampton or Marseilles, or wherever the real journey could be said to begin. Their route was as rigidly mapped out as a Cook's Tour, for he felt that it was desirable to avoid that premature boredom which may fall on ill-assorted fellow-travellers. It was arranged that the Duchess should travel with one of the girls and Lord Launceston. The other girl should go with Lord Appin, Lady Lucy, and Mr Astbury. Lady Amysfort and Mrs Wilbraham should accompany Mr Lowenstein, while Hugh was given the escort of Mrs Yorke and Lady Warcliff. Considine and Graham, it appeared, were at that moment hunting near Lake Rudolf, and would be summoned by messenger so as to arrive with the rest of the party. The various detachments should start at different times, one lingering for a few days at Cairo, another at Mombasa, but all should meet at Musuru in time for dinner on the Twelfth of August.

"Last Twelfth," said the Duchess meditatively, "I was entertaining for Bob at Glenumquhill. Fourteen men and not a woman besides myself. And this year I am to try to keep the peace among seventeen maniacs, eight of them female, on a mountain in the Tropics. After this who shall say that I have not the courage to make any sacrifice for the cause!"

CHAPTER 1

THE present writer is ill-equipped for the task of describing great houses, but Musuru demands that he should dedicate his slender talents to the attempt. From a wayside station on the railway between Mombasa and Port Florence a well-made highway runs north along the edge of the plateau through forests of giant cypress and juniper. To the east lies the great Rift valley, with the silver of its lakes gleaming eerily through the mountain haze. After a dozen miles the woodland ceases and the road emerges on a land of far-stretching downs, broken up into shallow glens where streams of clear water ripple through coverts of bracken and lilies. Native villages with bee-hive huts appear, and the smoke from their wood fires scents the thin upland air. Now the road turns west, and the indefinable something creeps into the atmosphere which tells the traveller that he is approaching the rim of the world. Suddenly he comes upon a gate, with a thatched lodge, which might be in Scotland. Entering, he finds himself in a park dotted with shapely copses and full of the same endless singing streams. Orchards, vineyards, olive-groves, and tobacco-fields appear, and then the drive sweeps into a garden, with a lake in the centre and a blaze of flower-beds. The air blows free to westward, and he knows that he is almost on the edge, when another turn reveals the house against the sky-line. It is long and low, something in the Cape Dutch style, with wide verandahs and cool stone pillars. The sun-shutters and the beams are of cedar, the roof is of warm red tiles, and the walls are washed with a delicate pure white. Standing, as I have seen it, against a flaming sunset, with the glow of lamplight from the windows, it is as true a fairy palace as ever haunted a poet's dream. Beyond it the hill falls steeply to the Tropics, and the gardens run down into the rich glens. Its height is some nine thousand feet above the sea, and its climate is always temperate; but three thousand feet beneath it is Equatoria, and on clear days a gleam can be caught of the great lakes. So the gardens, which begin with English flowers, fall in tiers through a dozen climates, till azalea gives place to hibiscus, and hibiscus to poinsettia, and below in the moist valley you end with orchids and palms.

Entering the house through the heavy brass-studded doors, you come first into a great panelled hall, floored with a mosaic of marble on which lie many skins and karosses, and lit by a huge silver chandelier. In a corner is a stone fireplace like a cavern, where day and night in winter burns a great fire of logs. Round it are a number of low chairs and little tables, but otherwise the place is empty of furniture, save for the forest of horns and the grinning heads of lion and leopard on the walls. The second hall is more of a summer chamber, for it is panelled in lighter wood and hung with many old prints and pictures concerned with the great age of African adventure. There you will find quaint Dutch and Portuguese charts, and altar-pieces gifted by a de Silveira or a de Barros to some Mozambique church long since in ruins. Brass-bound sea-chests, tall copper vases of Arab workmanship, rare porcelain of the Indies, and rich lacquer cabinets line the walls, and the carpet is an exquisite old Persian fabric. Beyond, through the folding windows, lie the verandahs, whence one looks over a sea of mist to the trough of the lakes. To the right stretch more panelled chambers—dining-room, smoking-rooms, a library of many thousand volumes, and as fine a private museum as you will find in the world. To the left are the drawing-rooms, hung with flowered silks and curious Eastern brocades, opening on a cool verandah, and lit in the evening by the same wild fires of sunset. Upstairs the bedrooms are masterpieces of arrangement, all fresh and spacious, and yet all unmistakably of Africa and the Tropics. From any window there is a vision of a landscape which has the strange glamour of a dream. The place is embosomed in flowers, whether growing in brass-hooped mahogany tubs or cut and placed daily in the many silver bowls; but no heavy odours ever impair the virginal freshness of the house. Luxury has been carried to that extreme of art where it becomes a delicate simplicity. It is a place to work, to talk, to think, but not to idle in—a strenuous and stimulating habitation. For on every side seems to stretch an unknown world, calling upon the adventurous mind to take possession.

Hugh dressed early, and, finding the hall empty, penetrated into the Green drawing-room, where he came upon Lady Flora Brune examining critically some Zanzibari ivories. They had met many times in London, and were on a footing of easy friendship.

"Well, Mr Somerville, I must ask the usual question. Had you a pleasant journey?"

"Fair," said Hugh, warming his hands at the fire. "We found Cairo a little too hot—at least Mrs Yorke and Lady Warcliff did, for I am a salamander. You were luckier, and stopped at Marseilles."

"Yes, and Aunt Susan behaved so badly. Poor Lord Launceston wanted to stay at home and write, and she dragged him about the whole Riviera, trying to find a house for next winter. He took it like an angel, but I am sure he thought a good deal. He provided me with a lot of books to read on the voyage, and I have muddled my brains so terribly that I haven't a clear idea left. I shall disgrace myself in this party, for it is to be very serious, isn't it?"

"Very serious, Lady Flora. But you and I are young, and the loss of our contributions won't matter. I am very stupid, too, since the elections—"

"You were beaten, weren't you?" said the girl, with wide sympathetic eyes.

"Handsomely. Four thousand of a minority instead of Seymour's majority of fifteen hundred. I hadn't a chance from the start. My work with Launceston was flung in my face, they shouted 'Indian labour' when I tried to speak about anything, and Nonconformist ministers went about the place in motor-cars telling the people that every vote given to me was a vote given against the Lord. They even accused me of being a Jew," said Hugh, stroking a very un-Jewish nose. "Besides, I was that strange wildfowl, a Tory free-trader, and another Unionist was run against me, who claimed the credit of such little Imperialism as was going. But on the whole I enjoyed the sport. I never once lost my temper, and I got a tremendous ovation after the poll. The men who had voted against me carried me shoulder-high to my hotel, and they all but killed the successful candidate. Englishmen at heart love a failure!"

"Are there any other victims here?" Lady Flora asked.

"Astbury lost by ten in a place which was considered hopeless, so he did well. Also Considine was turned out, but as he never went near the place, and left his wife to do his electioneering, perhaps we need not wonder. But all that is dead and buried. I hear people talking. Let's go and find the others."

The rest of the party had gathered in the inner hall. The young men—Hugh, Astbury, Considine, and Graham—wore ordinary smart London clothes. Carey, as was his custom, had a soft silk shirt and a low collar, above which his magnificent throat and head rose like a bust of some Roman emperor. Mr Wakefield had arrayed himself in that garb which seems inseparable from Colonial statesmen—a short dinner-jacket and a black tie. The tall figure of Lord Launceston stood by the fire, deep in conversation with Lord Appin, whose robust form and silver head contrasted strangely with the bent figure and worn, old-young face of his companion. Mr Lowenstein, a very small man, with untidy hair and bright eager eyes, wandered restlessly between Mrs Wilbraham, who was absorbed in the contemplation of Lord Launceston, and the Duchess, who was considering a plan of the dinner-table.

It was the rule at Musuru to disregard the claims of precedence. Hugh was sent in with Mrs Yorke, and found on his other side Lady Lucy. An English butler was the one concession to the familiar, for the meal was served by Masai boys, far defter and more noiseless than any footman, dressed in tunics of white linen with a thin border of blue. Hugh had scarcely time to look round the great half-lit room and admire the exquisite harmony of silver lamps and crimson roses, when he found his attention claimed by his right-hand neighbour.

"Please tell me who the people are and all about them," she begged in her pretty exotic voice. "I know you and Margaret Warcliff and the Duchess and Lord Appin and Mr Carey. That is Lord Launceston, isn't it, over there? I do think his deep eyes and haggard face just the most wonderful thing in life. How happy Charlotte Wilbraham looks talking to him! I know they are devoted friends. Who is sitting by his other side?"

"Mrs Deloraine. Don't you know her? She has many claims to be considered the most beautiful woman in England, but she is rarely seen in London. She lives in a wonderful old house in Shropshire, and writes what many people think the only good religious poetry of our day. What a contrast her Madonna face is to Lady Amysfort's!" Hugh looked across the table to where that great lady, with her small head and bright eyes, like some handsome bird of prey, was entertaining Lord Appin.

"Of course that is Lady Amysfort. I have seen her often, but you know one never can recall her face—only a vague impression of something delightful. I suppose that is the secret of her power, for no woman remembers to be jealous of her. Now tell me the others. Who is the pretty fair-haired girl sitting next Lord Appin?"

"Lady Flora Brune, the Duchess's niece. And then comes Sir Edward Considine, the man who has gone from the Cape to Cairo, and from Senegal to Somaliland, and has killed more lions than I have partridges. He and Graham have just come off a hunting-trip, and that explains why they are so gorgeously browned. That is Graham on your right, sitting next Lady Warcliff—the little man with blue eyes and a fair moustache. He went to Klondyke before it was fashionable, and has been in half-a-dozen wars, and is a Lieutenant-Colonel, though he is only thirty-five. He is the mainstay of that precarious institution, our Intelligence Department."

"Speak low," said Mrs Yorke, "and tell me who the people are on our side. Who is the big man next me? He looks like a lawyer."

"I expect you have heard his name in the States. He is Wakefield, the man who was Premier of Canada, and now devotes his life to preaching imperial unity. He is a scholar as well as a publicist, which is rare enough in these days. Do you know his neighbour?"

"The pretty dark child with the earnest eyes? No. Yes,—isn't she Laura Haystoun's girl?"

"Quite right. And now," said Hugh in a whisper, "you know everybody, except the people on my left. The first is Lady Lucy Gardner. Extraordinarily handsome, I think, though she is no longer young, and has been through all the worst climates in the world. Her husband is the Governor of East Africa, and is now taking his leave salmon-fishing in Norway, while his wife lends official countenance to this gathering. On the whole she is the bravest woman I know, and one of the cleverest. The man between her and the Duchess is Mr Lowenstein, whose name you must have seen in the papers. He is the whipping-boy of our opponents—why, I cannot guess, for a more modest, gentle soul I never met. You may have heard his story. He made a great fortune when quite young, and married a very beautiful girl, the daughter of a Scotch peer. People said she sold herself for his wealth, for he is, as you may observe, a Jew, and not very good to look upon. I believe, however, that it was a real love match, and certainly they made a devoted couple. Then she died suddenly, two years ago, and he got rid of all his houses and pictures, and tried to bury himself abroad. Carey saw his chance, hunted him out, and managed to put a new interest in life into him. Now, as you know, he is hand and glove with him in all his schemes. He is said to be one of the first financial geniuses alive, but he has no courage or nerve, and these Carey supplies in the partnership."

"I like his face," said Mrs Yorke thoughtfully; "there is a fire somewhere behind his eyes. But then I differ from most of my countrymen in liking Jews. You can do something with them—stir them up to follow some mad ideal, and they are never vulgar at heart. If we must have magnates, I would rather Jews had the money. It doesn't degrade them, and they have the infallible good taste of the East at the back of their heads. No Northerner should be rich, unless he happens to be also a genius."

"Genius, I suppose, means some consuming passion which burns up the vulgarity. We are talking about wealth, Lady Lucy," Hugh said, turning to his other neighbour. "Mrs Yorke will only permit it in the case of the elect. Otherwise it offends her sense of fitness."

The lady cast a glance over the room. "This house, for instance. It is so flawless and therefore so refreshing. And yet, when I think how much it must cost to have such a palace in the wilderness, I grow giddy. I am not sure if we have any right to be so comfortable."

Lord Appin caught the last words, and leaned over the table. "Surely that is an exploded heresy," he said, in the rich and exquisite voice which had made him *par excellence* the Public Orator of England. "I thought we had long ago given up the idea that austerity of mind depended upon discomfort of body. The Simple Life is the last refuge of complicated and restless souls. For myself I know no such stimulus to action as a good dinner, and to thought as a beautiful room."

"I am not certain," said Hugh. "It may be some tincture of Calvinism in my blood, but I confess I never feel quite happy unless I am a little miserable. When I am doing work I detest there is a glow of satisfaction about me which I miss when I am swimming along in something which is quite congenial. You remember Bagehot's account of Lord Althorp, who gave up hunting after his wife's death, not because he thought it wrong, but because he felt he had no business to be so happy as hunting made him. I am sure that we are happiest when doing something difficult and unpleasant. The cup wants a dash of bitters to make it palatable, for if taken neat it is sickly."

"How true that is," sighed Mrs Yorke. "Happiness lies only in a divine unrest; and if you are lapped in comfort you stagnate and miss it."

"That is the worst piece of fallacious Stoicism I have ever heard," Lord Appin said firmly. "It means nothing but a low vitality. If you are so morbid as to be dominated by your surroundings, then what you say is true enough. But to the philosophic soul environment matters nothing. He is happy alike in camp, court, and cottage. He will even preserve a modest gaiety in the House of Lords."

"That is not my nature," said Lady Amysfort with conviction. "You may be right—as a counsel of perfection. But which of us attains to that austere height?"

"I frankly confess I don't," Lord Appin replied. "I have just been saying how much I owe to a good dinner and a pretty room. But some of us do. Carey does, I think—and of Launceston I am certain. What is your view, Teddy?"

Sir Edward Considine had been explaining to the appreciative Lady Flora the plan of his recent shooting-trip; but both had been drawn by Lord Appin's proximity to listen to him. His soft voice when he spoke was a strange contrast to his hard, weather-worn face.

"It is all a question of that romance which most of us spend our lives looking for. Luxury is nothing in itself, but in its proper setting it can be an inspiration. A week ago I was perfectly happy. Graham and I were living in the most beastly discomfort, but then we were on the move and we had the excitement of sport, and we never thought about it. To-night, also, I am perfectly happy; but if all this had been in London, and I had been having months of it, I should probably have been miserable. You may imagine what it is to jog on all day through the hot bush with the dust of weeks on you, and your clothes in rags, and no food but tinned stuff. And then suddenly this afternoon we came to the gates of this place, and paid off our caravan-boys, from a hundred miles north—and in five minutes exchanged barbarism for civilisation. I wallowed in a bath, and my man was waiting with clean English things, and here I am, like the prodigal son after the husks, clothed and in my right mind. I call that romance, and there is no keener pleasure. But you must have the contrast."

Lady Flora nodded approval, recalling apparently kindred experiences in her short life. But the discussion was put an end to by Carey's voice from the head of the table. He began a little nervously, as if he were proposing a toast and had doubts how it would be honoured. For so massive a figure his voice was singularly high-pitched and small, so that he was the predestined victim of mimics. But there was a force behind it which arrested the ear.

"I think," he began, "that this is the time when I ought to say something about why we are all here. You don't need to be told that your company is in itself a sufficient delight to me. But this is not meant to be an ordinary party. Things have moved very fast lately in politics, and most of us have got our eyes a little dazzled. We want time to collect our wits, and think things out,—not only politics, but our whole scheme of life, our ambitions, the things which at the bottom of our hearts we care most for. We are all agreed, more or less, and we represent different sides of experience, so that we can supplement one another's deficiencies. For the moment the fates are against us, and I thought that, like the Apostle Paul, we should come out into the wilderness and reflect a little. We are only spectators at present, and it is an excellent chance to get our minds clear about what we want while we are looking on at the comedy which others are going to play for us."

Carey paused to sip his wine, and Mr Wakefield, who had a talent for trite quotation, declaimed with gusto the well-known lines of Lucretius:—

"*Suave, mari magno turbantibus aequora ventis,*
E terra magnum alterius spectare laborem;
Non quia vexari quemquamst jucunda voluptas,
Sed quibus ipse malis careas quia cernere suave est.
Suave etiam belli certamina magna tueri
Per campos instructa tua sine parte pericli."[1]

"Translate, please," Mrs Yorke whispered to Hugh.

"It means that it is great fun to have a good seat in the stalls and watch other people making idiots of themselves on the stage."

"We have seen many strange things in the last months," Carey went on. "Our creed has been dragged in the mire, and by those who professed to reverence it. Every decaying interest which wanted help has been told that in it could be found its peculiar salvation. Every vulgar feeling in the whole treasury of our national vulgarity has been enlisted in its support. Small wonder that England is a little sick of the very name of Empire. The result, of course, is a return to tradition. The lack-lustre creeds of fifty years ago have acquired a kind of splendour in contrast with the dullness of our faith. The old armoury has been ransacked, and the rusty flintlocks have all been burnished up. They make an imposing show on parade, and people have not yet begun to think what will happen in the day of battle. For the moment England is insular again, and the past three centuries have been forgotten."

Lord Appin was in the throes of a quotation. "'Little England, which was our reproach, has become our glory,'" he interrupted,—"'the little England of Shakespeare and Milton and Cromwell has conquered the Greater Britain of Baron Steinberg and Mr Bernstein.' The words, I need scarcely say, are not my own, but those of a bright young Liberal journalist, whose contributions to the daily press afford me much innocent pleasure."

"So be it," said Carey cheerfully. "The phase will pass, that we well know. As a philosopher you realise that, to use your barbarous jargon, Being can only develop through non-Being and the Infinite through the negations of the Finite. We have a living creative faith, and we are not disheartened because the people for the moment blaspheme their deities. But, as I have said, it is the occasion to examine ourselves and find the reason of that faith which is in us."

"We need a definition," said Hugh, who had been studying attentively the sphinx-like face of his host. "I call myself an Imperialist, and so does the noisy fellow at the street corner; but if I am pressed to explain I can give no summary statement of my creed."

"Is not the reason because it is not a creed but a faith?" Lady Lucy's clear voice had a peculiar power of compelling attention. "You cannot carve an epic on a nutshell or expound Christianity in an aphorism. If I could define Imperialism satisfactorily in a sentence I should be very suspicious of its truth."

"No," said Carey, "we don't want a definition. By its fruits ye shall know it. It is a spirit, an attitude of mind, an unconquerable hope. You can phrase it in a thousand ways without exhausting its content. It is a sense of the destiny of England. It is the wider patriotism which conceives our people as a race and not as a chance community. But we might take opinions. Let us each give his or her own description, beginning with Mrs Deloraine."

The lady looked a little confused. "I call it an enlarged sense of the beauty and mystery of the world."

"How true!" said Mrs Yorke. "May I have that for my definition too, Mr Carey?" There seemed a general agreement on this among the women.

Lord Launceston smiled a little sadly. "I don't yet see my way to any summary. It is a spirit moving upon the waters, a dumb faith in the hearts of many simple men up and down the world, who are building better than they know—

'Not till the hours of light return,
All we have built do we discern.'"

Lord Appin, who was eating grapefruit, looked up quizzically. "I call it, in the language of my hobby, the realisation of the need of a quantitative basis for all qualitative development. It is a hard saying, which I shall expound later."

"For Heaven's sake let us keep out of mysticism," broke in Mr Wakefield, who detested Lord Appin's metaphysics. "I define Imperialism as the closer organic connection under one Crown of a number of autonomous nations of the same blood, who can spare something of their vitality for the administration of vast tracts inhabited by lower races,—a racial aristocracy considered in their relation to the subject peoples, a democracy in their relation to each other."

Mr Astbury nodded. "I take Mr Wakefield's definition for mine."

"And I," said Considine, "call it romance. I have no head for political theories, but I have an eye for a fact. It is the impulse to deeds rather than talk, the ardour of a race which is renewing its youth. It is what made the Elizabethans, and all ages of adventure."

"For my part," said Lady Amysfort, "I think it simply Toryism under a new name—the Toryism of our great men, Bolingbroke, Pitt, Canning, Disraeli. Toryism was never Conservatism, remember. It was a positive creed, both destructive and constructive. Liberalism is a doctrine of abstractions, right or wrong, which bear no true relation to national life. Toryism has always held by the instincts and traditions of the people, and when our island became an empire it became naturally Imperialism."

"As a Liberal Imperialist, Caroline," said the Duchess with some asperity, "I profoundly disagree. I wish George were here to say what I think of your history."

Mr Lowenstein's restless eyes had been wandering from one speaker to the other, and he had several times opened his mouth as if to say something. Now he was about to begin when Miss Haystoun forestalled him.

"I should like to define it in very old words," she said shyly, in her low intense voice. "It is the spirit which giveth life as against the letter which killeth. It means a renunciation of old forms and conventions, and the clear-eyed facing of a new world in the knowledge that when the half-gods go the true gods must come."

"That is beautifully said," murmured Mr Lowenstein.

"Indeed, Marjory, I think it is almost blasphemous." The Duchess, who had been fretting for some time under the turn the conversation had taken, had at last succeeded in catching Lady Amysfort's eye, and the ladies rose to leave. Immediately the men reassorted themselves according to their preference. Astbury took his port round to the vacant chair next Mr Wakefield; Carey, Lord Appin, and Lord Launceston formed a coterie by themselves; Graham and Considine revelled silently in the novel luxury of good cigars, and Hugh joined Lowenstein, by whom he was cross-examined concerning the names of his fellow-guests.

It was not Carey's habit to linger at table, and the sound of a beautiful voice singing a song of Schubert drew the men soon to the inner hall, where Mrs Deloraine sat at the piano. At each end of the apartment log-fires burned brightly; outside the white verandah gleamed chill in the frosty moonlight; and the place was lit only by the hearths and two tall silver lamps beside the piano. A soft aromatic scent—the mingling of flowers and wood-smoke—filled the air.

Lord Appin took his place beside Mrs Deloraine. Carey stood in the centre of a great fireplace, and the others resorted to chairs and couches. Hugh, finding a very soft rug, settled himself at Lady Flora's feet.

The lady at the piano finished "Der Wanderer" and began the song from *La Princesse Lointaine*. It was a melody of her own making, very wild and tender, and in the dim light her wonderful voice held the listeners like a spell.

"Car c'est chose suprême
D'aimer sans qu'on vous aime,
D'aimer toujours, quand même,
Sans cesse,
D'une amour incertaine,
Plus noble d'être vaine,
Et j'aime la lointaine
Princesse!"

When she ceased there was silence for a little. The place and time were so strange—there among delicate furniture and all the trappings of a high civilisation, looking out over the primeval wilds. Savage beasts roamed a mile off in that untamed heart of the continent. The most sophisticated members of the company felt the glamour of the unknown around them. Lord Launceston rose quietly and walked to the window, where he gazed abstractedly at the starry sky; Lady Lucy was looking into the red glow of the fire; Marjory Haystoun and Lady Flora sat, chin on hand, in a kind of dream. Only Graham and Considine were unconscious of the spell. Months of hunting and going to bed at sundown had spoiled them for civilised hours, and they had dropped off peacefully to sleep in their chairs.

Carey broke the silence. "Here we are in Prester John's country," he said. "He may have had a daughter called Melissinde, and she may have been the Far- away Princess to some Portuguese adventurer who left his ship at Mombasa and wandered up into the hills. Do you realise how strange it is to be sitting here? Thirty years ago this was bush, with lions roaring in it, and the pioneers who may have camped here were three hundred miles from a white man, with hostile tribes around them, and the Lord knows what in front. I remember when I first came it was from the west. I had been trekking for months in Uganda, right across from Albert Edward and the Semliki to what is now Port Florence. I had had a bad dose of fever, and when we crawled up into the foothills I was as weak as a cat. We stayed here for a bit to recruit our strength, and, when I could stand, I went one evening, just about sunset, and looked down into the Tropics. That hour is as clear to me as if it had been yesterday. There was a fresh, clean wind blowing, which put life into my bones, and I stood on the edge and looked down thousands of feet over the little hill-tops to the great forest and on to the horizon, which was all red and gold. I knew that there was fever and heat and misery down below, but in the twilight it was transfigured, and seemed only a kind of fairyland designed for happiness. I was a poor man then, poor and ambitious, hungering for something, I did not know what. It was not wealth, for I never wanted wealth for its own sake. It was a purpose in life I sought, and in that moment I found it. For I realised that the great thing in the world is to reach the proper vantage-ground. I learned that things are not what they seem to the fighter in the midst of them; that the truth can only be known to the man on the hill-top. I realised that the heavenly landscape below me was far more the real Africa than the place of dust and fever I had left. And in that hour I saw my work, and, I think, too, the ideal of our race. If we cannot create a new heaven, we can create a new earth. 'The wilderness and the solitary place shall be glad for us; the desert shall rejoice and blossom as the rose.'"

The Duchess got up. "Marjory," she said, "you are nodding, and as for Alastair and Sir Edward, they have been asleep for the last half-hour. I think we are all ready for bed after our long journey."

As Hugh lit her candle at the foot of the staircase, she whispered to him confidentially, "When Francis begins to talk in blank verse, I always feel a little nervous. I think it is quite time for the women to say good-night."

CHAPTER 2

MORNING at Musuru came as a surprise to those who remembered the hot noontide of the previous day. For the air was as bitter as an English winter, and, looking from the windows, they saw the valleys filled with cold mist and the lawns whitened with hoar-frost. The result was that all the women breakfasted in their rooms. And of the men, only Hugh, Astbury, and Mr Wakefield appeared in the dining-room, where a roaring wood-fire gave the early risers a sense of comfort to temper their consciousness of virtue. That consciousness, however, was rudely disturbed by the discovery that Graham and Considine had breakfasted at least two hours before and had gone out heroically into the chilly morning.

Mr Wakefield stood warming his back at the fire, in the attitude of a Master of Hounds before a hunt breakfast. He had arrayed himself in Harris tweeds, and his legs were clothed with new buckskin gaiters. Hugh and Astbury, who knew something of the Musuru climate, had put on thinner shooting suits.

The elder man helped himself to mealie-meal porridge and cream. "We had an interesting talk last night, and I hope during our visit we may reach some valuable conclusions. But I foresee trouble ahead unless we can keep Lord Appin away from Hegel and put a stop to Carey's infernal mysticism. In my opinion, also, there are too many women for a really helpful discussion. We must, above all things, be practical. Now, I have here a kind of syllabus which Carey gave me last night—a list of the subjects we are to consider, and the order we are to take them in. To-night we are to begin with contemporary English politics and the present position of parties. Well, at any rate, that is relevant, if dull. Then we go on to the constitutional apparatus of Empire, the question of our tropical possessions, the economic and administrative problems. All these are very much to the point. But I notice at the end the sinister announcement that the concluding days are to be spent in talking about the ethical basis of Empire, and its relation to intellectual and aesthetic progress. That means, I fear, more of the unpromising mysticism of which we had a taste last night. We must keep Imperialism out of the clouds, or how on earth is it to commend itself to business men? I speak from a wide knowledge of the Colonies, and I assure you that what they want is a business proposition. We have, of course, our own ideals, but they are framed in a different language from yours, and I need hardly tell you that a common ideal, held with a difference, has proved in the past the most potent of disruptive forces. Let every man add his own poetry to the facts, but for Heaven's sake let us get the facts agreed upon first."

Mr Wakefield's eloquence was checked by his appetite, and by Hugh's warning that the word "Empire" was tabooed in the daytime. "Carey and I agreed," said he, "that we should degenerate into a debating society and get bored to death with each other unless we placed strict limits to our enthusiasm. So our discussions will not begin till dinner-tune. Before that we are at liberty to think as much as we please, but we must not talk about it. The resources of this place are limitless. We can shoot and fish and ride and walk; there is an excellent library; the finest scenery in the world is at our door. In the daytime we are flaneurs, without a thought except how to amuse ourselves. In the evening we can devote ourselves to your 'business proposition.'"

Mr Wakefield acquiesced a little reluctantly, and, having finished breakfast, ensconced himself in the library with a box of cigars and a French novel. Astbury went off to do some writing, and Hugh devoted an hour to his neglected correspondence. Meanwhile the mist was clearing, the sun had come out and burned up the rime, and, as he looked from the window, he saw a pale blue sky, which promised heat, and all the mystery of bright colour which a tropical morning displays. So, after going to his room for a book, he found a long wicker-chair on the verandah, and, lighting a pipe, settled himself for a peaceful forenoon.

He found it hard to read, however. The wide landscape shimmering below him, the calling of strange birds, the wafts of strange scents from the garden distracted his thoughts. By-and-by a trim white figure in a large sun-hat came along, and he said good-morning to Lady Flora.

The girl refused a chair, and seated herself on the parapet of the verandah.

"I am all alone, so I must come and talk to you, Mr Somerville. Aunt Susan and Lady Amysfort and Mrs Yorke are not down yet. Charlotte Wilbraham has taken Lord Launceston for a walk, Lady Lucy and Mr Lowenstein are talking business, Marjory and Mr Astbury are talking politics, and Barbara Deloraine is looking at a big botany book with pictures. I found Colonel Alastair and Sir Edward in the stables skinning beasts, and they were so covered with blood and the place smelt so horribly that I could not stay. Lady Warcliff is writing hundreds of letters about some of her emigration societies. I am sure she fusses far too much about her work. She behaves always like a weary Atlas holding up a world which doesn't in the least want to be held up. Last of all, I found Lord Appin deep in a big German book, but he told me to be a good girl and run away. So you are my only refuge. Tell me what you are reading in that little book with so many pencil markings in it."

"Plato," said Hugh. "I am taking advantage of my idleness to renew my acquaintance with the great masters. But it's very hard to find the proper book for such a morning."

"Nearly as hard as to find the proper clothes. When my maid called me she said it was 'freezin' 'ard,' so I put on my thickest tweed skirt. When I had finished dressing I saw the sun coming out, so I put on a lighter one. And when I came downstairs and went out on the verandah and saw that it was quite summery, I had to go back and change into summer things. Two changes in a morning are really enough to upset one. I feel as if I had been inconstant."

Hugh shut his book and began to refill his pipe. "I think I'll talk to you instead of reading Plato. What would you like to talk about?"

"This place, first of all," said the girl. "Did you ever see anything to match it? I am so glad Aunt Susan brought me. I fancied we should be living in a log cabin with Kaffir servants, and I seriously thought of leaving my maid at home, as I did last year in Norway. Instead, I find the most beautiful and comfortable house I ever dreamed of. And I like the idea of our party so much. We are going to talk high politics, and I am sure we have got some very clever men to talk them. It is such a refreshing change from the ordinary 'cure.' My first two seasons I went with Mother to stupid German places, where one saw the same people who had bored one in town and talked the same foolish gossip. It is a blessing to be in a place where one can talk about better things than other people's love affairs."

Hugh laughed. "You are growing old, Lady Flora, if that topic has ceased to amuse you. Have you had a hard Season?"

"Pretty hard, and I suppose I am growing old, for people are beginning to pall on me. Three years ago, when I first came out, I was tolerant of everything and anybody. But now I seem to have too much of it all. I want a little peace to get my mind clear and to know what I like and who are my friends. Didn't some one say that the art of life was to make up your mind what you really and truly wanted? I am afraid I shall soon be that deplorable young woman, 'her name was Dull.'"

"You have been reading the 'Pilgrim's Progress,' and you are afraid that you are one of the citizens of Vanity Fair?"

"I am horribly afraid. At the bottom of my heart I would really live almost anywhere else—even with the tiresome old Interpreter or the spinsters of the House Beautiful. Where do you live, Mr Somerville?"

Hugh shook his head doubtfully. "Various places up and down the Way. A good deal in the Valley of Humiliation. Now and then in Doubting Castle. But not much, I think, in Vanity Fair."

"No," said the girl, "I don't seem to have seen you about so much lately. Have you grown tired of the world?"

"I have so many things to think about nowadays. As you were saying, the secret of life is to find out what one really wants, and I have discovered that a little of Society goes a long way with me. I only liked it because of the romance which it has for us all at first. When I grew up properly and the gilt was rubbed off I found it hard and stupid: so like a wise man I seek my romance elsewhere. You are growing up, too, and finding the same thing."

Lady Flora climbed off her perch and leant over the balustrade, looking down into the infinite blue distances.

"At any rate we are both in the Delectable Mountains now," she said, "and we have the Shepherds, too, and they may teach us something. But I wish we were going to talk about a more helpful subject. Of course I believe in Imperialism, and I canvassed a great deal for cousin Charlie at the election. He was beaten, poor boy, and he said it was largely my fault, for I always agreed with anything anybody said to me. And I am much more interested in the Empire than in England, for all the nicest people I know are in Tibet, or Nigeria, or some remote place. But at the same time I can't help feeling that any politics are rather a far-away thing to me."

"And yet I don't see why they should be," said Hugh, rising and looking over the balustrade beside the girl. "We are all citizens,—I am giving you the kind of answer an elderly paternal person would give,—and we have long got over the old foolish idea that politics were only a game for men, and for a few men at that. What we are going to talk about is the whole scheme of life which a new horizon and a new civic ideal bring with them. It affects the graces as closely as the business of life, art and literature as well as economics and administration. Suppose a small tribe lived in a cave and never saw the daylight. One day the barriers at the door fall down, and they look out on a blue sky and meadows and a river, and are free to go out to them. It wouldn't be only the modes of tribal government that would be altered by the illumination."

"No, I suppose not. But the whole thing is still very unfamiliar to me, and I cannot understand the language you all talk in. I've never been able to follow even Lord Appin's jokes, though he's a relation, and Mr Carey speaks like a very impressive but very obscure bishop. Perhaps Lord Launceston may be simpler. He is so kind and wearied and sad, and his face is so like a Burne-Jones knight, that some day I shall certainly kiss him, if I am not too afraid of Charlotte Wilbraham."

"You would prefer that we should sit in conclave on the profound subject: How is a young lady of twenty or thereabouts, who is a little tired of being frivolous, to attain satisfaction in life? Upon my soul, I think that is a much more difficult question than the other."

"You are very tiresome, Mr Somerville," said the girl. "You think I am only a butterfly. I may be, but I can at least look beyond my cabbage-leaf, and I am very very discontented."

"Why not try good works?" Hugh asked.

"'Journeys end in mothers' meetings!' No! I've tried them in an amateur way, and the works aren't really good. You make yourself miserable, and only fuss and patronise the poor, so nobody is a penny the better."

"Well, then, there is the intellectual life?"

"I haven't the brains. It is all very well for Marjory, who has read everything, and finds life far too short for the things she burns to do. I don't live at white-heat like her. More by token," said Lady Flora, peering into the garden, "she is at this moment discoursing with Mr Astbury among the oleanders. Bareheaded too! I wonder if she knows that this is mid-day in the Tropics. She'll be cut off in the pride of her youth and beauty."

"There only remains falling in love and marrying," said Hugh solemnly.

"Oh, Mr Somerville, I never expected to hear you say anything so banal. As if any short cut to happiness lay that way! If you can't find a philosophy of life before marriage, you won't find it after. It is shirking the question, not solving it."

The girl swung round and revealed a laughing face and dancing eyes. "I am a better actress than I thought, and you were quite taken in. I am really blissfully happy, happier than I think I've ever been before. But I want to make the most of this place, so I have a scheme to offer. Why should we not have a special conference on our own account? The discussions in the evenings will be the voice of age. Let us have the voice of youth—you and me—in the mornings. I shall want to ask so many questions and have so many things explained to me. Besides, I may contribute really valuable suggestions in our *tête-à-tête,* which I should be much too shy to launch at the dinner-table. Shall we make it a bargain?"

As they shook hands on the compact the gong—aforetime the war-drum of a neighbouring tribe—sounded for luncheon.

Conversation at dinner was begun by a speech of some length from the Duchess of Maxton. In the afternoon she had been driven by Carey in an American buggy round a settlement of some fifty families from England. Enthusiasm was not commonly her *rôle,* but as a practical woman and a practical farmer she had been carried out of herself in admiration of the success of his experiment. She had tried the same thing on her husband's Suffolk estate, where it maintained a precarious life, fed by frequent doles from her own purse. Her first impression, therefore, had been that this was but another of Carey's extravagant hobbies, and she had been greatly astonished to learn that it paid him six per cent on his outlay.

The vast fields of tobacco and maize, the strips of lucerne, the orchards, the plain substantial houses, the well-made roads, the schoolhouse, the buxom contentment of the women, the healthy colour of the children, and the hard well-being of the men—she did not know what the most to admire. "How do you do it?" she had inquired, and had been told simply, "Management."

"Where did you get the people from?" she asked at dinner.

"Some from my old home in Devonshire—small farmers who could not make a living in England, young shepherds who wanted to be on their own, and a younger son or two who were not above labouring with their hands. But I wanted all sorts; so you will find South Africans and New Zealanders and Canadians in the settlement. I made a point of having none but men who had got the love of the soil in them. I don't think of the place as an emigration experiment. I wanted my estate farmed to the best purposes, and I hunted about for the best tenants. It is true that in time all will own their own farms, but even as freeholders they will still be in a real sense my own people."

"The danger I foresee in all such work," said Mr Wakefield, who found Lady Flora and Lady Amysfort, his two neighbours, a little inattentive to his conversation,—"the danger is that too much depends upon the will of a single man. One man like you, Carey, is a godsend; a hundred would be a calamity. For, when all is said and done, you are feudalists and aristocrats at heart. Now I maintain that the basis of empire is a democratic one—that is to say, empire as understood in the free Colonies, which are its real support. Africa, if I may say so, has been too much monopolised by 'men of destiny'—Rhodes, for example, and yourself. In Canada, in New Zealand, in Australia, you are inconceivable. I appreciate your work as much as any man, but I feel that it creates a false precedent. It is a precedent, I admit, which has small chance of being followed," he added, smiling.

Carey nodded and looked across the table to Lord Appin. "Mr Wakefield has brought us to the subject which we had arranged to discuss to-night. I think you will all agree that it is our first business to look at the condition of political thought in England, and incidentally at the position of political parties. England, even Mr Wakefield will admit, is still the imperial centre of gravity. Our creed is, of course, not identified with any party formula, but we Imperialists must work through existing agencies. It is most important, therefore, to know what materials we have to deal with."

"May I make a suggestion before we begin?" Mr Wakefield interrupted. "I agree with you, Carey, about the importance of the subject. But it is one which lends itself most readily to a barren speculative treatment. As ours is a practical inquiry, I suggest that we keep very close to facts and disregard what I believe is called the metaphysical basis of politics. I mean that in discussing Liberalism we should not ask ourselves what Liberalism may imply in its ultimate analysis, but merely what it means to the several millions who have voted Liberal at the polls. Otherwise we shall talk in a language which few of us can pretend to understand. We are not all philosophers like Lord Appin."

Lord Appin mildly dissented. "If I may say so, we are all philosophers, even Lady Flora, though we don't all of us know it. To be a philosopher it is not necessary that you should have formulated your creed in a system; it is sufficient if it governs your thought and conduct. I could label you all with your appropriate badges. I myself, for example, with certain private reservations, am a follower of Hegel. You, Mr Wakefield, I should class without hesitation as a disciple of the much-esteemed and lately deceased Mr Herbert Spencer. Lord Launceston, if I recall his Oxford reputation rightly, agrees with me. Our host is as fine an instance as I know of the Transcendental Idealist, though I don't suppose he has ever read a page of Fichte. Hugh, I think, is one of those peculiar people who go back to Kant and misunderstand that great man's meaning. Mrs Deloraine is a Platonist, and my sister is in her methods a crude Baconian. Even Sir Edward has a creed, and worships, with Nietzsche, the Superman. Did you ever hear his name, Teddy?"

"Yes," said that gentleman pensively; "and I once read a book of his—something about 'Zarathustra'—which my wife gave me for a birthday present. I liked it so much that I called a horse of mine after the author—won the Oaks in '99, you may remember. There was rather a muddle about it, for it was ridden by a jockey called Neish, and the sporting papers confused the two, and made him the horse and the other fellow the jockey."

"To return to what I was saying," continued Mr Wakefield with some slight asperity of tone, "I do earnestly beg of you all to keep on the hard highroad of facts. We have enough political metaphysicians in the world, and their works are to be found in the leading articles of the halfpenny Radical press. Our *raison d'être* is that we look more squarely at the realities of life. We have ample knowledge in our party to reconstruct the policies of the globe. For Heaven's sake let us keep off windy generalities."

Carey smiled benevolently during the interruption. "I am not a practical man. If I were, I should still be managing a little mine on the Rand. But I agree with Mr Wakefield up to a point—we must take full account of the data we have to work upon. That is why I propose that we should begin with the state of politics in England to-day. On this I have one remark to make, with which I think all will agree. The old creeds which still appear in the text-books are as dead as Julius Caesar."

The Duchess looked uneasy. Born of high Tory stock, she had married the head of a great Whig house and had zealously adopted its politics. "I do not admit that Liberalism is dead," she said. "On the contrary, it was never more alive than to-day. It has won a victory unprecedented since the date of the great Reform Bill."

"Nevertheless, Susan, I maintain that it is as dead as a door-nail. And to appease you I will add that Conservatism—for Lady Amysfort's sake I will not say Toryism—is in the same position. I propose to ask Lord Appin, who still reads the newspapers, to quote to us definitions of Liberalism, prepared both by friend and foe, and then I will ask you if the thing has not long been decently buried, though its wraith still walks the earth. Lady Amysfort will be kind enough to provide us with some account of that peculiar faith which she calls Toryism and proposes to identify with Imperialism. When we know what are the avowed creeds of the parties, we can fairly consider how much or how little of the vital spark is left in them. Then we can talk of Imperialism and those new doctrines which are its real rivals. Our country is hungering and thirsting for a living faith. We are all like sick folk by the Pool of Bethesda, waiting for the angel to descend and trouble the waters."

"I think, Francis, we might wait for the angel in the outer hall," said the voice of the Duchess. "It is very cold to-night, and that place is my ideal of comfort. Let us all go and have our coffee there and talk."

CHAPTER 3

THE great log-fire in the outer hall threw strange shadows upon the walls, and made the lion heads grin like outlandish ogres. Lamps were lit on the email tables, and the company settled in deep chairs, within the glow of the fire but outside its disquieting warmth.

Lord Appin, who had seated himself near the centre of the circle, produced a little volume in which newspaper extracts were pasted.

"I am, as you know," he said, "a connoisseur of public opinion. In my belief no statesman can afford to neglect the ingenuous manifestations of it which from time to time appear in its popular organs. There you will find the will of certain classes of the community stated, no doubt with imperfect grammar and more imperfect taste, but still with all the frankness and confusion of the original. So I subscribe to several press-cutting agencies, and my secretary, who knows my desires, keeps for me the more characteristic extracts. I ought, however, first of all to define what I mean by public opinion. Properly understood, it is the bed-rock, the cardinal fact of all democratic politics such as ours. It is the sum total of the instincts, traditions, and desires of our race, created not only by reasoned beliefs, but by those impalpable forces of persuasion which no contemporary can hope to diagnose. I am no despiser of the average man. What he thinks at the bottom of his heart, when he thinks at all, is what is sooner or later going to happen. Now creeds are not necessarily public opinion. They are the attempts to interpret it made by its official interpreters—preachers, journalists, and politicians. When I quote from the Press, therefore, I do not profess to be quoting public opinion in its real meaning, but an interpretation of it which has a vogue among a certain section of the interpreting class.

"Let me begin with a definition of the creed which has just won so conspicuous a victory. The bright flamboyant style betrays its source:—

"A sigh of thankfulness and hope is heard throughout the land. England with no uncertain voice has turned her face against Toryism, with all its moral *défaillance*, its insincerity, its opportunism, its lack of seriousness, its narrow and trifling sophistries, its unabashed class interest. The white soul of our people turns towards its true sun. Once more the large and generous spirit of Liberalism is abroad. We are on the threshold of a new era, and behind us lies nothing but confusion. Foreign affairs have been conducted from hand to mouth without any perception of large issues; domestic affairs have been dominated by an obscurantism which, under the influence of momentary panic, blossomed forth into ill-considered experiments in reaction. The heart of the nation needed a solemn purification, and by the grace of God that purification has come.

Men go about in the streets to-day with a new light in their eyes—poor men who see at last a hope for their starving households, earnest men who have fretted in secret at the long reign of apathy, young men who have now before them a career of civic usefulness. From warder to warder runs the challenge,'Brother, is it well with the State?' and the answer comes, 'It is well!'"

Lord Appin paused. "It is a charming picture of a national renaissance. But let us look," he continued, "at what Liberalism has to give:—

"The policy of Liberalism is clear. Men's minds have been too long dazzled by the jingo generalities of empire. Imperialism battens on the basest attributes of humanity, the lust of conquest and power, the greed of gold, the morbid unsettlement and discontent of a degenerate age. It is for Liberalism to bring back the people to the paths of political wisdom, which are also those of peace and pleasantness. Purity of character must be insisted upon in our public men. The heresies of a decadence must be expunged, and we must return to the sober and rational orthodoxy of our fathers. The House of Commons, the People's House, must be restored to its old prestige. The overgrown burden of armaments must be reduced, and England must appear before the world as the herald of a truce between nations. The cost of administration must be lessened that the private comfort of the citizen may be increased. Provision must be made for the old and feeble of the land; the slums—that eyesore of our civilisation—must be opened up to the wholesome air and light; the workman must be placed on a level with the master in the economic struggle, and for that purpose raised above the caprice of juries; in the exploitation of her neglected assets, the State must find work for those who are squeezed out of the capitalist mill. For each class of the community the way must be made plain for that development which is its due. Education must be freed from the blighting influence of clericalism; the liquor traffic must be curbed in the public interest; capitalism and the servitude it entails must be checked with a strong and earnest hand. In a word, Liberalism must lift again its old banner, on which its great master inscribed its never-to-be-forgotten creed—'Peace, Retrenchment, and Reform!'"

"It is a spirited piece of prose," said Lord Appin as he concluded, "though I am afraid it is mostly made up of what logicians call 'identical propositions.' Notice, too, the refrain throughout, 'Return,' 'our historic creed,' political orthodoxy.' Somehow it does not strike me as inspiring, but I think it is a not unfair statement of what a great many of the interpreting class wish the nation to believe. I propose to read as a pendant some remarks of my friend, the editor of the 'International Review.' With him the English language is a spiked mace, and perhaps some of the spikes are too long and sharp for my liking:—

"Triumphant Liberalism has promulgated its creed, and we trust that the world is edified. For ourselves, we can only see pathos in colossal travail with a *ridiculus mus* as the fruit of it. We have waited for a sign, and behold! we are referred to an ancient, vulgar, and half-effaced street-poster; we ask for some new thing, and we are given the oldest of pot-house cries. A contemporary, which claims to be the exponent of the new gospel, has given us a long and turgid exposition, in a style adorned by imperfectly remembered fragments of the Sermon on the Mount and the culture of the Mechanics' Institute. And the result? It is our old friend Gladstonianism with a more pronounced Nonconformist accent. The prophet of the future, it appears, is that poisonous politician—we dare not misuse the word 'statesman'—who, with the morbid conscience and purblind eyes of the egotist, was ready to sacrifice his country's honour to a fetish begotten of his own vanity. England, it seems, is to put her pride in her pocket and go whimpering among the nations as an apostle of peace, bleating about the grievous cost of her army and navy. The poor are to be elevated by tinkering expedients of re-housing and pauperised by doles from the Exchequer, while the law will be so amended as to give carte-blanche to mob violence. Education will once more be flung into the hands of clerics, only the frock-coat will take the place of the cassock, and the snuffle of Little Bethel will oust the more scholarly tones of the Church. The prestige of the Parliamentary "talking-shop," which all thinking men have long ago come to disregard, is to be revived and increased. An egregious economy will play havoc with our revenue system, and the deficit will be made up by the plunder, not of the rich parvenus, but of the unfortunate owners of ancestral lands. Our Empire, won by the blood and sweat of our great progenitors, and maintained by that class which alone is worthy of the name of Englishmen—our Empire, which gives to generous youth its only horizon, is to be lightly cast aside to satisfy the whimsies of a few dropsical pedants. Not one constructive idea emerges from the chaos of absurdities. Not once do the propagandists dare to look at the facts of a living world. Let us re-shuffle the cards, they say; let us pull down a little here and add a little there; but for God's sake do not tell us that conditions can change, for we know that our great leader has laid down once and for all the principles of our English policy. Let no man lay a finger upon that Ark of the Covenant!"

Lord Appin looked up from his book. "There is a great deal more, but that is the gist of my friend's criticism; and though I deplore its intemperance, I am inclined to agree with it. Liberalism, so far as I can judge, is correctly described as a shuffling of the cards. One further quotation I cannot resist. My friend goes on to show that the

Conservative party is equally barren of ideas, and he gives far from flattering portraits of some of those leaders—he calls them 'Mandarins'—who have just gone out of office, and in many cases out of Parliament. 'Oh for one hour,' he exclaims, 'of Randolph Churchill!' Then he turns to myself:—

"Lord Appin stands in a different position. He is, at least, untouched by the administrative incompetence of his former colleagues. He may choose to play the grand seigneur out of office, but once in the toils of a department he shows an industry as unwearied and a mind as acute as any statesman who has risen by merit alone. But he is cursed with a fatal temperamental weakness. He is intolerant of mediocrity, impatient of the pedestrian and the dull, and his shining gifts of intellect and character are available only in emergencies. His metaphysical habit of mind interposes a veil between him and the will of the people. He will not condescend to join in the dusty squabbles amid which the political life must be lived. He will do brilliantly in the field if he is permitted either to issue orders from a luxurious tent in the rear or to charge some desperate position at the head of the Maison du Boi.... But he will neither fight in the ranks nor in their immediate vicinity. The result is that he has fallen out of the battle line of public life. He might have ruled England as Disraeli ruled her, but he has chosen to make elegant speeches and write agreeable books. He has, definitely and of set purpose, given up to a coterie what was due to the Empire. He might have been a second Pitt; he has succeeded in becoming a second Lord Houghton."

The quotation was received with amusement by the company, with the exception of Mr Wakefield, who had listened to it with serious approval, glad of support for the views he had aired at the dinner-table.

"I have given you the current interpretation of Liberalism," Lord Appin continued, "and I have here a long extract containing the creed of the new Labour party. I do not propose to read it to you, for it is very long, and the gist of it can be put in a few words. It is written by Ainsworth, and is an excellent piece of work."

The Duchess made a mouth of disgust. "I do not see how one can attach much value to the views of a man like Mr Ainsworth. He washes so seldom and so imperfectly. Oh yes, Flora! I know that your mother was foolish enough to take him up, and that she pretends to admire and understand him. But I have no patience with such a course. If the man hates us and is going to destroy us and all our belongings, then let us treat him as an enemy and not as a tame cat."

"But, Aunt Susan," said Lady Flora, "he is really quite a dear. When he came to stay at Wirlesdon he wrote his letter of thanks on our own notepaper, and left it on his dressing-table."

"The gist of Ainsworth's argument," Lord Appin resumed, in a tone of mild expostulation, "is more or less what Imperialists say themselves. He claims that none of our old creeds are applicable, because the conditions have changed, and he asks for a fresh analysis. We shall, of course, differ from him profoundly as to the nature of the new conditions and the principles which govern their interpretation, but our general attitude is the same. Provided the whole Empire is taken as the battle-ground, I am quite content to see Socialism and Individualism fight out their quarrel unhampered. So there remains for our present consideration only the wide word 'Conservatism.' The elder Toryism, we shall all agree, is dead. Indeed, I am far from certain if it ever existed to any large extent in modern times. I am afraid that it was in the main, like the doctrine of Innate Ideas, a fiction of its opponents. It still makes an excellent Aunt Sally to knock down on the hustings, but a modern Lucian would have to go far afield to find an honest exponent of it. In the depths of the country, in vicarages and manor-houses, one or two very old or very stupid men and a few innocent women may still hold to it. There is, however, a Conservatism—I beg Lady Amysfort's pardon, a Toryism—which is a more living creed, or perhaps we had better call it an attitude of mind. Lady Amysfort is going to be very kind and read us her confession of faith."

The lady thus appealed to flung away her cigarette and, lying back in her chair so that the glow of the lamp was behind her head, opened a small manuscript.

"I ought to say," she began, "that I wrote this originally as an address to a meeting of Primrose Dames. You know the kind of thing—the local mayoress, the wives of rising tradespeople, and a sprinkling of the female clergy. But Henry Parworth, who read it, said that it would break up the Primrose League altogether, so I had to give them a chapter of 'Sibyl' instead." She adjusted her head and began to read in slow, clear accents:—

"Where shall we discover the path of the Statesman?" asked the Stranger in the 'Politicus,' and the question has often returned to pull up the hasty politician. We hear much about administrative reform, the clearing out of this office or that, but our political charwomen give us no clue to the constructive principles of statecraft. We see both our traditional parties seeking the will-o'-the-wisp of the moment, making their bow to the Dagon of to-day and the Baal of to-morrow, till it is hard for the unprejudiced spectator to detect wherein lies the difference in the articles of their faith. Yet the difference exists, we are told by Liberal writers. The Liberal party is conspicuously the possessor of a creed, of principles; if they accept a new doctrine it is because in some occult way it is part of their historic policy, and if they reject it the reason is the same. They are the party of a continuous intellectual development, while Conservatives are hand-to-mouth office-seekers, attendant upon the movements of the traditional cat.

"It is this current and facile view of Conservatism which I wish to combat. The old creed of the party is by universal consent no longer binding. The Tory country gentleman who believed as his fathers taught him and held all reform the invention of the devil is an extinct being, though he may maintain a shadowy subjective existence in the minds of a few Liberal journalists. But if this belief be gone, have we anything to take its place? Are our principles invented in the morning and discarded at the going down of the sun? Are our tenets bound up with no rational philosophy of human society, but merely the hasty maxims of clever adventurers? Mr Morley, in his book 'On Compromise,' has granted us some shadow of a creed, but our gratitude is moderated by the fact that it is not the creed of modern Conservatism. Those principles to which he bids us be true, if we would call ourselves honest men and women, are so archaic, so tenderly romantic, that not even Disraeli in his youth could have wholly accepted them. But unless we are to court the charge of frivolity, it is necessary to provide some theory of Conservative statesmanship and the Conservative attitude. On us lies the burden of definition. The fact of the Conservative temper in the nation is beyond cavil: it is for its upholders to show that it is not unreasonable. If we shrink from a noisy confession of faith, there is all the more need for a recognition of the meaning of our attitude. We decline to dogmatise about politics, but we are compelled to dogmatise about our attitude towards them. We must define our critical standpoint, though we hazard no further definitions, lest we fall into the old silliness and erect in our market-places altars to an Unknown God.

"My first remark concerns the vexed question of the relation of ethics and politics. Liberalism may be said to have devoted itself to the special cult of the political moralist. Now, to my mind, there is a vast distinction between conscience and conscientiousness, and that distinction is based upon the calibre of the accompanying intellect. If a man appeals to his conscience, I am entitled to inquire if it be the conscience of a man or the conscientiousness of a fool. Moral earnestness, if accompanied by intelligence, is worthy of all respect; but, if not so attended, it is merely a pathological state, like hysteria or delirium. I find, however, that the moralist in politics is apt to put a value upon conscience in itself. He pleads for a kind of finesse in ethics, a terrible finicking consistency, an abstract devotion to a very abstract creed. He refuses to allow the conscience to be ruled and directed by the mind: intellectual considerations, he says in effect, have no relevance in this sphere. We maintain, on the other hand, that the primary condition of statesmanship is what Hilda Wangel calls a 'robust conscience.' By this I do not mean an obtuse mind, and still less a dishonest one. I mean the temper which allows the sense of right and the practical intelligence to go hand in hand, never subserving the former to the latter, but interpreting the one by the other. It is the temper which looks at the essentials of virtue and not at its trappings. 'No great country,' Horace Walpole wrote, 'was ever saved by its good men, because good men will not go the lengths that are necessary.'

"Now mark what the word 'good' means. This is no plea for the unscrupulous man who sinks morality in statecraft. But it is a plea for the statesman who can sink himself in his people, who is less concerned with trying to save his soul than with trying to save his country, who can look at the great issues of life with eyes undimmed by any metaphysic of morality. It is a protest against the saint in politics, that worthy, hypercritical, and useless type of mind which is incapable of single-hearted action. '*La petite morale,*' in Mirabeau's words, '*est l'ennemi de la grande.*' When the Emperor Charles the Fifth, as we are told on good authority, appeared before the Throne of God, the Devil's Advocate had a long list of burnings, sackings, and slaughterings to bring against him. But his Guardian Angel argued thus: 'This man has lived a hard life among men, and not in the cloister or in the desert. He must be judged by fitting standards, and if on the whole he followed righteousness we must forget his stumblings.' And history adds that this view was accepted and Charles permitted to enter Paradise.

"The first point, then, in the Conservative attitude is that it insists upon a robust and practical mind. The second is that such a mind must think and feel in accord with the traditions of the national character. In this character there are certain clearly defined features. It is a temper naturally conservative, prone to keep up the form of things, though the spirit has gone, till they crumble to pieces from sheer age; slow to think; distrustful of novelties; intolerant of brilliance—the temper which in the individual spells mediocrity, but in the mass a kind of greatness. Against this great rock of English conservatism the spirits of a Bacon, a Cromwell, a Bolingbroke, a Canning, a Disraeli, like so many ineffectual angels, have beaten their wings in vain. But the majority of them, being wise in their generation, recognised their barriers and turned their prison-house into a wall of defence. It is not like the conservatism of the Liberal, an absorption in a barren dogma; it is the conservatism of a national temperament, and therefore upon it true statesmanship must build as upon its foundation. Ultimately, as most political thinkers have urged, the people in a blind, dumb way work out their own ideas, and these ideas are always right. There is a cant maxim among Liberal politicians that the statesman is the servant of democracy. So be it. But let a statesman serve the people by penetrating to their real interests and their real desires, and not by obeying any casual knot of agitators who clamour that their unintelligible patois is the voice of God.

"The third item in our definition is that Conservative statesmanship must be positive. When the great wave of reaction produced by the French Revolution had subsided, the era of Industrialism set in. New inventions lessened the cost of production. Manufacturers and mine-owners saw wealth, colossal wealth, in the near future. But there was the labouring class to be considered, a class to some extent tainted with the French restlessness, demanding better pay, shorter hours, happier conditions of life. It was a unique chance for a constructive statesman, but Canning died and the Manchester school succeeded. With a creed made up of a few tags from dissenting ethics and a few dubious economic maxims, this school was in the main composed of capitalists and employers of labour. To secure a free development for the new industrialism was their aim, but in the meantime sops must be thrown to the Cerberus of the proletariat. So they passed the Reform Bill of 1832, that harmless excursion in academic reform, and they repealed the Corn Laws, which put money in their pockets, silenced for a moment the cries of labour, and effectually ruined agricultural England. Against Chartism, which was a crude but genuine scheme of reform, they fought with tooth and nail! Reform for reform's sake, provided it be not radical, change for change's sake, provided it be unnecessary—such has been the lofty tradition of this vicious and destructive theorising. And thus the so-called Radicalism has advanced, professing a high ethical purpose, pandering to every fad of every clique of agitators, taking in vain the sacred name of Progress. And Conservatism? It, too, has forgotten at times that doctrine of positiveness which Canning taught, but throughout its moments of error and forgetfulness it has never quite lost sight of its ideal. As the party which professes no abstract creed, but bases its duty upon a knowledge of national character and a conception of practical good, it has maintained that reform when it comes must be real, and that a trifling with change for its own sake is the last and fatalest heresy.

"In 'positiveness' then the true *raison d'être* of Conservatism is to be found. But, indeed, I object to the word Conservative. I should prefer to call myself a Tory. The former word implies that the centre of gravity lies in a dull conserving of institutions and creeds which may have outgrown their usefulness. 'Tory,' I am told, meant in the beginning an Irish robber, and the attitude of the Irish robber in life seems to me preferable to that of the hide-bound formalist who worships a Church and State which are no more than names to him. Toryism is not the path of least resistance, but a living and militant creed, offering tangible results and based upon the vital needs of the nation. I have read many 'Pleas for Unprincipled Toryism,' which were attempts to defend our supposed lack of a theoretical basis. But we have no need of such a defence. We have our basis, we have our principles, and they are none the less principles because we are not so arrogant as to confuse them with the laws of Sinai.

"One word in conclusion. It seems to me that there is another duty incumbent upon the Tory party, which is perhaps of all its tasks the most arduous and the most vital. In our modern world we have Been inaugurated the reign of a dull bourgeois rationalism, which finds some inadequate reason for all things in heaven and earth and makes a god of its own infallibility. Old simple faiths have been discredited, a spirit of minor criticism has gone abroad, and the beliefs of centuries are now in a state of solution. It is not a promising mood. 'Provincial arrogance and precipitate self-complacency' are not the stuff of which a strong nation is made. National prejudices, deep inborn convictions for which no copy-book justifications can be found, are after all the conquering forces of the world. The French Revolution destroyed the cult of Church and King; but it inspired an equally blind and passionate worship of certain civic ideals, and with these in their soul the raw levies of France conquered Europe. To the Tory the instincts of the people must always seem truer in the long-run than the little-reasoned disquisitions of a few professors. To the Liberal this is heresy; he demands a creed which shall approve itself to his superb intellect, for Liberalism is essentially the faith of the intellectual. Against such an attitude it is the duty and the highest privilege of Tory statesmanship to wage implacable war. It may take many forms—attacks upon institutions which still fulfil their purpose though in a narrow way their basis may seem irrational, dogmas in economics and theories of reform which have only a speculative validity, a system of ethics made in the study or the lecture-room. I know of few finer words in literature than those in which Burke swept away the sophistries which sought to abolish patriotism and defend certain vague cosmopolitan rights of man, or those in which Disraeli in the theatre at Oxford in '64 scourged the money-changers of popular science. And so in our analysis of Conservatism we come back to something which is not unlike the beliefs of our grandfathers. Conservatism in their view was sworn to defend Church and Throne, in our view it is sworn to defend the things which lie at the back of Church and Throne, the instincts of a people, the character of a nation. It is conservative, this attitude, but it is also reforming. A people develops unconsciously, and this development is on far other lines than the progress of Liberal illuminati. It is its duty to foster this popular development as against the vagaries of a clique or a caucus. It is its duty to conserve, while there is reason, and to destroy ruthlessly and finally when the justification has passed. And it has a right to this attitude, for it bases its conduct upon the 'instant need of things' and upon no *a priori* creed. Its opponents, fixing their eyes upon falling stars, have no leisure to study the ground they walk on. Mistaking their own clientele for the nation and themselves for Omnipotence, they wander like children in the dark, and instead of the narrow path to the Celestial City follow the primrose path to that sinister personage who, as a great authority has told us, was the first Whig."

Lady Amysfort's cool accents had scarcely ceased before Mr Wakefield, who had listened with some attention, said loudly, "My dear lady, there is a great deal of sound sense in that and a great deal of nonsense. I detest your obscurantism, but on the main point I entirely agree with you. We must be positive and practical in our work, and the metaphysician is every bit as bad as the Liberal doctrinaire."

The Duchess had had her temper considerably ruffled by the matter, and still more by the manner of Lady Amysfort's discourse. She had an intense dislike of the Primrose League, and a suspicion of Disraeli, who had once said of her husband that his air suggested an "inspired rabbit." Looking round the circle she saw no one disposed to take up the cudgels for her much abused party, and Lady Amysfort's attitude, as, slim and exquisite, she leaned over a lamp to light a cigarette, annoyed her by its suggestion of the supercilious. She therefore fixed her opponent with an austere eye, and advanced to the attack.

"There is much that I could say, Caroline," she began, "but I will confine myself to one point which is common to you and the writer of Bob's second extract. You both maintain that we Liberals are hag-ridden by formulas, and declare that the Conservatives are the only people who can look squarely at facts. To begin with, I think that you very much overstate your case. Heaven is my witness that I do not love the style of the Radical press. I detest its loudmouthed generalities, and I think the way it drags the most sacred words of Scripture into its arguments simply blasphemous. It resorts so consistently to immense appeals on trivial occasions, that when the great occasion arises it has nothing further to say. But in spite of all this folly you cannot maintain that you can do without dogma altogether, or that the dogmatism of the two factions differs otherwise than in degree. Take again this question of facing facts. I think the Liberal point is a perfectly good one. Things have gone hideously wrong under a Conservative Government, simply because it did not look at facts. We may choose—foolishly, I think—to cloak our return to common-sense in Nonconformist language, but what we really mean is that our opponents did not understand their data, and we are going to try to understand them. We are not really quarrelling about principles but about facts, and it is only a bad debating trick to pretend otherwise. I do not say that we shall read the facts correctly, any more than you did, but our sole justification is that we intend to try. When you maintain that the Conservatives look at facts, and the Liberal clings to principles, all you mean is that the different sides have different arts for capturing the popular fancy. We are apt to claim a monopoly of the purer virtues, you of practical common-sense; but we both aim at common-sense, though my side invests it with the glamour of high principles, yours with the charm of an historic past. I honestly think that is the fairest way to look at our political records. I quite agree with you that the difference at bottom is one of temperament. I have heard Bob's voice shake with emotion when he spoke of Chatham, and I have seen tears in Mr Calderwood's eyes when he spoke of Eternal Justice. I will confess that I would rather have politicians pat a little history book familiarly than the New Testament, but both are legitimate forms of appeal. Our faiths spring from the same source. You think us foolish; we think you stupid; while the truth is that we are both rather foolish, rather stupid, and in the last resort rather wise."

The Duchess's remarks met with the strong approbation of Lord Launceston, who had been crossing and uncrossing his long legs nervously while Lady Amysfort read.

"I think what you say is most true," he said. "All parties have a common basis now. They preach the same faith though in different accents. And all parties tend simply to shuffle the old cards at any crisis, instead of making a new analysis of the facts. It is the business of clear-eyed people to prevent this natural inclination. Our common basis I should call democracy—English democracy, that is, with all its historical and racial colouring. It is not a dogma, but a fact, or rather the recognition of a fact—that under modern conditions Everyman governs. Now democracy is the great destroyer of shams. It clears out the rubbish and leaves the truth tolerably plain to the single-minded inquirer. Besides, it opens up the way for superiority. I do not say that it means always an enlightened rule, but it gives scope at any rate for the true enlightener when he arrives. It is the best, indeed the only, basis for building anew on. And here, curiously enough, it reaches the same result as Toryism. It used to be the old boast of the Tory party that it was loyal, and would always render faithful service to any leader who could capture it. The Liberal party, it was said, was too individualistic, too split up by the differences which come from honest but incomplete thinking independently, ever to make a good following. Democracy does the work of Toryism on a wider basis. The people have no intellectual arrogance. They think slowly, not very clearly, and always on broad and simple lines, but when they once grasp a conception they are invincible."

"We are agreed, then, on one important point," Carey took up the conversation. "Both of our great parties purport to look at facts, but both tend to get into conventional grooves and neglect their duty. However, in the democracy which lies behind them both, there is a permanent instinct under proper guidance to revise the data of policy. And here I may anticipate what I think Lord Appin intends to say. The new Labour party, which claims to be specially in touch with democracy, urges as its chief *raison d'être* the duty of revision. We may differ from them on what constitutes the data, we may differ still more profoundly on the interpretation, but our general attitude is exactly theirs."

"I have always maintained," said Lord Appin, "that they were our natural allies. I opened a review the other day and found an article on their programme by one of their leaders. He advocated a mission of labour delegates to the Colonies in order to confer with the Labour parties there and arrange a common programme. I confess that the proposal, crude as it was, cheered me greatly, as showing some kind of sense of imperial solidarity."

"So, if the hooligans of Mile End sent a deputation to consult with the larrikins of Sydney and the toughs of Montreal, you would call that an effort in the cause of imperial unity?"

Mr Wakefield spoke with an asperity which for the moment left the company silent. The tension was relieved by Lady Flora, who, with an innocence not destitute of tact, inquired if a larrikin was the same as a bush parrot, since a pair had just been sent her. Upon which, with a paternal gravity and some humour, Mr Wakefield proceeded to explain to her in an undertone the exact distinction.

"My point is very simple," Lord Appin continued. "Even a class policy, which recognises that success can only be won on the stage of the whole Empire, has a certain statesmanship in it. For it recognises one cardinal truth, the enlarged basis of our problems."

"Now, Hugh," said Carey, "you shall have that definition of Imperialism for which your soul yearns. It is simply looking at all the facts instead of at only a few of them. We begin by realising that we are not an island but an empire, and therefore, in considering any great question, we take the whole data into account. Imperialism, if we regard it properly, is not a creed or a principle, but an attitude of mind."

Lady Flora caught the last words in the midst of her lecture on bush parrots. "That is exactly what Cousin Charlie said when Uncle George found him at Monte Carlo when he should have been at his Embassy. Uncle George said it was a disgrace that he should be seen in such a place, and Charlie said it wasn't a place but an attitude of mind."

"We are all Imperialists at heart nowadays," Carey went on, "except Lady Flora, who is a wicked girl. Every party is more or less resigned to the fact of empire. Some kick a little against the pricks, some are half-hearted, others burn with zeal; but all have the same conviction that it is inevitable. We have not begun yet to work out the details seriously, but we have won the first position. And that is as it should be. The Empire must be accepted, like the Monarchy, as a presupposition in politics which is beyond question. Any inclination to use it for party ends should be as jealously condemned as the occasional attempts to drag the King's name into current controversies or to assume that patriotism is the monopoly of one side. We shall, of course, always differ on particular questions, but there should be no difference on the ideal. Indeed, I honestly think that there is little among ordinary sane-minded people. The average man may be described as a confused Imperialist. He wants to make the best of the heritage bequeathed to him; his imagination fires at its possibilities; but he is still very ignorant and shy, and he has no idea how to set about the work. The first of imperial duties is to instruct him."

"And yet," said Mr Astbury, "I find many people openly contemptuous of the ideal. I daresay this contempt is due to imperfect understanding, but we have to face the fact that many are not only apathetic about the things we care most for, but actively hostile."

Lord Appin reopened his scrap-book. "True enough. We have some honest opponents, and a few indifferently so, and I have been at the pains to collect their opinions. I think I can distinguish several types. There is, first of all, Mr Luke Simeon, who surrendered his fellowship at King's to 'labour,' as he says, among the masses. He is eminent at Browning halls and university settlements, and has done much, I believe, to civilise the East End by the distribution of indistinct reproductions of Giotto and Botticelli. He is a pale, earnest, well-meaning, and rather silly young man, who should have remained in the church of his clerical forefathers. He attacks Imperialism as the 'worship of force.' It represents, he says, that tendency of a decadent age which may be observed in the Roman ladies who took their lovers from the prize-ring. Up to a point I agree with him. The worship of brute force, of mere conscienceless power, is the most certain sign of degeneration. His fallacy is that he really condemns force altogether, whether exercised for a beneficent purpose or not, and he hides his bias under the assumption that Imperialism means power without ideals or conscience. He has a temperamental shrinking from certain of the hard realities of life, and he flatters his weakness by investing it with a moral halo. He lives in a little world of artistic and literary trifling, and he has consequently no perspective, so that he will quote you a bad artist on some point of foreign policy and a minor poet on some problem of economics. His shallow aesthetic soul is revolted by three-fourths of life, so he dubs it evil and rejects it. He is not a young man whom it is worth taking pains to convert, but his stuff has its vogue, and he has disciples. We have but to expound the moral purpose in our creed to take the logical ground from beneath his feet, for, though he desires it in his heart, he is not prepared for an absolute condemnation of power. Then we have our Benthamite friend, Mr Wrigley of Manchester, who is one of the few remaining exponents of the old Radicalism of the 'forties. War is his special dislike, and commerce his idol. He is averse to empire partly because his mind is full of Rome and Carthage and he has not the imagination to conceive a new model, partly because it gives scope for energies which are only by accident utilitarian. His ideal State would be a community of Samuel Budgetts and Worldly Wisemans. The answer to him and his kind is that their doctrine is built on a false conception of human nature, and that in tranquillising life they would denude it of all that makes it worth having.

'*Summum crede nefas animam praeferre pudori,*
Et propter vitam vivendi perdere causas.'[2]

For good or for ill humanity has long since decided against him. Next, there is the school of which we may take Mr Chatterton as a representative. In theory they are full blooded and masculine enough, though their heroics smack of Peckham. They love to rhapsodise about 'Old England' and the Elizabethans, and beer and cricket, and heaven knows what. Their complaint is that a spacial extension means a weakening in intensity of the national life, and they also will throw Rome and Athens at your head. They are all for the virility of England, they say, as against the neurotic restlessness of the Imperialist. With them, again, I have a certain sympathy, though the taunt of 'neurotic' comes ill from gentlemen whose style is so explosive and delirious. The answer to their arguments depends upon the question of the value of space and of the whole material basis in any spiritual development, and in deference to Mr Wakefield we will leave that over till a later day. Lastly comes an honest fellow for whom I have a great regard. You all know Ambrose by name. He lives on twopence a-day and slaves at his philanthropy. He objects to empire because imperial questions distract the attention of the nation from urgent matters of home reform. And he is perfectly right. As long as we make 'national' and 'imperial' water-tight compartments, there must be this jealousy. What we have to show him is that the whole is one great problem, and that his own interests cannot be realised save by the help of the other interests which he despises. And then he will be on our side, for at heart he is one of us."

"You have omitted," said Mrs Wilbraham, "the greatest source of opposition—the folly of some of our own people. Why is it that many of us—myself for one—grow nervous when the word 'Empire' is mentioned, and get hot all over? Human nature is so hopelessly silly. A dear creature, whom most of us know, started a league last year to ensure that women throughout the Empire should be reading Shakespeare at the same time every evening. 'How sweet,' she said, 'to think that every night at half-past nine the whole English-speaking world would be repeating immortal words,' and she was very angry with me for saying that the English-speaking world would be much better employed dining. And then, what is to be said about our poetry? I had a collection of imperial songs from the works of popular poets sent me this summer. One had the chorus, '*We can all do our little bit for England.*' Another was an invocation to empire—'*Empire, the very thought of thee!*' And, worst of all, there is Sir Herbert Jupp. You know how ambitious he is to be a great orator, so he has had many elocution lessons, and he speaks whenever he is invited. It is the most dreadful stuff, and he winds up always with a tag from some bad poet, which is enough to make one cry. One could believe that he was hired by our opponents to make our case ridiculous. I almost think that, more than any other party, we suffer from a defective sense of humour."

"Tut, tut," said Mr Wakefield, heaving himself from his chair and straddling into the firelight. "It will never do to be hypercritical. It is only a dying cause which can attain to perfect taste. A living creed is sure to have its extravagances and its crudities, but it can afford to be absurd. After all, we must have our subalterns as well as our marshals, our Garibaldis as well as our Cavours and Mazzinis. The more silliness in Imperialism the better, say I! It shows that it is getting on terms with human nature, which is deplorably silly. Of course our poetry is bad, of course our rhetoric is tawdry, of course we show no sense of the ridiculous! And the reason is simply that we are in earnest. If we once become self-conscious, then we may as well shut up shop and pull down the sign.... Carey, my soul longs for a whisky-and-soda!"

CHAPTER 4

HUGH had found a comfortable chair in the lee of an acacia thicket, whence he looked over a stretch of low bracken to the lawn which swept from the house along the edge of the escarpment to the home woods. The sunshine lay warm around him, but the clear air had none of the sultriness of noon. Rather it burned like some dry ether, with an aromatic freshness in its heat. In accordance with his good resolutions he was renewing his acquaintance with the classics, and was reading aloud to himself the exquisite cadences of Theocritus's Seventh Idyll.

"I am the foul fiend, Flibbertigibbet!" said a voice at his elbow, and Lady Flora, with an armful of books, sank upon the mossy turf beside him. "No! Stay where you are. I want to sit here. Poor Mr Somerville, I've come to disturb you again. But it is our compact, you know. What have you been reading?" "Greek," said Hugh, holding out his book.

"Poetry! Well, so have I—all the morning. We played such a good game, which Charlotte Wilbraham invented—making comic imperial poetry. It is quite easy. You simply get all the names of places you can think of and string them together, and then put at the end something about the Flag or the Crown or the Old Land. Mr Wakefield was rather cross at first, but he was soon pacified, and he played very well. I thought the first night he was a dreadful old thing, but he is really very kind, and quite amusing."

"I want to hear your poem," said Hugh.

"Oh, I couldn't write any—at least nothing fit to read aloud. I'm too stupid for clever games. But I carried off Marjory's, in spite of her protests." The girl took a paper from between the leaves of a book and read the following verses:—

"'Rests not the wild-deer in the park,
The wild-fowl in the pen,
Nor nests the heaven-aspiring lark
Where throng the prints of men.
He who the King's Path once hath trod
Stays not in slumbrous isle,
But seeks, where blow the winds of God,
His lordly domicile.
Where 'neath the red-rimmed Arctic sun
The ice-bound whaler frets,
Where in the morn the salmon run
Far-shining to the nets;
Where young republics pitch their tents
Beside the Western wave,

And set their transient Presidents
As targets for the brave;
Where through th' illimitable plains
Nigerian currents flow,
And many a wily savage brains
His unsuspecting foe;
Where gleam the lights of shrine and joss,
From some far isle of blue,
Where screams beneath the Southern Cross
The lonely cockatoo;
(The last word may be 'caribou.' Marjory wasn't sure whether a caribou or a cockatoo was likely to scream most.)
Where in the starlit Eastern night
The dusky dervish sleeps,
Where the lone lama waits the light
On Kangchenjunga's steeps;
Where Indian rajahs quaff their pegs
And chase the listless flies,
Where mazed amid a pile of kegs
Th' inebriate trader lies;
There, o'er the broad and goodly earth,
Go seek th' imperial soul.
Broken the barriers of his birth,
Th' eternal heavens his goal.
In wind or wet, in drink or debt,
Steeled heart no fate can stir,
He is the Render of the Net,
Th' Immortal Wanderer.'"

"It is long," said Lady Flora, when she had finished, "but, like the White Knight's poem, it is very, very beautiful. Charlotte said it had the true ring of colonial poetry. Do you know, Mr Somerville, of all the discussion last night I scarcely remember anything except that Imperialism has nothing to do with being a Liberal or a Conservative, and that it means we must begin all over again. Also I remember that it is not a creed, but an attitude of mind. I thought a good deal about that when I was having my hair brushed this morning. Somebody once told me that according to philosophers everything is only an attitude of mind—you and I and the sun and Musuru and the butterfly over there. Is that true?"

"Of course," said Hugh. "We are all creatures of the Red King's dream, but till he wakens up we pretend we are real."

"I wish," said the girl pensively,—"I wish I could believe that Aunt Susan was only an attitude of mind. She has arranged a picnic for this afternoon, and I did so want to go for a gallop over the moor we passed through the first day. Don't you think, Mr Somerville, we could slip away by ourselves? You've been here before and know the country, so we shouldn't lose our way. I've been round the stables, and there is a little white Arab I have set my heart on."

It was impossible to refuse a request that so chimed with his own wishes, and Hugh readily consented. At luncheon their path was made easy, for the Duchess had a headache and did not appear. Accordingly about three o'clock they found themselves cantering up a grassy ride among the woods, scaring the small buck and the bush pheasants, the white Arab bucking furiously, and Hugh's sedate Africander pony shying at every rustle in the trees.

At the end of the wood a great swell of downland lay before them. They gave the ponies their heads against the slope, and settled down for a long gallop. Soon the heat of the day had gone. A wind of their own creation sang in their ears, the scents of the moor, distilled by suns and dews, rose in waves to greet them, the horizon disappeared, and they saw only the misty fleeting of the ground beneath them. The ponies knew their country and never stumbled. Jumping little streams, plunging through tufts of fern, and scrambling cat-like among broken rocks, they never lost the same easy delicate motion. It was pure ecstasy, the very essence of physical well-being, and when after some two miles they stopped with lathered mounts and scarlet faces on the top of a long ridge of hill, they looked into each other's eyes in frank and cheerful comradeship.

Hugh jumped from the saddle and helped Lady Flora to dismount. "Let us sit down," he said, "and look at the view. We are on the backbone of the plateau. Musuru is 200 feet below us; and look! there is the lake quite clear."

He pointed where far to the west and deep down in the great trough shone a gleam of water.

The girl, still panting, looked where she was bidden and then closed her eyes.

"It is pure paradise," she said. "What have we done to deserve it? I have to pinch myself to remember we are not galloping on some Sussex down. What lies to the north?"

"Some hundreds of miles of unknown bush and then the foothills of Abyssinia."

"East I know. West there are the great lakes and the Mountains of the Moon and the Congo forest, I suppose. And south?"

"The plateau runs down for some hundreds of miles to German territory, and then you get into Nyasaland and the Shire Highlands, and in the end you come to the Zambesi."

"My imagination faints. Please, don't tell me any more. And we are here as pioneers, except for the Musuru colony. Savagery is on every side, and yet in half an hour's ride I can get back to my maid and a French chef and the latest English novel. It is too much, Mr Somerville; I am not worthy of it all."

They were sitting near the edge of one of the native tracks which intersect the moor. As Lady Flora spoke a party of natives on trek came along, blankets on shoulder, the men carrying spears and shields, and the women with babies slung on their backs. They saluted by raising their hands high above their heads, and Hugh acknowledged the greeting.

"They look like some of the northern tribes who have been down at the railway selling cattle. Their home is probably near Rudolf. There, if you like, is the romance of Empire. Here is a young lady in a blue habit riding after luncheon and exchanging courtesies with aborigines from the heart of Africa."

The girl rose to her feet and disentangled her reins. "Let us go on, please," she said. "I feel so full of life and adventure that I cannot sit still. Where shall we go? Let us visit Prester John and demand tea. I'm sure Melissinde must be charming, and I'm dying to make her acquaintance. Or shall we try Soria Moria Castle in the Mountains of the Moon? Nothing is impossible this afternoon. The names of the places are like tunes—Musuru, Ruwenzori!"

"What about the imperial poetry you parodied this morning?"

"I recant, please, at once and for ever. The worst geographical verses are full of poetry, and I shall spend the rest of my life writing them. The ponies are rested, and we can have another gallop along the ridge."

A couple of miles off was a small kopje crowned with a few trees. To this they raced, and the girl was an easy victor. For, coming suddenly upon a narrow rocky watercourse, she took it flying, while Hugh's more sober pony insisted on scrambling down and up the banks. At the kopje the plateau was cut into by a long glen running up from the west, and they looked down from their eminence on steep bush-clad sides ending below in a dark evergreen forest. A soft purple haze hung over the depths, and from far down came the music of a waterfall.

For a little Lady Flora was silent with delight. She made a charming picture as she reined up her Arab on the edge of the slope, the sunlight in her hair, while with one hand she shaded her eyes and looked out to the horizon.

"I never realised before what space meant. Of course I have been up mountains, and I once camped in the desert for a week, and I've been several times on the high seas, but I seemed always to carry my own atmosphere with me. But here everything indoors and commonplace and conventional is a million miles behind. I suppose I am the first woman who has ever been here, and I feel as if the place had been created for me and had been waiting for me since the beginning of time. What an egoist I am!"

On these uplands in mid-winter the dark comes swiftly, and already the sun was going down behind the far hills in a riot of crimson and amethyst. The heat had gone, and a chilly freshness was creeping into the air.

"We must be making for home," said Hugh. "Let us canter back gently, for an East African twilight is not a thing to hurry through. So you are getting the sense of space into your blood! Well, that is Imperialism, you know, or at least the foundations of it. We all get stuffy sitting tight in our old creeds. We live, most of us, in gardens which are very pleasant and well-watered, but sleepy and not overwholesome. And we grow old and stale before our time—the old age of decay, not the honest old age of being worn down with the friction of life."

"But how hard it is for a woman to avoid it! Men have such a wide world compared with ours. Our business is only to adapt ourselves to things as they are. Men can mould them as they please, and if they find the shades of the prison-house closing on them, they can put their packs on their shoulders and shake the dust of civilisation off their feet. How I envy you all!"

"That is one way, but not the best way. A man can always run off, but the best of them won't. Their business is to try and shape things according to a better plan. Our lives are like a lot of separate circles scattered about in space. Sometimes they are cut by others and then we have friends, and talk of this man or woman 'coming into our lives.' I have heard you use that phrase at least a dozen times since I came here. Now and then one circle largely overlaps another, and then people are in love. Once in a blue moon, perhaps, two circles almost coincide. And then you have what is commonly known as a happy marriage. But the circles always remain the same size, so for restless souls love and marriage and even friendship are no solution, as you very wisely observed yesterday. And it is no remedy to remove the circle from London to Polynesia or the Klondyke, for you do not make it any bigger by changing its site. The only thing to do is to draw a larger circle with a wider radius. Only," said Hugh sadly, "those who do that often fail to complete it, and leave only a broken arc to show how vast their design was."

"I like that metaphor," said the girl musingly. "Of course it is quite true that you do not get any nearer satisfaction by shifting your dwelling. But how hard it is for *us* to stretch the compasses and describe a wider circle."

"It is getting easier every day. Our great-aunts had a code of rules laid down for them which nothing could break through. They left the schoolroom for a year or two of sentiment and gaiety, and then married and became good housewives; or perhaps they didn't, and steered a precarious course on the high seas of scandal. Our grandfathers thought that the only choice lay between Amelia Sedley and Becky Sharp. They had not discovered Diana Warwick."

The sun had gone down, and a soft mulberry afterglow filled the western heavens. The ponies stepped sedately over the rough veld, till the woods rose black in the twilight, and they entered the long ride which led to the house.

"I think," said Lady Flora, "that our circles are being widened for us. I know that in the last three days mine has expanded so far that London is only a little patch in a corner. I suppose you would say that we women are citizens now and not shepherdesses in porcelain."

"Yes, that is a part of the truth. I was in Paris at Whitsuntide, and went to see Père Antoine. He is very old and blind, but he talks wonderfully, and his mind gets clearer with age. He said that the chief fact of the modern world is that humanity is drawing closer together. The State is taking the place of the old Church, and politics are acquiring a new meaning. Classes and ranks are being broken down, and men are beginning to find not only their duty but their happiness in community. They feel and think corporately, and not as atoms. It is something like this which the whole string of 'isms from Comtism to Marxism has been trying to expound. A political creed was once a list of dogmas which meant nothing to the ordinary man or woman. Now every creed—ours as well as others—must spread its roots into all the interests and affections and aspirations of our life. Another saying of his impressed me a good deal. He declared that the worst modern vice was 'spirituality,' and that the most crying need was that the world should awake to the value of its great temporal heritage—'*nôtre grand heritage temporel!*' That means much from a man who all his life has preached a mystical religion."

The hall-door appeared before them with a glow of firelight shining into the chilly night. A groom led away the ponies, and soon the riders were warming cold hands at the hearth.

Lady Flora called Heaven to witness her enjoyment of the afternoon. "And how serious we grew! I suppose it was the twilight, which always makes me sad and sentimental. After tea let us go and find Colonel Alastair and Sir Edward, and play games on the billiard-table. I think we both want a bear-fight to bring us out of the clouds."

The library at Musuru was a long room, panelled in some dark sweet-smelling wood, with the bookcases sunk in the walls. As with Gibbon's

Emperor Gordian, so with Carey: sixty-two thousand volumes attested the variety of his inclinations. It was a working-room, as the maps and papers piled on the desks bore witness, and its strenuous air was increased by the absence of any ornaments or pictures. But it was also a pleasant place for talk, for the shaded light gleamed cheerfully on vellum and morocco, and the low chairs round the great fireplace invited to comfort and conversation. The Duchess's headache continued, and her niece had gone to sit with her. The rest of the party disposed themselves about the hearth in a circle, while their host stood as usual planted squarely on the hearthrug.

"Our conclusion last night," Lord Appin began, "was that Imperialism cut across parties and demanded a revision of all traditional dogmas in face of a new body of fact. This, of course, does not mean any breach in our historical continuity. We have a vast deal to learn from all the traditional creeds; only they must be re-thought, as it were, and presented in a new system and a new language. This process, we also agreed, involved a change in our attitude of mind—indeed this change, if I remember aright, we defined as the essence of Imperialism. Instead of being negative, temporising, and unscientific, we must show ourselves positive and constructive. We have now to work out some of the details of our creed, so far as they are clear, and like philosophers we begin with the widest category. Our host commands us to-night to consider the question of the constitutional apparatus, the machinery of imperial union."

Lord Appin, as if aware of the gravity of the undertaking, selected a large cigar from his case and carefully lit it.

"First let us repeat all the platitudes," he continued, "and get done with them. The pivot of the Empire is the Crown. In the last resort all our units, colonies and dependencies alike, submit to the sovereign executive power. We have also, roughly speaking, one law, for though I believe—Mr Wakefield will correct me if I am wrong—that at least five great legal systems and many smaller codes exist within the Empire, yet we have one ultimate tribunal of appeal, and therefore some continuity of interpretation. As I remember once hearing Mr Wakefield say, 'To have the power of construing colonial laws and customs is to have the power to guide and restrain, to have, in effect, control of development.' Now these two common possessions are a stupendous machinery of union, if properly directed. The trouble is the modes in which the sovereign authority is exercised. Its functions have been in practice delegated to the British Cabinet, and therefore, indirectly, to the British Parliament. Now clearly such Cabinet and Parliament must have two aspects—a national one, for the British Isles, and an imperial one, in which they control the Empire. But with the grant of self-government to so many colonies there can be no direct control, and so the doctrine of trusteeship has been brought into being. I think it historically correct, and it has the further merit of exactly covering the existing practice. A government rules England and the dependencies directly, but as regards the autonomous colonies it acts as a trustee for their welfare—that is to say, it provides for their defence, and reserves the right in the last resort to veto any of their legislative acts which it thinks dangerous to the Empire as a whole. This might be a perfectly satisfactory arrangement if our Cabinets or Parliaments were not human, and the magnitude and number of imperial questions were not beyond their power. A Parliament confronted with a great quantity of local problems can only give a perfunctory attention to most imperial matters, and in any case cannot hope to make itself sufficiently well informed on them to give its decisions much weight. Hence we get dissatisfaction on both sides. A Canadian who attends the debates in the House of Commons may wait for days before one imperial consideration emerges, and may see the Government which controls his destinies turned out of office on some business of English education. And the Englishman may justly complain that his own affairs are scamped because the men who were elected to look after them have to give their time to some Indian frontier question. The Home reformer and the Imperialist alike tend to grumble against a doctrine which seems to impose upon certain old-fashioned machinery a task too heavy for its performance. Have I stated the difficulty correctly, Mr Wakefield?"

The gentleman appealed to nodded his approval, and Lord Appin continued—

"We have to try and find some way out of the difficulty. I shall leave that to others who have made the subject their own. But I have one word of caution to give. Before dinner I looked into Bismarck's Memoirs, and I was much struck by certain sayings of his which Busch reports. He had to face the problem of finding some constitutional machinery for the new German Empire. There were plenty of legalists around him to prepare formally perfect schemes. But Bismarck most wisely counselled patience. 'Let us take,' he said, 'what we can get, what the States are freely willing to give us. As long as we have the impulse to unity in the soul of our people, almost any scheme will work. But if we once begin to squabble about details and impose a cast-iron constitution no scheme on earth will work. We cannot coerce the national life into narrow channels, but if we foster that life it will make in time the proper channels for itself!' There, to my mind, spoke the true creative statesman."

Lord Launceston, whom the company seemed to expect to take up the tale, straightened himself from the depths of a long chair, where he had been studying the fire, and looked deprecatingly towards the last speaker.

"Are we not rather putting the cart before the horse?" he inquired mildly. "Yesterday we agreed upon the meaning of our attitude—a frank recognition of new conditions. But that is merely a formal definition, and we want to know the nature of the spiritual change and the new principles which are born from it. And now you suddenly ask me to consider a piece of practical detail, and minute detail at that—the kind of constitution we propose for our State. Is not that a little premature?"

"There are two reasons for the arrangement," said Carey. "One is that it seems wise to sketch the ground-plan of our new republic tentatively, since that is only another way of looking at the data which must be our basis. When we see what we have to work with, we can go on to deal with principles. The second is that Wakefield is so notoriously intolerant of metaphysics, or anything approaching them, that we thought it wise to go gently with him and burn a little incense before his shrine in the shape of practical details."

Lord Launceston acquiesced, and continued—"I have had the ideal of federation before me ever since I began to be interested in politics, and I suppose I have read of or discussed almost every scheme that has been propounded. I own I am not very enthusiastic about any. They all begin with what Bismarck reprobated, asking too much. The chief—the scheme of legislative federation—need not detain us. Its principle is home rule for each unit and a central imperial legislature to govern and make laws for the Empire. It is an ideal fit enough for a small and compact empire, but to one so immense and scattered as ours, it is for the present, at any rate, wholly inapplicable. I do not dogmatise on what the future may bring forth. Distances have shrunk since our great-grandfathers' time, and we are nearer to Toronto and Cape Town than they were to Rome, but the difficulties of space and time are as yet insurmountable. I have other objections to legislative federation besides its impracticability. I question if it is the most suitable ideal for an empire which contains on the one hand self-governing colonies, and on the other dependencies where autonomy is eternally impossible. The Tropics will always be a bar to a type of union which belongs essentially to white men and the Temperate zones. Again, it means the creation of a new representative body, and in face of the growing impotence of representative assemblies constructed on the old lines, I doubt if it would be wise to experiment with another. Besides, in all the units of a federation there must be a fairly uniform development. All must have attained to a certain height of self-conscious national life, so that they can enter the federation on equal terms. But can we maintain that such uniformity exists with Britain at one end of the scale and, shall we say,

South Africa at the other? Lastly, unity must precede union. There must be imperial solidarity in fact before it receives formal recognition. The Empire is a living growth, and any forms we impose upon it must correspond to its living movement; otherwise, instead of chain-mail we shall have a strait-waistcoat. Any rigid scheme of federation applied prematurely will either be inoperative, and so bring the ideal into discredit, or it will curb and choke the life and produce monstrosity instead of growth."

"For the time being," continued Lord Launceston, "I do not see either the feasibility or the merits of federation in the common sense. Our conditions are not the conditions on which the ordinary federation is constructed. But," he added cheerfully, "there is no reason why we should not develop a type of our own to meet our special requirements. There is no need to cumber ourselves with the irrelevant precedents of other empires. Let us make the most of the elements of consolidation we possess. Our primary merit is our elasticity. Our ideal is that of Virgil:—

'*Non ego, nec Teucris Italos parere jubebo,*
Nec mihi regna peto: paribus se legibus ambae
Invictae gentes aeterna in foedera mittant.'[3]

We have our free nations and our protected states, and in them all the one bond of union is the ultimate executive power. Any attempt at federation must proceed, therefore, on the executive side. The legislative side may be left cheerfully to the care of the 'trustee' doctrine, as Lord Appin has called it. But since we have services common to the whole Empire, expert knowledge is demanded, and we must have some machinery for calling to our assistance the practical wisdom of all our component States. We want, that is, a Council, and if you must have an epithet, I should prefer Imperial to Federal I have considered in my day many proposals for such a Council, and I cannot say that I have yet made up my mind on any one of them. That, however, is not important. We are not now drafting the Act to establish such a body. If we are agreed upon the principle, it does not pass the wit of man to devise the details. I have no doubt that Mr Wakefield is ready with some admirable device."

Mr Wakefield was about to speak when he was forestalled by Lord Appin, who murmured dreamily—"What a conception! An Imperial Round Table to which colonial statesmen should flit like halcyons over the waters!"

These words did not please Mr Wakefield. "I fail to see the suggestion of comedy," he said warmly.

"Comedy?" said Lord Appin soothingly. "I should not dare to hint at it. But you will have a considerable intellectual admixture. Our own

Parliaments contain a confusion of types, but we have never before ransacked the globe for variety."

Mr Wakefield was only half appeased, and began in a slightly aggrieved voice—

"The chief fact we have to reckon with," he said, "is colonial nationalism. All the self-governing colonies look upon themselves as nations—new national types with a specific national future. They began life under different conditions from England, and brought to their new lands only a light baggage of English traditions. Those new lands are themselves a great moulding force as regards national character. The boy who grows up in the backwoods and the boy who goes the conventional round of Eton and Oxford will become different men, though they may be the sons of the same father. A colony begins with a struggle for bare life, scarcely conscious of her own existence, only of her needs. And then success comes, and more success, and one morning she wakes to find that she has become a nation and can call the older people cousins. She has no standard of comparison, and begins by being extremely self-confident and bumptious. Take a young man and plant him with a wife in the wilds and tell him to make a home. So soon as he has done it he will begin to brag, and the harder the struggle the finer the fellow he will think himself. For, mind you, it is all his own—he owes little or nothing to borrowed capital,—so he writes 'Alone I did it' above his shanty, and looks down his nose at Creation. We call him a braggart, but we are wrong, for he is something subtler than that. He is a child, supremely ignorant, supremely courageous, crowing over his first triumph. And as it is with the individual, so with the people. As soon as they can straighten their backs and look around, and see a very good and entirely new earth, they pronounce the benediction of the Almighty in Eden, and swagger outrageously. Everything they have is the finest in the world, and they themselves are the last word in human perfection.

"Well, that is all natural and proper, for it is only a stage, and does not last. The man finds himself prosperous, but fragments of his early recollections come back to him, and he begins to want to know something about his forebears. He used to plume himself on his isolation: now he wants to be related to somebody. He suspects that he is badly educated, and he tries to correct his deficiencies. By-and-by a tremendous fit of humility seizes him. He has made an estate for himself and his children, but he wants some of the graces of life. He sends his boys to European schools, or he hunts up his kin in the old country, or he imports old furniture and pictures for the decoration of his new house. It is the second stage—when he begins to recognise that he cannot isolate himself, that he is bound by ties of kinship and race and inherited culture to a larger world. Once again what happens with the individual happens with the colony. She has attained to a fuller self-consciousness, and is aware not only of her merits but of her defects. On one side, therefore, she is conspicuously humble. She wants to learn all the wisdom of the ages that the old world can teach, but when she has learned a little she will brag once more, and say that she discovered it for herself, and then she will be humble again and want to learn further. On the whole she will show, if considerately treated, a real intellectual docility. But remember, she will never abate one jot of her national pride. The colonist, who is eager to get the best that England can give him, and will sit at the feet of teachers, is yet perfectly certain at the back of his head that he is a monstrously fine fellow, in no way inferior to any man whose advice he asks and takes. This pride rubs off a little with experience, but at first it is raw and nervous, and terribly quick to take offence. It is in her early stages that a colony is most difficult. When she becomes perfectly sure of her foundations and looks around the world with calmer eyes, she is no longer so intolerant of criticism and eager to scent out insult.

"Colonial nationalism is built up on the basis of this temperament. The chief element in it is pride of achievement and a readiness to fight the world to compel acknowledgment. It may be a little irritating at times, but the statesman will view it approvingly, for it is the spirit which makes a strong people. It will accept advice, but never dictation. At all costs it demands the right to work out salvation on its own lines."

Mr Wakefield paused to relight his cigar, which had gone out in the process of his argument.

"If there were no other elements," he resumed, "then we might say good-bye to any thought of a United Empire. But, joined with this local pride, is the feeling I have already described, a sentimental attachment to the parent race, an eager desire to acquire those other elements of civilisation which their new land cannot give them. In a sense, therefore, this national pride becomes the chief incentive to union. They admit themselves second to no other people, but, when they look round, their practical good sense tells them that, as isolated nations, they are separated by centuries of development from the greater Powers of the world. They can only realise their ambition by the assistance of the other branches of their race. They wish for union, because it involves no sacrifice of pride. They believe, rightly or wrongly, that they can give as well as receive. If they have less wealth, they can show a high level of sterling manhood. If they have a smaller weight of political thought behind them, they are free from the less worthy accretions of tradition. The contact with mother earth, the struggle with nature in her wilder moods in a land of sunshine and winds and great spaces where man can breathe—surely it all must enable them to think freshly and clearly, and to recognise some of the simple and eternal truths which are clouded over in a more sophisticated life."

"That," said Lord Launceston, "I am very ready to admit."

"Good. Well, then, any scheme of union must reckon with this nationalism. It is on the constitutional side that it is most jealous, for to a free colony her constitution is a kind of visible sign of her independence, the very Ark of her Covenant. You must, therefore, devise some scheme which leaves their autonomy for the moment intact, for any change must come as a concession from them and not as a mandate from England. I look forward to the day when the Colonies of their own accord will surrender to the central executive many matters which are now in their complete discretion. But that executive must contain their own members, and the reform must be mooted by some body representative of the whole Empire.

"And now I come to the practical question of methods. We want a Council, which shall involve no harsh break with our present policy, and shall also do no violence to colonial nationalism. Remember what our aim is. We have an alliance—for that is the real relationship—and we want to make this alliance closer and more organic, and to devise bonds which shall be enduring and yet elastic, expanding with the growth of our corporate life. Now a mere advisory council is good, but it is not enough. It is the form suitable to an alliance, but we want something more. Our Council should therefore be given certain executive functions. Faithful to our principle of making use of existing machinery, we might begin with the Cabinet. Why should not the King on the executive side sit in imperial as well as in national session? The Cabinet at its normal meetings might deal with the affairs of the British Islands; but in imperial session it would deal with questions common to the Empire—the army and navy, foreign affairs, commercial treaties, the conflict of laws, currency, postage, shipping, naturalisation,—there is no end to the list. At present the British Defence Committee has power to summon Colonial representatives to its deliberations. Carry the practice one step further. Give the Cabinet the same power, and let Colonial privy councillors sit in its special session, not merely as advisers but as members of the executive, and you have the nucleus of a true Imperial Council."

"It is a nucleus, certainly," said Hugh, "but if the point about our nucleus is its indefinite capacity for expansion, you have omitted one vital provision. How are your Colonial representatives to be chosen? If, as at present, they are only summoned by the King on the advice of the British Cabinet, that Cabinet will remain the sole real executive."

Mr Wakefield smiled indulgently. "You have raised the very point I was coming to. The Colonial members must be representative, otherwise they can claim no mandate from their people. I propose to extend the principle of the triennial conferences of Premiers. Why should not they take place more often,—say every second year,—without any great inconvenience. The Premiers would be Cabinet Ministers ad hoc, and would attend the Cabinet in its imperial session. Few of the greater imperial questions are so urgent as not to be able to wait for such sessions, certainly not the great questions of policy. The Imperial Cabinet would have power to vote money, the Colonial representatives voting according to the proportion of Colonial contributions. As the Colonies grow to their full stature and assume more of the imperial burdens, these contributions will become larger, and their power of control proportionately greater. The Premiers would have a mandate in a true sense from their colonies, for the subjects discussed in the Cabinet would already have been discussed in their own parliaments, and might even have been at issue in the previous elections. In time Colonial officials would be appointed to the great executive posts in the Empire, and we should attain to the only practical form of imperial federation—one central and representative imperial executive. I would also suggest, as a supplement, a permanent committee of the Privy Council, with advisory functions, to discuss imperial questions between the sittings of the executive, and a permanent Imperial Intelligence Department to keep in touch with any new developments. Such is a rough outline of a scheme which seems to me both possible and desirable. It may be amended in detail, but I think it is right in its main lines."

"I would like to ask one question," said Mr Astbury. "To what representative body would your Imperial Cabinet be accountable?"

"In the first instance to the British Parliament, though the Colonial representatives would of course be accountable to their own parliaments also. If at some future time there should come any form of imperial legislature, then the Cabinet would naturally account to it."

Lady Warcliff had hitherto borne small share in the discussions. Her extreme mental energy was accustomed to take the form of restless organisation rather than the speculations of debate. Since her arrival at Musuru she had been busy investigating every detail of the management of that immense household, and had all but driven the Scotch major-domo into lunacy. She had mastered, too, the principles of the agricultural settlement, and was engaged in the somewhat hopeless task of convicting Mr Lowenstein of error in certain financial methods he had employed in his philanthropy. She had sat through the previous discussions with half-closed eyes and an air of elegant isolation. Now her preoccupation with other things seemed at an end, for she took up Mr Wakefield's parable with a surprising vivacity.

"I quite see the merits of your scheme, but you will permit me one criticism. An imperial executive, such as you propose, would no doubt do admirably all the work of the Empire which concerned the mother-country and the free Colonies. But what about the dependencies — India, Africa, and the Far East? I have always regarded them as in a special sense the domain of England, in which the Colonies had no manner of interest. Would they not, with their fetish of independence, resent the very existence of protectorates, or in any case give them a very perfunctory attention?"

"Your objection, my lady," said Mr Wakefield, "springs from a misunderstanding of democracy, and especially colonial democracy. If the people are ever to rule they must learn to trust their servants. At present, I grant you, they are apt to be childishly suspicious of the proconsul. But that suspicion is no true democratic product. The only justification of democracy, as Lord Launceston said yesterday, is that it clears the way for superiority. Until it is realised that its mandate, once given, carries with it complete confidence it will never be a governing creed. And this is beginning to be realised. It is the labour leader who is the best disciplinarian, and the demagogue who is given the most rope. Besides, our democracy in the Colonies is a very curious thing, and I look to it to counteract the vices of the home-grown variety. It advocates conscription and colonial navies, and it is inspired throughout with national pride. If it had its own people sharing in the government of India or Egypt, do you suppose it would talk about 'satraps' and 'prancing proconsuls'? It would think of the protectorates as God-given trusts and fields for the vitality of our race to exercise itself in. Remember, our democracy is a white man's democracy, and we are not moved by any foolish Rousseauism about the rights of man. It is otherwise, I know, in England. When I was there this summer I made it my business to see people of all shades of opinion. At a meeting in the Queen's Hall I heard Mr Corley-Pratt declare that India was an incubus, a wen, a lifeless weight, a stain upon the conscience of the British people, and everything else that could be metaphorically mixed. I read a protest by some University professors against the annexation of Situnga, on the ground that to keep a people in political tutelage was to be guilty of slavery. I found many good men who still clung to the Gladstonian view that any rising of fanatics was an effort of a people 'rightly struggling to be free.' These gentlemen would have all the possessions of England redistributed by some International Labour Congress. I tell you that such infernal nonsense would not be tolerated in the Colonies for one instant, and the man who talked it would be lynched. No, madame; we have our race pride, and any insult to it by professor or politician is hotly resented. Our democracy is the creed of men and not of sentimentalists."

Lord Launceston had listened a little anxiously to Mr Wakefield's closing words.

"I grant its merits, but it has its dangers too. A high-handed Bismarckianism is as much a risk to the well-being of our dependencies as any academic cult of the rights of man. But I agree with you that democracy will find in itself a cure for its weaknesses, and that it will not endanger those great realms we hold in trust for races who are unfit to struggle singlehanded in the arena of the world. In these questions I am what you call a 'mugwump.' I lay down no canon, and only ask that our grave responsibility be recognised, and that each problem as it arises be determined on the facts, illumined by reason and conscience. But to return to your Council, with which I am wholly in sympathy. I think that on the whole your account of Colonial feeling is just. There is no doubt about the reality of the impulse towards union. At present our machinery is adequate, but it will not always remain so, and what is right in an alliance will be futile in a more intimate relation. We must recognise this tendency and prepare for change; very cautiously at first, for we are dealing with *life*, remember, and no dead matter which can be coerced into any mould we please. The reform, we are agreed, must begin on the executive side. We have our Empire, and it is right that its common services should be administered as efficiently as possible. There we are on solid ground. As I have said, on the question of legislative federation I am very doubtful. I am not at all certain whether the world is not passing away from the doctrine that legislation should proceed only from a representative body. So certain German legalists think, and there is a good deal to be said for the view. But at any rate we can neglect that question for the moment, and trust to time to bring its own solution. But the other is a question for the present. There is no need for haste, but a beginning must be made, and the ground prepared for development. It is well to begin early to lay down the lines of the vessel into which we are to change, for if we wait till our present ship goes to pieces we may find ourselves in the water. You cannot improvise an army in the hour of need, and it is no easier to improvise a constitution."

Mr Wakefield had lit another large cigar, and, pleased with the ready acceptance of his views, turned a cheerful face to the company.

"There must be no *undue* haste, but we should not waste time. As you know, I strongly believe that the moment has come for a reform of imperial tariffs so as to create a system of preference within the Empire. If we delay, the Colonies will make separate treaties with other countries, and where the treasure is there will the heart be also. Further, certain industries which might yet be preserved to us will pass to other hands, killed in British hands by protected rivals abroad. I will not argue the matter, for our host, who does not agree with me, has vetoed the subject as foreign to the purpose of our conference. But my point is that the thing can only be settled by some representative Imperial Council—not a mere conference of Premiers, but a Council with a mandate from the whole Empire to consider and decide the question, and with all the material for decision at its call. Moreover, it could only be worked in practice by an imperial executive. I agree with our opponents to this extent, that without some such machinery it would be madness to elaborate any preferential system. Take again the business of defence, on which Colonel Graham may have something to say."

Graham, who was still suffering from the drowsiness begotten of hours unwontedly late, hastily collected his wits, and asked for the question to be repeated.

"It is a matter I have thought a good deal about, and I have bombarded the War Office with my schemes. Generally speaking, I want to affiliate colonial levies to the regular army for training purposes, and also for mobilisation in time of war. The last war showed that we fought as an Empire, but the difficulty is to organise all our splendid fighting strength so as to give it the maximum of force in a crisis. I will not trouble you with any of my schemes, which are long and intricate. But the rock we shipwreck on is the question of colonial contributions, and this obstacle will remain until we get some kind of joint executive. We cannot get the Colonies to put their men under our control unless they have a share in that control, and no one blames them for the feeling. They want to run their own show themselves, but they would be perfectly content to be affiliated with us if they had a say in the management. The same thing appears in the contributions to the navy. No colony likes to vote a sum and have no voice in expending it. It is the old question of taxation without representation. A common executive would get us over the difficulty, for then it would be the whole Empire which asked for men and money and directed the use of both."

Lady Flora had slipped silently into the room and perched herself upon an arm of Marjory Haystoun's chair. She looked a little bored with the discussion, and was preparing to depart again when the stern eye of Mr Wakefield arrested her. Apparently addressing his words to her, though in reality unconscious of her presence, he declared that Colonel Graham had spoken excellent good sense.

"Our main obstacle after all is the insularity of England. The Colonies are insular too, but that does not matter, for it is with England that the motive power still lies, and from her must come the chief impetus. At this moment London is the centre of gravity for the Empire, perhaps for the world. But how long will that continue? England owes her predominance mainly to two facts. First, she has been outside the arena of European strife, and has not been for centuries the cockpit of wars. Her development, political and economic, has been allowed to proceed unchecked. Again, by the gift of Heaven, she was the fortunate possessor of certain means of production, such as coal and iron, and was able to get a long lead in the industrial movement. But how long will all this continue? Already her lead is shortening. In time her coal and iron supplies will decline. She owes her large population mainly to her industrial pre-eminence, and the loss of it will mean starvation and bankruptcy. She cannot hope to compete with countries which feed themselves and are self-contained towards the world. But where she fails as an island, she may succeed as an empire, for the Empire has within its bounds every ingredient of national wealth which other peoples can show. In time to come the centre of gravity will change according to natural economic laws. If electricity should replace coal as the motive force of the future, a country such as Canada, with her immense water-power, will be far better endowed by nature than England. Or some undreamed-of force may be discovered by science which will make some other colony the predominant industrial partner. Further, manufacturers will in the long-run migrate to the site of the raw material, and Birmingham and Lancashire will not always keep their prerogative. At present, again, London, from her position and her vast accumulated wealth, is the financial centre of the globe. But every European nation is turning her eyes to the development of her outlying possessions; and, moreover, we have Japan and the United States, and in the near future China, to carry that centre out of Europe. I can foresee the day when Sydney or Vancouver will be far more eligibly situated than London for transacting the business of the world. Well, if all this will happen some time or other, surely it is wise to make early provision that it shall happen smoothly and comfortably. If you can arrange that industries shall have the chance of transference on natural lines throughout the Empire, and that population shall follow them, you have no need to fear any economic *débâcle*. At present you have forty millions of people to our ten, but what will be the proportion in a hundred years' time? We must provide for some elasticity in our interests, and this can only be secured by thinking of the Empire not as England plus a number of poor relations, but as one organic whole, whose centre is to be determined by the evidence of time. This is no new doctrine. Adam Smith, who will not be suspected of wild-cat dogmas, preached it as the logical corollary to any policy of colonisation. In the early centuries of the Christian era the great Councils of the Church were held, now in Spain, now on the shores of the Bosphorus; and such mobility, which is the fruit of true cohesion, must be the ideal of our Empire if it is to survive. We are connected at present, but it is to the interest of us all, and especially of England, to be more closely related if we are to be secure against the future. Insularism must cease to dominate British policy, and be left only to the obscurantists and reactionaries. Such constitutional union as I propose is only a small and formal beginning, but it will make broad the path for the true spiritual change."

"Imperialism, then," said Lord Appin, "is to be defined from the English point of view as a kind of national old age pensions scheme?"

But Mr Wakefield, having had his say, and having secured, as he believed, the assent of his audience, was not to be disturbed by any epigram.

"I accept the definition gladly," he said. "That is Imperialism on the business side. The other sides—and I grant you they are many—I leave to people more competent to deal with them."

Carey walked to one of the shelves and took down a book.

"Do you remember," he said, "a passage in which John Davis, the Elizabethan seaman, held out a prospect for his countrymen? I fear he was actually talking of the North Pole, where his dreams have not been realised; but we can apply his words to the ideal of a united empire:—

"'How blessed may we think this nation to be, for they are in perpetual light, and never know what darkness meaneth, by the benefit of twilight and full moons, as the learned in astronomy do very well know; which people, if they have the notice of their eternity by the comfortable light of the Gospels, then are they blessed, and of all nations most blessed. Why then do we neglect the search of this excellent discovery, against which there can be nothing said to hinder the same? Why do we refuse to see the dignity of God's creation, since it hath pleased the Divine Majesty to place us the nearest neighbour thereunto? I know there is no true Englishman that can in conscience refuse to be a contributor to procure this so great a happiness to his country, whereby not only the prince and mighty men of the land shall be highly renowned, but also the merchants, tradesmen, and artificers mightily enriched.'

"You see what an old creed ours is, and how catholic in its application. You will find cover under these words, Wakefield, for your practicality, and Marjory for her transcendentalism, and Teddy for his romance. I think we may close our discussion for the evening with John Davis, who makes a good tail- piece. For the next two days we shall let the matter rest, for some of us are going hunting. On the evening of the day after to-morrow I propose that we take up another question of detail, and a very practical one—our tropical possessions."

Considine rose and marched resolutely from the room. "If you and Alastair," he said to Hugh, "expect to be ready at four to-morrow morning, you had better get to bed."

Lady Flora looked at him with stern disapproval. "Am I to be allowed to come?" she asked.

"My dear child!" said Mrs Yorke. "They are going after lions! Besides, what about the conventions?"

The girl shook an impatient head. "You have broken our compact at the very beginning," she whispered to Hugh. "If I were not such a Christian and such a lady, I should be seriously annoyed. But you are quite wrong if you think that you'll have any adventures as good as I shall have here. I am going straight off into the wilds on the white pony to make friends with Prester John."

CHAPTER 5

THE stars, which had been shining with a frosty brilliance, were paling towards dawn before Hugh was sufficiently awake to see where he was going. He had been routed out by Alastair Graham in the small hours, and had somehow found himself on a horse, in a great blanket-coat, with half-a-dozen dusky figures trotting alongside. He had been jogging on for half an hour before he finally rubbed sleep out of his eyes, and, drinking long draughts of the electric air, roused himself to some interest in life. The sky was changing from black to some ineffable shade of purple, and the track among the mimosa thorns was beginning to glimmer ahead in a fantastic grey. Soon remoter objects distinguished themselves—a kopje, a big tree, a jag of rock. And then over the crest of the far downs came a red arc of fire, and the heavens changed to amethyst and saffron, and, last of all, to a delicate pale blue, where wisps of rosy cloud hung like the veils of the morning. They were near the western edge of the escarpment, and, looking down into the trough, Hugh saw over the great sea of mist the blue fingers of far mountains rising clear and thin into the sky. The air was bitter cold, and the cheeks tingled with the light wind which attends the dawn. Lines of Theocritus—the *alektor kokkuzon napkaisi* of the Seventh Idyll—ran in Hugh's mind from his reading of yesterday. He realised that his senses had become phenomenally acute. His eyes seemed to see farther, his ears to mark the least sound in the bush, while the scents of the morning came to his nostrils with a startling freshness. Pungent, clean, yet with an indescribable tropic softness in it, was the air of the desert, which he sniffed like the Scriptural wild ass. He looked round at his companions. Graham, a burly figure in a sheepskin coat, rode somewhat in the manner in which Napoleon is painted as retreating from Moscow, sitting squarely in the saddle with a meditative chin on his breast. Considine's long lean figure on a blue roan seemed wholly in keeping with the landscape. He wore an old khaki suit and a broad-brimmed felt hat, and sat his horse as loosely as a Boer. He leaned forward, peering keenly about him, whistling some catch of song. In civilised places he looked the ordinary far-travelled sportsman, a little browner and tougher, perhaps, than most. But the Considine of the Turf Club and the Considine of the veld were different beings. The bright eyes, set deep in the dark face, and the sinewy strength of his pose gave him the air of some Elizabethan who had sailed strange seas to a far country. To Hugh at the moment he seemed the primal type of the adventurer.

Soon the travellers were greeted by the most comforting of all the scents of the wilds—the smell of a wood fire, and the faint odour of roasting coffee. Their boys had made their breakfast-camp in the crook of a little stream, where the forest ended and the long downs of the northern plateau began. In a few minutes Hugh was sitting luxuriously on a pile of rugs, drinking excellent coffee out of a tin mug. The Trappist silence of the early ride was over.

"You'll get none of the luxury of Musuru here, my boy," Considine said. "We are going to have the same fare as Alastair and I enjoyed a week ago—tinned stuff and what we kill. You've hunted yourself, and know that to eat potted meat with your fingers out of a tin after a hard day is better than a dinner at the Ritz. Akhub," he cried, "what about the beats?"

The chief shikari—Zanzibar! Arab, ex-slave-trader, and heaven knows what besides—bowed gravely, and informed his master that he had arranged for Graham to go due east into the down country, where buck and rhino were plentiful; Considine should keep on to the north, where he had a better chance of a good eland head; while Hugh was to remain on the edge of the escarpment, where lay the best chance of lion.

Considine nodded. "You'll want your Mannlicher for buck," he said to Hugh, "and your '400 cordite express. For pity's sake don't go into the bush after lion without the express. Akhub is going with you and will look after you. I want you to get a lion, but remember he is worth taking pains about, or he may get you. I've twice been clawed by them, and it's no sort of fun."

Breakfast over, the parties separated, and Hugh with the shikari and five boys set out along the rim of the plateau. A pleasurable excitement, with just a shade of trepidation in it, flavoured his morning pipe. He yearned to get a lion, but he had some nervousness lest he might show up badly in a tight place, having never before faced anything more dangerous than a sleepy Norwegian bear. He was a good shot enough in a Scotch deer-forest, but a situation where a miss meant not annoyance but mortal peril was new to his experience.

The cold morning changed to a hot noonday, and at two in the afternoon Hugh sat down to lunch, in a better frame of mind. He had got two hartebeests with fair heads, and in a marshy place a really fine waterbuck. His anxiety, he found, had not impaired his steadiness, and he was recovering his composure. He was still soft from civilised life and tormented by a thirst which several cups of hot tea barely assuaged. Lunch was perforce a short meal since he had to meet the others at a certain point which Akhub declared was three hours' riding ahead, and if he wished for more hunting there was no time to be lost.

The afternoon's trek was hot and dusty, and he had little sport. Green doves and a white-tailed hawk were the only signs of life in the bush, which seemed to lie torpid in a universal drowsiness. By-and-by they entered a timber tract, where large acacias and junipers made glades like an English park. It was drawing towards evening, and according to Akhub's calculations another half-hour would bring them into touch with the rest of the party. Hugh had almost abandoned the thought of sport, when a sudden cry of *'ngatun-yo* from the boys made him look down a tributary glade. He saw a great yellow beast, like an overgrown dog, go lolloping across into a thicket of trees, and with a beating heart he recognised that he was at last in the presence of a veritable lion.

Earlier in the day he had carefully planned out his conduct. He would quickly yet calmly take the express from the bearer, and circumspectly yet swiftly reconnoitre the ground for a shot. Alas for good resolutions! At the first sight of that tawny back Hugh was off in pursuit down the glade at full gallop, while an agitated boy waved the neglected weapon in his rear. He had his Mannlicher on his saddle-bow, and almost unconsciously he slipped in cartridges while his eyes searched the environs for a sign of his quarry.

Suddenly he saw him a hundred yards ahead trotting along a narrow native path. He was going slowly, unconscious apparently of the proximity of man. Hugh dismounted, hitched his well-broken horse to a tree, and sent a flying shot at the beast, which had the effect of making him halt for a second, look round, and then turn into the shade of the trees on the right. Hugh ran up to where he had entered, and a little nervously looked into the sparse bush. There was the lion well in range, so, kneeling down and aiming carefully, he fired. A shot from behind is never easy, and as it chanced the bullet went low and shattered the left hind leg. The beast stopped with a growl of pain, turned slowly round and looked at the intruder, lashing the low bushes with his tail.

The moment had come for a second shot, and Hugh got it in full on the chest, but a little too high for the heart. An express bullet would have stretched him out, but the little Mannlicher had no such power. The great beast roared in fury, caught sight of his enemy behind a tree-trunk, advanced a pace, and then gathered himself for a charge.

With a nervous hand Hugh had managed to slip in fresh cartridges, and as the lion moved he fired. It was a clean miss, and Hugh had a confused sense of something yellow and evil-smelling flying through the air as he leaped aside. Whether consciously or unconsciously, he had fired his second barrel, and the next he knew he was picking himself up, unhurt but shaken and blood-stained, from beneath a branch which the lion had broken, while the creature himself lay stone-dead a yard off. The last shot had by a miracle found the heart.

Hugh's first impulse was to make assurance sure by firing into the body, but a moment's inspection convinced him that there was no life left. Then his mood became one of insane jubilation. Alone and with the wrong rifle he had killed his lion. He felt three inches taller; he longed for Akhub, for Considine, for any one to come and see. And then a growl behind him made him turn his head, and he forgot his pride in abject terror. For there, about twelve yards off, was a second lion, bigger and darker in the mane, glaring at him wrathfully with his ugly jaws half-open.

His hand went to his cartridge-belt, only to find it empty. He felt his pockets, but not a cartridge remained. They had dropped out in the fall and lay some yards off beyond the dead beast.

Hugh did the only thing possible, and sprang for the nearest tree. He was not a moment too soon, for as his quaking body was swung up to the second branch something tore at his leg, and the next moment he was contemplating boot and gaiter ripped off at the back and a long scratch in the flesh. In the same second he seemed to hear a shot ring out—no ping of a Mannlicher, but the honest thunder of an express—and the long dark face of Akhub appeared in the glade.

It was a very chastened hunter who descended the tree to receive the congratulations and reproaches of the chief shikari. It was abundantly clear to him that he had done an unpardonable thing, and, but for the activity of his boys and the near neighbourhood of the tree, might have been stretched torn and dying beside his quarry. But the mood could not last. The exhilaration of a successful adventure came back to him. After all, he had walked up his lion with a small-bore and killed him unaided. With huge pleasure he now saw that his own animal was the finer and bigger of the two.

He lit a pipe and jogged on in the deepening twilight, his whole soul filled with the joy of conquest. This was life indeed, for, say what we may, there is no satisfaction so intense as victory over some one of the savage forces of nature. Better for the moment than vice-royalties or Garters or millions is the joy of making the first ascent of some hard peak, or sailing a boat home through a tempest, or seeing some wild animal fall before your own courage and skill. In that hour Hugh would not have changed places with Launceston or Carey.

Soon he came into the glow of a big fire. Lanterns were hanging from the boughs of a huge juniper, and beds were being got ready underneath. At little fires close by the boys were cooking supper.

The others welcomed him with a great shout. "Well, what luck?"

"Two lions," said Hugh, with studied modesty. "One mine and one Akhub's—and a few buck."

"Gad! you've had the cream of the day," said Considine. "I got nothing but a hartebeest. And Alastair never had a shot. How did you get your lion?"

Hugh told his story to a disapproving audience.

"You foolhardy young devil! Though, after all, I suppose I've done the same thing in my time. How's your leg?"

"A scratch. Only wants a simple dressing. I've learned my lesson all right, for I never was in such a blue funk in my life. You don't find me stalking lion with a Mannlicher again. For heaven's sake, old man, give me a drink."

Considine, following the bushveld ritual, doled out to each a small whisky-and-soda. "Keep that in mind, Hugh, when you next go on trek. After a long day you want a pick-me-up before you dine, or you can't eat; and if you can't eat you can't sleep, and if you can't sleep you get fever as sure as fate. Never touch the stuff in the daytime, and I'm against it at dinner, but as a pick-me-up there's nothing like it."

They sat down with tremendous appetites to that best of meals, a hunter's supper. There was tinned soup, which they drank out of mugs, curried guinea-fowl which Alastair had shot, venison-steaks stewed with onions, and a species of tinned plum-pudding which was the joy of Considine's heart. Coffee and peach brandy completed the courses, and then the three got into sleeping-bags, had more logs put on the fire, lit their pipes, and prepared for the slow talk which merges gradually in slumber.

Hugh snuggled into his kaross with a profound sense of comfort. He felt warm, satisfied, and indomitably cheerful. Never had his pipe seemed sweeter; never had he felt his mind more serene or his body more instinct with life. The wide glade was lit up by the fire, and the high branches made a kind of emerald canopy picked out with the golden points of stars. The boys were singing monotonous native songs around their bivouac, and through the wood came the eerie rustling of night winds. A zareba of thorns had been built round the camp, close to which the horses and mules stood patiently champing their fodder. The camp was a miniature city, with its fortifications and its watchmen, and Hugh felt himself in a new world—the hunter's civilisation, the oasis which he makes anew for himself each night in wilds which are careless of human life. For a moment his mind travelled back to Musuru, where at that hour delicately clad women would be sitting down to rich food amid flowers and silver and white linen. The contrast was so piquant that in the catholic mind it awoke the spirit of comedy.

"What are you cackling at, Hugh?" Considine asked. "Fling me your tobacco- pouch like a good chap, for mine's empty. Lord! how often I've lain like this and smoked and looked up at the sky. And how many good fellows have done the same and are at it still! It's all very well for Wakefield and the rest to theorise about Empire. I daresay it is logical and scientific enough. But you can't get the feeling of all it means till you've got very close to the bones of the old Earth, and heard her muttering to herself, and realised what a tough old fiend she is and what a job it is to get even with her."

"*Si jeunesse savait!*" said Hugh. "That's the tragedy of life—that the men who do the things can never tell about them or quite understand them. They only feel dimly that they are in the grip of some gigantic destiny. I don't suppose the Three Hundred when they combed their long hair for death before Thermopylae ever thought what a gorgeous game they were playing. If they had, they would have gone into battle drunk with pride and walked through Xerxes' army. It seems a law of mortality that the instinct for deeds and the guiding and understanding brain cannot be equally matched, except once in a thousand years in a Caesar. The world is full of dumb, blind people, doing admirable work and faced with wonderful sights, and all the time without a glimmering of an idea of the magnificence of it."

Sir Edward Considine was in ordinary life a gentleman of cultivated manners, who spoke the English tongue with reasonable purity. But in the bush he developed a style of his own, and talked a slang culled from four continents, which the present writer cannot hope to reproduce. He tossed Hugh's tobacco-pouch back to him, raised himself on one elbow from his couch, and shook his head emphatically.

"They understand," he said, "better than you or I can tell. I've made a special study of the scallywag, and what I don't know about him ain't worth knowing. Most people make the mistake of thinking that he is always of the same type. There are a hundred types of him, and only one thing common to each—they are all dreamers."

"But for your infernal noise I should be one now," said Graham sleepily from the far bed. Considine picked up a boot, landed it neatly in the midst of the heap of rugs, and continued—

"I've been stuck up in half a dozen parts of the world with fellows who hadn't been home for years. Most of them used to talk Johnsonian English simply because they had forgotten when they last spoke to a white man, and thought of English only as a book language. None of them talked much, and it was the devil's own job to get them to speak of themselves. But they were the salt of the earth for all that, living hard, working hard, and ready to sell their lives any day in the way of business. Do you think that kind of man is only a mill-horse, jogging on in his round because there is nothing else for him to do? I tell you every man-jack of them has got his own private dream. He knows he has got his race behind him, and that he is the advance-guard, and the thought bucks him up to rot away in swamps and shiver with fever, and in all probability be cleaned out in some obscure row. Nobody knows another man's life, but we get glimpses now and then of his inner soul and take off our hats to it. You remember Lacey, who was at Eton with Alastair and me? Ask Alastair about him."

"What? the fellow who was killed somewhere up Chitral way?"

Considine's boot had brought Graham to attention. "Yes; he held a border fort with a dozen men for five days against several hundred ruffians. He fought so well that they wanted to spare him at the end and made him all kinds of offers. But he stuck it out, and they only got in over his body. When we found him he had about fifty wounds on him."

"I remember the story," said Hugh.

"Well, I was a pal of his, and he had made me his executor. I got his diary that he had written up till the day he died. If I hadn't seen that book I would have sworn that Lacey was the ordinary stupid fellow who fought because he liked it, and that he had stuck it out more from obstinacy than from policy. But the diary changed my mind. I found that he had carefully considered the whole question of surrender. Overtures had been made to him, and apparently they were such as he could have trusted. But he concluded it was a case for the white man's pride. He reasoned it all out. If he kept his head up to the last, he thought that the moral effect on that particular part of the border would be so great that there would be little more trouble. He deliberately chose death because he fancied it was his duty. And of course he was happy. The last pages of that little book, all grimy and blotted with blood, were one long paean of triumph. He couldn't spell, and he had very little idea of writing, yet the end of that book was the purest lyric of joy. The sacrifice was not in vain either, for, as you know, it ended the war, and now the blackguards who killed him burn offerings to his shade at hillside shrines."

"I don't for one moment deny that the great spirits—the leaders—have a clear ideal before them. But surely the same thing doesn't apply to the ordinary rolling-stone who wanders into adventures because he cannot keep out of them, and hasn't an idea in his head except that he likes to knock about the world."

"I never yet met the man without an idea in his head," said Considine; "but I give you up the ne'er-do-well, who has something rotten about him in heart or brain. I mean the wanderer who likes the wilds better than civilisation, and therefore is what civilised people call an idler, simply because the only things they recognise as work cannot be done in the kind of places he frequents. I know the breed, for he belongs to my own totem, and in defending him I am more or less justifying myself. My game is exploration, and I work at it pretty hard, though it's what you might call an intermittent profession. Another fellow's is natural history or mapping or prospecting or something else. We're devilish unsatisfactory people to our wives and families, I know, but, still, we don't rust. We keep our minds keen and our bodies active, and I scarcely call that idling. We're the least frivolous kind of man on the planet, and the least vulgar. Look at the ordinary industrious citizen. He wants to 'get on' in his beastly trade, and to have a house in Mayfair and a place in the country, and marry his daughters well, and get into Parliament and have a title to clap on to his squalid name. Or perhaps he wants to be applauded in the papers and be treated as a personage wherever he goes. I ask you if these are ambitions for a white man?"

Considine filled his pipe again from Hugh's pouch, and lit a match with difficulty. A light wind had got up which flickered among the high branches.

"Last time I was at home I went with Blanche to a ball at the Templetons. It was a big affair—royalty and ambassadors and a brace of foreign grand dukes, one of whom once hunted with me in the Selkirks. I stood for about half an hour beside a pillar and watched and meditated. The noise round about me was just like the jabbering of monkeys in a Malayan forest. None of the people looked you squarely in the eyes, and the women had all faces like marionettes. I saw my aunt's head bobbing and grinning, and her talk was some scandal about her oldest friend. Two fellows were standing near me—one was in the Cabinet and the other was a tremendous legal swell—and they were laughing at some of Manton's last sayings. Hanged if I could see any humour in 'em! One of the two came and spoke to me afterwards, and said he supposed the scene must be a pleasant change to me after the Congo. I told him it wasn't much of a change, only the monkeys were caged instead of running wild on the tree-tops. He laughed as if I had said something funny. After a bit I got very sad and sober. Young girls passed me with romance still in their eyes, and others, a little older, with the romance dead. I seemed to be looking on at a vast puppet-show, and I began to wonder if anybody was alive except myself. And then the comedy of it struck me, and I laughed to myself till people turned round to look at me, and Blanche came and asked me if I was ill. Of course, it was a game, and a good enough game, but yet to most of the people it was a tremendous reality, all they knew of life, and they would have shrieked in holy horror if I had told them that they represented not the last word in civilisation but a return to a very early stage of barbarism. The rough fellow clearing trees with an axe for his home was miles farther up the scale of being than they.... And then old Thirlstone drifted towards me. I daresay you know him, Hugh?"

"The man who was made an Under-Secretary the other day?"

"Same fellow. I used to know him long ago in the Service, and he was the hardest-bitten devil I have ever struck. He was in Tibet with Alastair, and he and I once had a try at getting into Kafiristan. Then his uncle died, and he became an enormously rich peer and had to come home and attend to his affairs. When he first came back he dined with us, and Blanche had a lot of people to meet him. He hadn't much to say for himself, and everybody thought him a bore, except me and a few of his own kind. Well, he settled down and married, and got into the ordinary rut, and there he was, still brown in the face but rather tired about the eyes. Blanche had told me he was much improved, so I knew what to look out for. All his roughness and shyness were gone, and he had the same kind of manner as the other monkeys, only he looked more wholesome. I wanted to speak to him, so we found a quiet corner in the supper-room. And then I put it straight to him, if he liked his new life. He said he did, talked a lot of rot about doing his duty in the sphere into which it had pleased God to call him, and about the fun of being at the centre of things; but there was not much conviction in his tone. So I began to tell him what had been happening to me, mentioned some places we had been together in and friends we had known. Soon I got him as keen as mustard. He dropped all his long words and fell into the honest slang of the backwoods. We had half an hour's talk of old times, and then his wife came in with the big boss of his party. You know Lady Thirlstone, I daresay. A pretty American with a figure and fine eyes, but neither complexion nor heart. Thirlstone got up to join them and looked at me rather sickly. 'I've got my wings clipped, old man,' he said. 'Wish me joy of my gilt cage, for if I weren't a gentleman I'd kick it to splinters to-morrow.'"

Somewhere in the forest a jackal barked and was answered from the far side of the camp. The fire was dying down, and a native boy came forward to heap on more logs.

"And yet," said Hugh, "what good is the *Wanderlust* in itself? You may have all manner of dreams, but you spend your strength in futility. I daresay Thirlstone sitting chafing in Parliament is playing a better part in the solid work of the world than Thirlstone gallivanting about the Hindu Kush."

"That's where you are wrong, my dear," said Considine. "We are the advance-guard, always pushing a little farther on and making the road easier for those who come after us, the serious solid fellows who make laws and create industries, and generally reap where we have sown. You cannot measure the work of a pioneer by the scale of a bagman. We keep the fire burning, though we go out ourselves. Our failure is our success. We don't found colonies and build cities, but unless we had gone before no one would have come after."

"Hugh," said Graham solemnly, "if you encourage Teddy, he'll keep on talking like a minor poet till daybreak."

"I like his minor poetry. Go on, and never mind that savage. You defend the adventurer because he keeps a nation restless?"

"True for you. He is the electric force in civilisation. Without him we should settle, like Moab, on our lees and rot. And you cannot measure him by ordinary results, because his work is spiritual and unworldly. Raleigh failed in everything he put his hand to, and went to the scaffold with all his schemes discredited. And yet he had set moving the force which was to make his dreams a superb reality. The pioneer must always be ploughed under, but only the fool considers him a failure. That Nietzsche fellow Appin was chaffing me about the other night has got the right end of the stick. The individual is tremendously important. We think of men as mere cog-wheels in some great machine, whose only value is as part of the works. Heaven forbid that I should deny the value of the great social machine in ordinary life. But there are many who have no share in it, and they have their value none the less, for, if you don't mind mixed metaphors, they somehow generate the motive power for the whole show. Take the case of Gordon. You may tell me that he was mad and a fanatic, that he ran his own head into the noose, that he had flaws in his character, that he was impossible as a colleague or a subordinate. I daresay that is all true, and I don't care. His failure and the manner of it were worth a dozen successful wars and a whole regiment of impeccable statesmen. It put new faith into the race, and screwed us up for another century.

"Remember," Considine continued, "that individualism is the keynote of our work. I have seen the French business in North Africa, and know their methods. There the State moves forward as one man, and not a step is taken in the advance till lines are laid from the base and the country is well held in the rear. Everything is centralised and officially directed. That is not our way. We send our younger sons out into the world, expressly forbid them to do things, disavow and discourage them, and then profit by their disobedience. As long as we have hundreds of young men who ask only the chance of danger, and are ready to take the whole world on their shoulders, we need have no fear for the future. When every one demands his price and asks to be shown some fair likelihood of success before he tackles his job, then we are morally bound to decay –

"My pipe is out, and I am getting sleepy. We've an early start before us, so I suppose we should compose ourselves to slumber."

Soon the world was quiet, save for the occasional crackling of a log and the deep breathing of the sleepers. Hugh pulled the furs about his chin, and watched the red heart of the fire glowing in the velvet dark of the night. He floated off into vague dreams, where lion-hunts ended in London ball-rooms, and almost in the same moment it seemed to him that he was awake again, with the fire black and the bitter cold gripping at his exposed neck and shoulders. He drew his coverings together, and sank into that light dreamless sleep which is the true luxury of the wilds. In another moment of time it was dawn, and, wide awake and refreshed, he was looking at a pale morning sky from which the stars were fading, and hearing the cheerful sound of the boys making early coffee.

CHAPTER 6

THE gardens at Musuru cover three thousand feet of a mountain-side, sloping steeply down from the lawns around the house to a tropical glen, where a brawling stream runs in thickets of palm and cactus. For Carey's guests it was a prescribed excursion to descend to the Tropics some morning, lunch in a summer-house, and make the best of an arduous return in the late afternoon. Such an expedition had its charm, for it was a stimulating adventure to climb down, as it were, in a few hours through many degrees of latitude, and witness in a brief day the scenery of twenty climates. But it had also its drawbacks, for in the morning when human energy is high the task was easy, and all the difficulties were reserved for that unhallowed season when lunch is a memory and tea a distant hope. So mules were provided for the women, and with the accompaniment of native muleteers and an Arab guide, the party assembled about eleven o'clock at the point where the road dipped into an avenue of cool cedars. Mrs Yorke, in a dress of delicate green muslin, carried a parasol, and sat her mule with the ease of one long at home in Southern places. The others, Marjory Haystoun, Lady Flora, and Mrs Deloraine, wore broad-brimmed hats and clothes of some serviceable linen stuff. Lady Flora refused to mount her mule, and tramped sturdily along with Mr Wakefield and Mr Astbury.

The garden was a labyrinth of paths, for the most part shadowed with trees, but coming suddenly at times to a kind of stage where the travellers had a wide prospect of the valley. At first the deep rooty fragrance of pines and cedars was all about them. Rhododendrons and azaleas formed the thicket, and there were stretches of mossy turf down which little streams fell in cascades to the forest below. Except for the greater heat of the sun, which the canopy of green scarcely averted, the road might have been a drive in some English park. Every now and then came patches of well-known English flowers, most of them past their first bloom, though the heath was still a gorgeous sheet of colour. Insensibly, however, the place changed to another latitude. Now it was some superb Riviera garden, where myrtles and syringas and shrubby geraniums crowded on the paths. At one halting place there was a parterre of flower-beds bright with a dozen species of canna and lily. A stream had been dammed to make a small hanging reservoir, where every variety of waterplant blossomed, and ducks of a curious burnished green swam among the white petals. Still they descended, and now the vegetation closed in, and instead of an avenue the path was a tunnel. Huge trees matted with vines and passion-flowers, tall forests of fern, broad-leaved wild bananas, and quantities of little palms, made a jungle which it seemed vain to hope to penetrate. Insect and bird life, which had been silent above, awoke in these regions, and the air was a-flutter with delicate wings. It was very hot, not the strong glare of the sun, but the moist warmth of rich vegetable life and a too generous earth. Mr Wakefield laboured in his tracks, the ladies on the mules ceased to gossip, and even Lady Flora looked flushed and breathless. Soon the noise of water rose above the hum of the forest, and suddenly through the blue and orange shadows of the trees gleamed the foam of a great torrent, as milk-white as any glacier stream. A well-made bridge of logs led across, and a few minutes later the party were seated in a little bungalow, with a floor of beaten earth, a thatched roof, and a shady verandah.

The sight of a cool luncheon-table with waiting servants in white tunics restored the travellers to comfort. They found a light meal of fruit and cold foods, while Mr Wakefield industriously set about the quenching of a very respectable thirst. After a while he recovered his composure, and had leisure to regard his companions.

"'If these things be done in the green tree,'" he said, "'what shall be done in the dry?' If I am out of breath coming downhill, how on earth am I to get up again? I have never understood why an all-wise Providence created the Tropics. They are full of noxious animals; their climate embitters life and is apt to end it prematurely."

Astbury, squarely built, fair-haired and ruddy, was also ill fitted for violent exercise in hot climates. A noted athlete and a mountaineer of high reputation, he could endure extremes of cold and exhaustion and only find his energy quickened, but in the Tropics he was apt to lose his restless activity and become an idle and good-humoured spectator of life.

"I want to know the answer to that question, too," he said. "What does the white man get from the Tropics? His strenuousness goes out of him, and he becomes a heavy-eyed cumberer of the ground. At Musuru I am always thinking about reforming the world, while down in this place the world can go to pieces for all I care. What do we get from living among palm-trees and gorgeous colours in the atmosphere of a Turkish bath?"

"Nothing," said Mr Wakefield. "The Tropics are a purgatory appointed by Heaven for the purging of our immortal souls. They are a sphere of duty in which for their sins many honest men are compelled to labour – nothing more!"

"I wonder if women are more Oriental than men?" it was Marjory who spoke. "Because, you know, all this makes me happy. I seem to get the creases out of my soul in this hot sun and this glory of flowers. In what people call strenuous weather I would much rather stay in bed. But to-day one really believes that veins of fire run through the earth, and that nothing is dead, not even the rocks. One feels the world so much bigger and fuller and richer and more mysterious. Don't you think so, Barbara?"

Mrs Deloraine, who had been gazing at a huge bouquet of orchids presented to her by one of the servants, lifted an abstracted eye.

"What an intoxication colour is!" she murmured. "Look at these scarlet bells and that great purple chalice. I had no idea such depth of richness could be found in the world. Our senses are starved in the north, with nothing but clean thin scents around us and pale rain-washed greys and blues. There is no passion in our Nature, for it is all too well subordinated to the needs of man. But here we have a world which has no thought of humanity. These scarlet blossoms flame for other than mortal eyes. You cannot think of Pan in one of our hazel thickets—the thought is almost indecent. But I can well imagine his slanted eyes looking out from behind that tangle of vines."

"I, too, feel that," said Mrs Yorke. "In the North the life-force in the earth is enough for our needs and no more, but here there is a generous overflow. I feel as if life were longer and kinder and easier, but also that I matter less in the scheme of things than I thought. I am a little home-sick, too, for I am a daughter of the South, and the hot air brings back my childhood." Mrs Yorke sighed with a tender melancholy.

"I feel the wickedness more than the kindness," said Mrs Deloraine. "It is an unmoral world, this warm-scented place, and there is a shrieking cruelty behind the splendour. Natura Maligna and Natura Benigna have walked hand in hand in these glens. Look at the flowers! No Wordsworth could read any lesson of peace in them."

Lady Flora arose and examined the bouquet; then, selecting a huge purple blossom, she fastened it in Mr Wakefield's coat. She walked a few steps back and surveyed her handiwork.

"I want you to look wicked, Mr Wakefield, but it's quite impossible. You only look benevolent and embarrassed. Barbara, you may wear orchids if you please, for I think you are the only one of us who could stand them. Letty would look a sorceress at once, and Marjory is one without them."

Astbury had wandered to the door and was looking up the steep slopes of greenery they had descended.

"What a Jack-and-the-Beanstalk business it is, and how little one would imagine a place like Musuru atop of it all! I think Miss Haystoun is right, and that the Tropics should increase our vitality, but we must be very vital beings to begin with. A hot sun or a keen frost will make a strong man stronger, but they will kill a weakling. So with the Tropics in my view. An eager fellow can live in them for years and be none the worse, but your waster dies. That is why a lean sandy-haired Scot is perfectly happy in West Africa, while a Portuguese sickens at once, though the one is a Northerner and the other a Latin. In my case, the Tropics make me sleepy, and I don't mind admitting it. But they also fill me with a vast bovine contentment, which I suppose is a kind of condensed and stored vitality. They are the only really restful places in the world, for you feel that your life is such a speck on the great wheel of things. I remember after the Boer War coming home by the East Coast in a cargo-boat and landing at a little port called Inhambane. There was a long sweep of white sand, a line of green palms, and a lot of whitewashed, green-shuttered, thatched houses in groves of bananas. I was rowed up a little river among quiet villages under palm-trees, where the people always seemed to be chanting a low, slow Arab song. It was very hot, and I lay comfortably in the stern, watching the oily current and the black arms of the rowers and the snow-white gown of the steersman and the deep blue sky between the feathery tops of the palms. And then I sank for two heavenly hours into Nirwana. I had never been to Nirwana before, but now I badly want to go back again. In London my working-rooms face on a dingy grey street with a mouldy old cab-horse standing at the corner. Sometimes, when I look out, that river at Inhambane comes over me so badly that I hardly know what to do. For, if you once get the Tropics into your blood, however much you may hate 'em and disapprove of 'em, you can't forget 'em. And some day you will go back."

Marjory, swinging lazily in a low wicker chair, announced her agreement. "I am of the belief of the old sailor who said nothing was impossible 'south'ard o' the line.' Your horizon is far wider and you live in touch with the great elementary things. Barbara, I am going to repeat some verses you once wrote. Listen, everybody:—

'In the ancient orderly places, with a blank and orderly mind, We sit in our green walled gardens and our corn and oil increase; Sunset nor dawn can wake us, for the face of the heavens is kind; We light our taper at even and call our comfort peace.

Peaceful our clear horizon, calm as our sheltered days
Are the lilied meadows we dwell in, the decent highways we tread.
Duly we make our offerings, but we know not the God we praise,
For He is the God of the living, but we, His children, are dead.

I will arise and get me beyond this country of dreams, Where all is ancient and ordered and hoar with the frost of years, To the land where loftier mountains cradle their wilder streams, And the fruitful earth is blessed with more bountiful smiles and tears,—

There in the home of the lightnings, where the fear of the Lord is set free, Where the thunderous midnights fade to the turquoise magic of

morn, The days of man are a vapour, blown from a shoreless sea, A little cloud before sunrise, a cry in the void forlorn—
I am weary of men and cities and the service of little things,
Where the flamelike glories of life are shrunk to a candle's ray.
Smite me, my God, with Thy presence, blind my eyes with Thy wings,
In the heart of Thy virgin earth show me Thy secret way!'"

The verses were received with a murmur of approval by Mrs Yorke and Mr Astbury. Mr Wakefield contented himself with observing that he was glad there was some one to say a good word for the Tropics, but that personally he should be unhappy till he was back at Musuru. As the afternoon had grown cooler a start was made, which was a little delayed by an attempt on the part of Lady Flora to explore with her mule a track which led down to the edge of the stream. The result was that she could not turn her animal, which had to be towed back ignominiously by the whole staff of the bungalow.

The ascent proved less arduous than had been expected. Mrs Yorke, stricken with humanitarian feelings, declined to burden her mule, and in the company of Lady Flora walked gallantly up the steepest part, with the face which her ancestors may have worn when they rolled the tea-chests into Boston harbour. As the air grew colder and pines and cedars reappeared, comfort descended once more on the party, and even Mr Wakefield ceased to puff. The scent of heath was so homely that the experiences of the day were forgotten, and each felt as if the walk had lain through some English wood with a conventional country-house to return to. But on emerging on the lawn from the long avenue the sudden sight of Musuru brought all to a halt. The glow of sunset was on the white walls, and the whole had the airy perfection of a house seen in a dream.

"What a place to stumble upon by accident!" exclaimed Mr Astbury. "Imagine a party of hunters who knew nothing about it and believed they were in the depths of savagery! Suddenly, climbing this long hill, they come on walks and flower-gardens. They think they are going mad, and look down at their dirty, torn clothes to reassure themselves. And then they reach the top and come in sight of the house. It would take a long time to persuade them that it was not an Aladdin's palace."

"Enter the party," said Lady Flora, pointing to three riders and a regiment of boys who had halted at the far side of the lawn. Presently three sunburnt men had joined the rest, and were assailed with inquiries, whose makers, like Pilate, did not stay for an answer.

"What sport?" Lady Flora asked Hugh.

"Good. Fifteen head of buck and two lions. I got one and Akhub the other, but I was chivvied by both. And you? Did you find Melissinde?"

"No. She doesn't live in the valley. We've been all day in the Tropics listening to Barbara's poetry. I want to see your lions, and you've got to give me a skin. Since you broke our compact you must pay toll, you know."

It was a milder evening than had yet been enjoyed at Musuru, and after dinner the party sat in the inner hall watching a young moon climbing that immense arch of sky which is only given by a hill-top prospect.

"I feel as if I were in a lighthouse," Lady Warcliff said, with an air which invited contradiction. "I almost expect to hear the horn of some great ship down below in the fog. If only each hot country had been given a habitable mountain, they would be the only places in the world to live in. On the ordinary upland you dominate the flat country because you are higher up, but here we also look down on the plain because we are wholesome and cool and sane and they are fevered. We are a lighthouse to the whole of Equatoria, and if there were fifty other lighthouses in the Empire there would be no tropical problem."

Lady Flora and Hugh had discovered a small couch out of the area of both firelight and lamplight and close to the windows, which were lit from without by the pale glimmer of the moon. Here they had a vantage-ground for seeing the faces of the others.

"I do so wish," whispered the girl, "that they wouldn't all talk in paragraphs. Either let them chatter in a friendly way or let Mr Carey or Lord Appin say all that has got to be said themselves."

"Hush," said Hugh, for Carey from the fireplace was beginning to speak.

"So far," he said, "we have discussed the relation of Imperialism to current politics at home. We have looked, too, at the essential features of the new constitution which must some day take the place of the old. And now we come to the details of administration, and the first and greatest of these problems is that of our tropical dependencies. For whatever the development of the free Colonies, they can never share in it. The central executive of the Empire will change its character, but it can never change its task. The direct responsibility for tropical administration will always rest with it. The burden of the Tropics can never be shared with local and responsible legislatures; for they can never be wholly settled by the white man, but must remain largely in the hands of races for whom autonomy is unthinkable, at any rate for the next century or two.

"If that is so, clearly the Tropics will furnish all the administrative problems which are not concerned with the common services of the Empire. The work of our imperial executive will be the joint problems of the whole Empire plus the day-to-day administration of our tropical dependencies in Asia, Africa, and America. This last will be no light business, and must be taken seriously. I am not a great believer in the cant of expert knowledge in politics. Efficiency is apt to be either a meaningless catchword or a stupid worship of professionalism. But our tropical administration must be based on expert knowledge, for in our everyday life in Europe we have no experience, no inherited body of ideas, which is in any way applicable. It is a thing by itself, governed by other rules than those which sway popular government.

"We have already decided that it will be the test of the capacity of democracy for empire if it can accept the abrogation of its claim over some part of the territory under its control and trust its servants. I do not believe that democracy will be found wanting. The danger, to my mind, is far more that its trusted servants may be inadequate to the task. For it is above all things work which demands a clear eye and a steady head, and in which supineness and pedantry will spell disaster. The great administrative questions of the future will be tropical questions. The Tropics will be the training-ground of our great officials. It is high time, therefore, that we tried to get at some scientific understanding of our responsibilities. If expert knowledge and not a mere handful of moral platitudes is to be our guide, we must take steps to systematise and develop that knowledge.

"We are not without precedents. Both France and Germany have set the example in founding schools of what they call "colonial science." And four centuries ago our own Hakluyt urged something of the same kind. The risk is that we allow ourselves to be misled by the case of India, where we have made a great success by a kind of accident. We send out raw boys to that service, and in a year or two they are efficient administrators. Yes, but the same rule will not hold everywhere. India is a long-settled country, which runs by herself. We control, amend here and there, give her the benefit of our protection, but we do not really interfere. The social machine in its essentials is independent of us. It is quite a different matter in lands where the fabric of civilisation has to be built up from the beginning. There you have no rules to go by, except your own wits; and knowledge is the only dividing line between success and failure. We must take up the business very seriously, and equip ourselves resolutely for the work. I do not propose to weary you with suggestions, for it is no part of our programme to burrow among details. But two points I would insist upon. The first is, that we must take steps to give our people the best possible training for the work they are going to. I want to see imperial colleges established where young men will be taught tropical medicine, and surveying, and natural history and ethnology, where, in a word, the long experience of the Empire will be concentrated into precepts. And the second is, that we must provide for reciprocity between the home and the foreign services, so that the man in the Colonial or the Foreign Office may have first-hand experience of his own to guide him, and the man at the outposts may know the ways of the home office, and may keep in touch with home politics. At present the two branches are cursed with a confusion of tongues, and speak a different language, though they may mean the same thing. A boy who goes into the civil service in England would under my scheme go out automatically in five years to a minor post in some dependency, and return after some years of service to a higher post at home. By this means our governors and our permanent secretaries would be of the same class, with the same training, each sympathising with and understanding the other's work. There would be some kind of solidarity in imperial administration, and when the wheels go smoothly they go faster and farther."

Lord Appin had joined the group at the window, and was gently pinching Lady Flora's ear.

"You know the Tropics, Francis," he said. "I don't suppose there is any hot country on earth you haven't been to. Tell me, are they ever going to change their character? Will white men and women ever be able to live in them in reasonable comfort? Or are they to be a permanent Purgatory to which we resort for our souls' good?"

"We discussed that question at lunch to-day," said Lady Flora. "Mr Wakefield said they were merely Purgatory, but most of us thought them more like the Garden of Eden. They make Barbara and Letty feel wicked, and Mr Astbury sleepy, and they make me very, very thirsty."

"Well, what do you propose to do with them, Francis?" said Lord Appin again. "Are they to be a kind of Botany Bay for penitential souls, or, in your own words, are they some day to blossom as the rose?"

Carey smiled. "I think Alastair and Sir Edward are the best authorities," he said. "We will ask them what they think. My own opinion is, that we can improve them all, even the worst parts, up to a certain point. That is to say, we can make them habitable by white men and women for a year or two at a stretch. But that is not enough to secure continuity in development, and here is where the doctrine of the vantage-grounds appears, which Sir Edward was explaining to me the other morning. Teddy, expound, please."

That gentleman rose courageously from a long arm-chair where he had been stretching legs wearied with the day's riding. Leaning against the mantelpiece, somewhat in the fashion of a giraffe against a palm-tree, he embarked on his explanation.

"I was much struck by what Lady Warcliff said after dinner to-night. She wanted a lighthouse like Musuru in every tropical colony, and she said that if you had such a thing their problems would be settled. Well, I mean the same thing, only I call it a vantage-ground instead of a lighthouse. We needn't trouble about the seaside strips of land, because either they are swamps and don't matter much, or the sea winds make them fairly healthy. We can also leave India out. It is fully developed, and we know exactly how much it takes out of the white man to plant him there. What I want to say concerns Africa mainly, since it is here that we have the great undeveloped speculative dependencies.

"Let us call our possessions in Africa four—north, east, west, and south. The first gives us Egypt and the Sudan hinterland up to Gondokoro; the second is the coast around Mombasa, this plateau, and the trough of Equatoria; West Africa is the coast around the Gulf of Guinea and the hinterland of Nigeria; South Africa is everything from Lake Nyasa and the Congo to the Cape. Now some of these are white men's countries, and in time are going to be colonies. Some day we shall have the federation of South Africa, and then the lowlands around the Zambesi—what we call North-west and North-east Rhodesia and Nyasaland—will fall to be administered by the federal government. So, also, we shall have the free colony of East Africa, with its capital on this plateau, administering the lowlands west and east of it. That is one possible development. The other is that the colonies occupy only the healthy country and leave the lowlands as dependencies under the central executive. It doesn't particularly matter to my argument what is going to happen. The point is that wherever you have an unhealthy tropical tract you have somewhere in the near neighbourhood a patch of white man's country.

"I expect you can all see a sort of map in your mind. Well, first of all, in South Africa we have high veld from the Cape to within a hundred miles of the Zambesi, and round the eastern coast we have the line of the Drakensberg running from Cape Colony right up to Manicaland, so that we are never far from healthy country. In Nyasaland we have the Shire Highlands, and in Barotseland we have long stretches of pasture, with bracken and hazels like England. I've hunted there, and seen it with my own eyes. In East Africa we have this gorgeous plateau as the vantage-ground for the coast strip and for Uganda. In North Africa we have Egypt as the vantage-ground for the Sudan. It is not an upland, but it is a place where Europeans can live and work happily for years. In West Africa we have nothing quite so good. But in a little while, when we have railways and better roads, and can house and feed our people better, there is no reason why all the Nigerian uplands should not be at least as healthy as the better parts of India, if we except the hill stations."

"But the presence of a few wholesome square miles in a territory will not prevent people from sickening in the rest," said Mr Wakefield.

"No, but it will give them a place to rest and recover in. Tropical administration must be spasmodic—we must make up our minds for that. But it need not be too spasmodic. If the land is to be properly governed, and any policy carried through to a finish, you must have the same officials resident in the country for a fair length of time. And, more important still, you must see that they retain the mental and bodily vigour which is necessary for all good work. Now these vantage-grounds of ours will enable us to secure this. By a merciful fate we have been permitted to bag all the most habitable parts of Africa. We have the great hot flats, where life is hard, but where, if some kind of civilisation is to penetrate, it must be through Englishmen who live and work there. And next door we have the health resorts where these Englishmen can go when their vitality ebbs and lay in a fresh supply, and where the greater administrative problems can be thought out. They will be what Simla is to India, the workshop of government. They are near enough to be within hail of the lowlands, but they are in another climate, and give a tired man the moral and physical tonic he needs."

"Allah has indeed been merciful," said Lord Appin. "But, my dear Teddy, your vantage-grounds will not settle the problem of the Tropics. You have to find the race of men who will tolerate your regime of alternate sickness and health. The average official will sigh too continually for the fleshpots of the vantage-grounds, and instead of carrying back with him to his station a fresh supply of force he will carry only an unsettled mind."

"Maybe. But he will be more unsettled if he has to go home, seedy, every eighteen months or so, and can never have his wife and family out. I assume that the men will be keen on their job. And this assumption is allowable, for the Tropics have a tremendous fascination of their own. It is only the loneliness which scares a man. If he had a chance of seeing his kind oftener, and keeping more in touch with civilisation, he would have little fault to find with his life. I have met scores of them, and a fellow has to be very stupid if he does not feel the romance of making a new country. In time he gets the place into his bones, and the danger then is not of his losing heart in his work, but his losing all interest in home. We must keep both fires alight, otherwise we become either like the Portuguese who forgot Portugal, or like certain French colonists who remember the boulevards all too clearly."

"I wonder how good a judge you are, Teddy," said Lord Appin. "You like the wilds, I know; but is it not rather in the way that the ordinary city man tolerates the discomfort of his Scotch shooting-box? He feels a certain pleasure in the sensation, because he knows it will not last long. But he would be a very sad man if he had to make a lifetime of it. You go off for a year or two, and enjoy yourself immensely, but I wonder how much of the enjoyment comes from the knowledge that you have always Hill Street and Considine Abbey behind you somewhere, awaiting your return?"

"I suppose I shall never make you understand," said Sir Edward dolefully. "Best ask Carey."

"Oh, Francis follows the simple expedient of turning the wilds into something much more delectable than England. He has no right to decide."

"I won't argue," said Carey, "because the point is unarguable. Also Mrs Deloraine is going to sing. But I live in hopes of converting Lord Appin to barbarism. After all a metaphysician should be an adventurer."

Mrs Deloraine had gone to the piano and was playing the opening chords of a Schumann air. To her Lady Flora fluttered like a moth to a candle, music having charms for her which were at no time to be resisted. Lord Appin had suddenly discovered a new Louis Quinze cabinet, and was devouring it with the keen eye of the collector. Hugh drifted into the nearest drawing-room, where he found the Duchess, and was impounded for a game of cribbage, a taste for which had always marked the noble house whose name she bore.

"So far," she said, "the Tropics are the least exhausting subject we have discussed. I suppose it is because we are in them and know so much by instinct that we can afford to leave most of the platitudes unsaid. I thought Francis and Sir Edward talked very good sense. But, you know, they only gave us the rudiments of their real opinions. Both of them want to make us all have houses on these vantage-grounds, as they call them, and live part of the year there, and regard them as much our home as England. Sir Edward preached me a long sermon about it last year, just after George had taken a new forest in Scotland. He wanted to know why he didn't go farther afield, to some part of the Empire, and set a good example. He said that only one profession was left for our class—to be the pioneers of a wider patriotism. I suppose he was right. But I am old-fashioned, and I cannot quite imagine myself an imperial lady. Till travel becomes easier I would rather stay at home most of my time, for running about the world, as Francis does, is wearing to a woman. I am middle-aged, and have very little vanity left, but I would rather remain as I am. I can see Sir Edward's imperial lady. She will have no complexion, her voice will be rather high, and her eyes always a little too bright. Not a very comforting creature to live with!"

"You prefer Lady Considine?" Hugh asked.

"No, indeed. I don't defend Blanche. Perhaps when we have reached a further stage of development women will be able to live up and down the world and yet keep their restfulness. But at present the nomad woman is still something of an excrescence. She is a 'sport,' outside our normal development, and therefore high-coloured and shrill. As for Blanche, she is a relic, marooned long ago on a little island of her own. Is she a friend of yours, Mr Somerville?"

"No. She asks me to dinner, but I don't often go, unless Teddy is at home. When I talk to her I never know whether to think her a doll or a vast and terrible eider-down quilt smothering the universe."

"And yet, if you had seen her ten years ago, you could not have escaped falling in love with her. Everybody did, even George, who is as blind as an owl to female beauty. She was the most exquisite girl I have ever seen. With her bright hair and melting eyes she floated through a room like a creature from another world. No one knew that she was stupid, for her face mesmerised everybody, even women. Sir Edward was the great *parti* of his time, and she naturally married him. Happily they are both miracles of good-humour, so they put up with each other fairly well. But they haven't an idea or a taste in common. She would like him to stay at home and get into the Cabinet, and give great parties at Considine, and generally move in the sphere of life where she is conscious of shining. He considers that Abana and Pharpar, rivers of Damascus, are better than all the waters of Israel. I used to think her a fool, but I am not so dogmatic now. She is intensely clever in her own way—an eider-down quilt, as you justly remarked. If Sir Edward were not a born Esau she would have smothered him long ago. Her whole life is one devout prostration before conventional shrines, with her orthodox opinions, her soft downcast eyes, her gentle voice, her elaborate and extravagant prettiness. If that marriage was made in heaven, the gods were in a comic mood. And yet they love each other after a fashion."

"Who love each other?" said Lady Flora, bearing down upon the cribbage- players like a privateer on harmless merchantmen. "I hope you mean Mr Wakefield and me, for I am going to propose to him to-morrow."

"I trust he won't accept you, my dear," said the Duchess, "for he will go to prison for bigamy if he does. He is married already—to an enormous American."

The girl sank upon the couch. "I never loved a dear gazelle," she began, when the gazelle in question appeared in the offing.

"To-morrow," said Mr Wakefield, in the tone of a dying gladiator, "we are going down to the lake and are going to cross in Carey's steam-launch. We are not to be allowed to content ourselves with theorising about the Tropics, but are to make practical experiments in them. The only consolation is that we shall get our mail at Port Florence. I am charged to say that the outgoing post leaves first thing in the morning, and that everybody must have their letters ready to-night."

CHAPTER 7

ABOUT noon of the following day the party found themselves shepherded on board a trim little vessel which lay moored a hundred yards from the jetty of Port Florence. Thick awnings warded off the sun; the deck, with its white wood and gleaming brass, was as trim as the parlour of a Dutch housewife; a light breeze ruffled the blue water and fluttered among the feathery palm-leaves on the shore. Steam had been got up, and five minutes after embarking they were gliding through the hot shallows to the mouth of the bay. The sound of ship's bells and the airy freshness of the deck delighted the guests with a mingled sense of homeliness and strangeness. The arrival of a large English mail provided abundant occupation for, at any rate, the early hours of the voyage.

The women wore the lightest of gowns and the men were in flannels. Lady Warcliff, as the daughter of an admiral, assumed a proprietary air when her feet trod a deck, though she was a bad sailor and abhorred the sea. Faithful to her duty, she carried off Carey on a tour of inspection, leaving her letters at the mercy of any vagrant wind which cared to bear them to the fishes of Lake Victoria. The Duchess, in a deckchair, opened her correspondence with the rapidity of a conjurer, and distributed fragments of information to Lady Flora and Mrs Wilbraham, who, having had small mails, were busy with a bundle of home papers.

"George is in Scotland. He says the weather is dreadful, and that he has had nothing from the river but three small grilse. How vexatious! I know exactly what will happen. He will get no more, and then he'll spend the whole winter doing calculations how many hundreds these grilse cost him a pound.... Pamela has gone to Ireland with Mary Daventer. Flora, I wonder what mischief your mother will do there? She is much too theatrical to be allowed to dabble in politics, for she would turn a parish council into a Guy Fawkes conspiracy.... Eve Nottingham has written a book, purporting to be the letters of a Japanese wife to her English mother-in-law. What will that silly woman be after next? She has never been outside Europe, so she picks out Japan for her theme. She might as well write the letters of a Coptic greengrocer to his Abyssinian grandmother. I suppose it will be the usual erotic outpouring, which the newspapers will call 'intimate' and 'poignant,' and well-brought-up girls won't be allowed to read.... The Prime Minister has made a good speech about either criminal aliens or Jerusalem artichokes—I cannot read Georgiana's writing,—and Violet Hexham is going to marry her chauffeur. Really, English news is very tiresome. How glad I am to be in Central Africa instead of at Cowes!"

Mrs Wilbraham arose with an air of tragedy, sombrely brandishing 'The Times.' "A disaster of the first magnitude has befallen the Empire! Sir Herbert Jupp has made a speech."

"Where did the horrid affair take place?" Lord Appin asked.

"At the annual dinner of the Amalgamated Society of South African Operators' Benevolent Fund, when Sir Herbert was the guest of the evening. He said—I quote 'The Times'—that 'we had suffered too long from the tyranny of the foreigner, and that it was high time we began to get a little of our own back. The Mother must summon her children around her knees and grapple them to her with hooks of steel' (it sounds as if the children were going to have a lively time of it). 'Against a united empire,' says Sir Herbert, 'no powers of darkness can prevail. We fling back the jealousy and hate of the globe in its teeth, content with the affection of our own kinsfolk. We have truckled too long before the insolence of Europe. Let the Island Race show a haughty front to the world, remembering its God-given mission and its immortal destiny. If the Lord be for us who can be against us!' What a crusader! I did not think Master Shallow had been a man of this mettle!"

Lady Flora had been reading a Liberal paper. "Here's another man who appeals to high Heaven. On Friday, August 2, in the Bermondsey Tabernacle, the Reverend Doctor Price-Morgan delivered what this paper calls an 'electric appeal, instinct with a certain fine quality.' I see that he describes the Empire as a 'blood-stained monument of human folly,' and he calls imperialists men 'without conscience, without honour, without patriotism, without God.' I hope you recognise your portrait, Sir Edward. 'Let us,' he says, 'destroy the accursed thing and return to the old simple paths whence we strayed.' Can he mean Elizabethan piracy? He concludes nobly with 'A nation without a conscience is like a man groping in the dark on the verge of a precipice.' Will somebody explain to me about the Nonconformist Conscience?"

"The Nonconformist Conscience, my dear," said Lord Appin, "is too big a thing to be defined casually at mid-day on a tropical lake. It is the name which most people give to the particular national failing from which they happen to be exempt. Under its shade the militant freethinker and the gentle pietist lie down like lambs together. Very often it has nothing to do with conscience. Certain people choose to defend certain things in which they believe by appealing to morals and religion, when the real reason of their belief is something quite different. In these cases it is a mannerism of speech rather than of thought. With many it is a condemnation of certain gross and robust shortcomings to which they are not inclined, by means of which they distract attention from their own less masculine vices of lying, dishonesty, and cowardice. With those of a particular religious persuasion it can best be described, I think, as the homage which a feeble present pays to a strong past. At one time with Nonconformists rested the liberties of England, and nobly they fought the battle.

"Their lives were one long protest against wickedness and folly in high places. But the times passed, and our own day of easy tolerance dawned, when the only disability which Dissent has to endure is a social one and the worst accusation brought against it is vulgarity. But the honest fellows still maintain their air of shrill protest and unwearying dissidence. The burning wrongs of their forefathers, which were also the wrongs of England, have become petty discomforts which it requires an acute mind to discover, but the rhetoric is as vivid as ever. The attitude may seem an anachronism and a parody, but I prefer to look kindly upon it as a belated concession to romance. It is the tribute of the prosperous middle-class, seeking to make the best of both worlds, to the grim Ironside and Anabaptist who relinquished all to win the Kingdom of Heaven."

"Why not call it hypocrisy?" said Mrs Wilbraham. "It is precisely the quality which makes us the contempt of our European neighbours—an austere creed with a practice limping far in the rear."

"Because," said Lord Appin, "no summary definition does justice to so complex a trait. It is the old desire to make an omelette without breaking eggs, and the curious thing is that we can discern in it both a firm intention to make the omelette at any cost and a sincere conviction that it is infamous to sacrifice a single egg in the process. Were both feelings equally strong we should be in a perpetual state of suspended animation. Only the inborn practicality of our race puts the weight on the former, and so—under protest— we advance. Till we learn to think clearly we shall always have the conflict between the two, yet till our vitality perishes the first will always carry the day."

Lord Launceston had come aft from watching the shore of the bay through a field-glass and had found a seat beside the Duchess.

"I differ," he said, "in rating most highly the confused moral instinct which you condemn. However illogical, however vexatious in its effects, I would not for worlds see it disappear from our national life. There may be hypocrisy in it, but there is also a tremendous reality. It is a concession not so much to tradition as to eternal principles of conduct, and in its essence it is not nonconformist but conformist. It is the force of social persistence, which counteracts the extravagant flights of our national energy. The result is that any new movement is compelled to carry with it this heavy ballast before it can succeed, and originality is made safe and practical. It is the underlying earnestness of the country, which, because it believes enormously in its creed, is conservative and eager to repel assaults. England is in consequence slow to convince; but once convinced, she moves with unique impetus, just as a strong stream may take longer to divert into a new channel than a rill, but when diverted is a far greater force at command."

"What value can there be in the attitude of some canting rascal of an employer who grinds down his workpeople and protests piously all the while against what he calls 'servile conditions' of labour in some other place?" Sir Edward sat on the bulwarks with a broad Panama hat on his head and a cigar in his mouth, his air suggestive of anything but nonconformity or conscience.

"No value in the man, who will certainly lose his soul, but much in what he stands for. The mere fact that a rogue pretends to a conviction is a sign that there is a preponderating majority of honest men who sincerely hold it. Cancel all the hypocrisy, and you will still find an immense deal of sound moral instinct. I grant you it is often wrong, hopelessly wrong; but the instinct is right, it is only the application that is faulty. The remedy is to educate and persuade, not to sneer and override. The truth will always prevail, if we can only put it with sufficient clearness."

Lady Amysfort's eyebrows had gone up during these words. "Is Saul also among the prophets?" she asked in that cool voice with the tinkle of ice in it, which was the despair of her enemies. "I little thought I should live to hear Lord Launceston defend Nonconformist ethics. To me the notion that any conviction must be respected merely because it happens to be honest is one of the many Whig superstitions that have been long ago exploded. Another is that you cannot kill a heresy by persecution, but must only encourage it. The truth is that you can stamp out a heresy for ever if you persecute it with sufficient vigour, provided it has none of the stuff of life in it. And equally our business is to ignore utterly convictions, however honest, unless they happen to be also intelligent. I am bound to say that in my researches in the dark place of Dissent I have rarely found the conjunction."

Lord Launceston laughed. "You give away your case, Caroline, by admitting that the heresy you are going to stamp out must not have the stuff of life in it. I agree. Crush out all the trumpery crazes as relentlessly as you please. Only beware of a living conviction, for it will be too much for you. I am wholly against the childishness that would flatter and cringe before fads which should be knocked on the head. All the more reason, therefore, why one should be respectful to the things that matter. If you were faithful to your Tory principles, you would recognise in this 'conscience' one of the abiding instincts of our race, which statesmanship, on your own admission, must reckon with. A very good working test, whether a conviction is living or not, is the number of people who share it. It is not an infallible rule, but if you find any large proportion of reasonable average men holding a view, it is worth while taking it seriously. And remember that this much criticised moral anxiety is a weapon which may be used on our own side. If your opponent has a sharp sword, it is wiser to annex it for your own use than to destroy it. Our business is to enlist this moral fervour on behalf of what we regard as truth and righteousness."

The luncheon-bell began to ring as Lord Launceston ceased speaking. As the heat of the sun was now very great, the afternoon found the company indisposed to exertion, physical or mental, and inclined to long deck-chairs in the shade and the lightest of romances. Towards five o'clock, however, there was a general awakening when it became clear that the yacht was approaching the farther shore. Lady Warcliff sat in the bows with a Zeiss glass, staring with eagle eye, like Cortes, at a wooded hill which began to loom out of the haze. A crowd of land birds—flamingoes, cranes, herons, and brilliant-backed ducks—played the part of sea-gulls, and thronged around the yacht. Land odours, chiefly the smell of wood-smoke, were drifted out to the travellers.

Carey, who had disappeared all afternoon on some private business, now came on deck and stood by the bulwarks looking at the sunset. Hugh joined him, and together they watched the riot of crimson and saffron in the sky kindle the olive-green forests till the tree-tops glowed like jewels. The marshes which fringed the lake were caught up into the pageant and smouldered with strange fires of tawny gold.

Carey drew a long breath. "It is Antony's dream come true," he said. "See, there are all the elements—the fantastic clouds,

'The forkéd mountain and blue promontory.'

Look, now, for you will see the colours wiped clean out of the world as the sun dips."

It happened as he said, for it seemed as if a great curtain were suddenly let down upon the landscape. The light and colour ran out of the foreground. Soon the waters were dull grey, though the forests still burned. Then the forests were quenched, though the highest trees had gold crowns and the far ridge of hills. These faded in turn, and in a grey world the yacht came to her moorings in the little bay of Entoro. The dinghies were lowered and the company went ashore.

They were met on the beach by the whole population of the place, led by a tall oldish man with grey whiskers, whom Carey introduced as the Reverend Alexander Macdowall, in charge of the Scotch Mission. He led them to a low, white, barrack-like building, which was an appendage to the mission-house, and which Carey used as a lodge on the occasion of his visits. It was found to be severely but comfortably furnished, and the yacht's servants having brought up plate and linen and some of the minor comforts of civilisation, the company were soon installed in quarters which might be regarded as luxurious in any tropical town. The mosquito-nets and the absence of fireplaces spoke of a climate very different to Musuru: but the night, as it chanced, was not unduly warm. Save for the humming of insects and that faint musty smell which is inseparable from houses on which for most of the year the sun beats hotly, the dinner, cooked by the yacht's servants, might have been served in some old-fashioned Scotch shooting-box.

To the meal came Mr Macdowall, splendidly habited in an antique suit of broadcloth. His weathered face, his sharp and kindly blue eyes set in a maze of wrinkles, and his spare, straight figure made up a picture which took the eye as something clean-cut and virile. His manner had the spacious ease which the wilds give to those who are not enslaved by them. He called Carey "Francis," and adopted the company at once into the circle of his friendship.

"I come from your own countryside, Lord Appin," he said, in answer to a question; "I have not been back for ten years, and I question if I could return. I have made my own place here, and I could not endure interference very readily again. I daresay at home I should even be falling out with the police. Besides, there's no need to go back. I have no near relations, and the thing I most cared for in Scotland was the fishing. But I can get that here now, and I'm quite content."

"What was the place like when you came?" Hugh asked.

"A den of cut-throats," said the missionary. "Tribe warring against tribe, the land raided by Arab slave-dealers, and no man knowing when he woke in the morning if he should see another. I lived through three massacres of Christians and half-a-dozen native wars, and by-and-by the place settled down. England began to hear about the lakes, and we had travellers and hunters visiting us, and things began to get a little better. Our work had been much blessed—not in the ordinary sense, ye understand, for there were few converts of the real sort, but we had driven some habits of industry and decency into the people. It was a hard life in those days, for we had little but native food, and our medicines often ran short. I had a good deal of black-water fever, and several times I was nearly dead with it. I remember all those days I could not get the thought of the Ochils out of my head—yon fine, green, clean country with a well-head in every howe. Out on the knoll where I had my hut I could see on clear days the long blue line of the Mau, where Musuru stands now. It used to comfort me to look at it. I knew there was a cool blessed country up there, and many a time I said over the psalm to myself, 'I will lift up mine eyes unto the hills, from whence cometh my help.' I was convinced that the regeneration of this place could only come from the heights."

"And did it?" some one asked.

"To be sure. Francis came, and at last we had a man in this feckless country. I am not going to bring the blushes to the cheek of my old friend, but you will believe me when I tell you that he put new life into the whole land. All the industries here are his starting. He has more influence among natives than any man since Livingstone. And then he has Musuru, that city set upon a hill-top, to which we can all go for advice and rest."

"The rainbow trout will be ready for you next month," said Carey.

"I'll be there," said the old man, chuckling. "This is Central Africa. And yet in two days I can get up to a Scotch glen, with bracken to catch your flies in, and I can get as good trout out of the pools with a black hackle as ever I got in the Devon. It is all the refreshment I ask for. Give me a day now and then with my rod, and I'm prepared to bide in this vineyard till my call comes."

Now it chanced that nearest Mr Wakefield's heart lay a passion for fly-fishing, and when the meal was over he claimed Mr Macdowall for a highly technical conversation. The party broke into groups: two rubbers of bridge were organised, and the others wandered into the verandah, beneath which the lake gleamed faintly under a young moon. Marjory Haystoun, fired with a sudden zeal for adventure, started with Mrs Wilbraham for the shore, regardless of a heavy dew and the thinness of her evening shoes; but the pair were summarily recalled by Mr Astbury, who spoke darkly of fever. By-and-by the bridge ended, and Mr Macdowall, tearing himself from a discourse on tiger-fish, made his farewells.

"I've done what you told me, Francis," he said to Carey. "The chiefs will come in early in the morning, and you can hold your palaver with them after breakfast. The white folk will be at the kirk at eleven to hear what you have got to say. I daresay I'm breaking my ordination vows—resigning my pulpit to a notorious heretic like you, but a little heresy once in a way does the world good. It's like an artificial flee, and excites the appetite if it does not satisfy the hunger."

The Duchess, who was a pillar of the Establishment, was relieved to learn next morning at breakfast that the whole party proposed to attend church, but she was a little dismayed to hear that the service was to consist of an address from their host. Her dismay was not lessened by the discovery that it was to be preceded by a gathering of native chiefs to present their respects to Carey.

"Surely it is scarcely work for a Sunday morning," she complained. "I dislike mixing up politics and religion. Besides, Francis is not in orders, he is not even a lay reader, and I know that he holds the most terrible opinions about the bishops. One of them told me that he always felt that Francis might pat him on the head if he said anything he agreed with, and tell him he was a good boy. I am not in the least afraid of natives, but I object to sit in the midst of a circle of hundreds. I shall feel too like an early Christian."

"Some time ago, Susan," said Carey, "I believe you occupied a conspicuous position on a platform at the Albert Hall. You were then in the midst of a circle not of hundreds but of thousands, and you showed no anxiety. You will find very little difference in the spectators to-day except that they have better manners, and are on the whole better to look at. I ought to say, however, that they will all be armed. I will not have these people meet me except as free men, and in this country it is the badge of a free man to carry spear and shield." The ordeal turned out to be of the mildest kind. The party were conducted to a spot a few hundred yards from the beach, where they found a semicircle of black warriors gathered around a little green hill. The chiefs stood to attention as they approached, and saluted in silence. But when Carey, who came a little later, ascended the mound he was greeted with a shout of welcome and a raising of spear-points skywards, which made the women shiver and flushed Lady Flora's cheek with excitement.

"That is the royal salute," Hugh whispered. "I wonder how many tribes in the continent give him that. He once told me he thought he had over thirty native names, and they are all flattering."

Carey sat down on a tree trunk, and the spokesman of the chiefs approached him. In the main he spoke their own tongue, but for those who used a special dialect he had a boy from the Mission to interpret. So far as the party could follow, the discussion was mainly about crops and stock diseases. There was some talk of a tribal disturbance on the western border, and once when a decision seemed to be questioned, Carey's slow, quiet tones changed to a sharp command, and the watchers saw his mouth harden. Sitting there among his own people, his massive figure and brooding face had a superb air of authority. All the men—Wakefield, Lord Appin, Lord Launceston, even Sir Edward—seemed to shrivel in the contrast, like beings out of their proper sphere.

"I never realised before how handsome he was," Lady Flora said to Hugh. "He came to dine with us in London in July, and I remember thinking that his clothes did not fit and that he carried himself badly. I could not help comparing him with a colonel in the Guards, who was also dining and who had the most beautiful straight figure. But out here he looks like a king. No one could be afraid of my Guardsman, but I cannot imagine any one disobeying Mr Carey. It is that massive head of his which overawes one like a mountain."

The business did not take long. Carey spoke a few final words slowly and impressively in a native tongue, there was a low murmur of applause, and the *indaba* was over. The party walked back silently to the mission-house, where they found the whole population of the settlement assembling. Besides the Mission staff there were a number of teachers from the industrial school, a contingent of local traders and planters, and a few Government officials. Carey knew every one by name, and was full of kindly inquiries. Most of them had been his guests at Musuru, and his greetings were those of a popular country squire with his neighbours at meet or market.

The little whitewashed mission church was filled to overflowing. The Duchess had rarely in her life felt at a loss, but the air of the gathering made her nervous. There was a Sabbatical hush in the audience, which suggested a religious service, but none of the accessories of church were present. Mr Macdowall entered and sat down on the chair commonly reserved for the choirmaster, where he proceeded to take snuff and gaze at the audience through benevolent spectacles. Then came Carey, who ascended the small pulpit, cleared away a Bible and a water-bottle which stood on the book-board, and, standing erect with his hands in his pockets, thus addressed his hearers—

"This is not a service, so we need waste no time in preliminaries. I have asked you to come here to-day because I wanted to meet you face to face and say certain things to you. We are all fellow-workers in one cause, though we call it by different names. I am older than most of you, and I have had a wider experience than most of you, so my views on the things which most deeply concern you may possibly be of some little assistance. I am not going to talk to you about theology, but what I have to say is vitally concerned with religion. Whatever our creeds—and I daresay Macdowall would scarcely credit me with any—we are all serious men, and in our various ways, as far as our imperfect light allows, we may claim to be seeking the kingdom of God and His righteousness."

"Ye're mistaken, Francis," Mr Macdowall interrupted; "ye're lamentably unsound in the faith, but I never denied that ye were a profoundly religious man."

Carey's face relaxed into a smile. "Well, then, I will take advantage of this testimonial, and talk to you in this church about secular things. Every country and every group of men have some special problem of their own. They have dozens of problems, of course, but there is always one which may be considered the centre of gravity, and on this it is their business to concentrate their attention, for on its settlement depends the settlement of all the others. Your business, on which everything else depends, is the wise management of the native peoples that live round about you. For every white man there are forty or fifty natives, and yet in your hands lies the administration and on your head is the responsibility for the future of the country. You have to fight against ignorance, stupidity, and barbarism. So has all the world; but you have the tremendous advantage that you have your foes in concrete shape before your eyes and know exactly what you have to get to grips with. In England we have the same enemies, but we cannot see them, and we have first of all to go and hunt for them; and there is a perpetual difference of opinion as to which is which—some calling ignorance honesty and stupidity wisdom. You are spared all this fuss. You know what brutality is and what decency is. You have got to convert the one into the other. "I am going to talk to you to-day about the two extremes we have to avoid. The first is the danger of underrating the status of the black man, and the second is the still greater danger of overrating it. As to the first, I know that most of you feel strongly about certain recent changes which have been made in the criminal law. Well, I was largely responsible for these changes, and I am here to defend and explain them. You argue, some of you, that the native is a child and must be treated as a child and punished at the discretion of his master, who stands to him *in loco parentis*. You maintain that to make native discipline depend upon the cumbersome machinery of a court of law is to make it a farce. Who, you ask, when his servant offends will be at the pains to take him before a magistrate? He will either take the law into his own hands, which will be bad for the discipline of the State, or he will let the matter pass, which will ruin the discipline of his household. That may be so, but if he follows the latter course he will have only himself to thank, and if he follows the first he will be punished. And the reason is that we dare not underrate the status of the native. You may repeat that he is a child, but the law must look upon him not as a potential but as an actual citizen, and must give him the dignity of such. He must stand before it as an equal with the white man—not a social equal or a political equal, but a legal equal. It is the State and not the individual that has the main interest in his development, and therefore to the State must be left the responsibility. To place it with the private citizen is to give him a burden more heavy than he can bear, and to expose him to those temptations towards brutality and injustice and caprice which may end in his own degradation. The State rightly refuses to allow such risks. With it rests the sole duty of punishment. But—and here I speak to practical men who will not, I think, misunderstand me—what after all is the meaning of law? It is the norm of conduct framed to suit average circumstances. A man must comply with it or pay the penalty, but sometimes it may be right to pay the penalty and break it. I may prevent a man in a public street from doing something disgraceful but not criminal, and I may be guilty of assault in the process. I am justified in breaking the law, and the law is right in fining me. There are a thousand conceivable cases when legal docility is a moral disgrace or a practical folly. Every man must have clearly before him his duty as a citizen. If he breaks the law he must be clear that his warrant is sound both as regards his own conscience and the State to which he owes obedience. Especially is this the case with the new law as to the rights of natives. It does not prevent a white man in emergencies from making a law for himself, but by its prohibition it compels him to be very certain about his justification. It will, I trust, put an end to caprice and encourage fair dealing, for he who breaks it can only appeal to the last and most rigorous of tribunals.

"The second danger is that you conceive of the native status as higher than it really is. This fault will be committed by the idealists among you, as the other will be the error of the practical man. And yet I have often found idealists and practical men alike doing homage to what I can only think is a false conception of native development. The native's mind is sharp and quick, his memory is often prodigious, and he has histrionic and mimetic gifts which may mislead his teachers. But for all that he stands at a different end of the scale of development from the white man. He represents the first stage of humanity, and he has to travel a long way before he can reach that level which we roughly call our civilisation. You cannot annihilate ten strenuous centuries by assuming that they have not existed, and inviting the native to crowd the work of them into a year or two. Between his mind at its highest and ours at its lowest there is a great gulf fixed, which is not to be crossed by taking thought. It is less a difference in powers—for he has powers as remarkable often as our own—as in mental atmosphere, the conditions under which his mind works, and consequently the axioms of his thought. He will learn gladly what we have to teach him, and you will imagine that the lesson of civilisation has been learned, when suddenly you are pulled up by some piece of colossal childishness which shows that that mind whose docility you have admired has been moving all the time in a world a thousand years distant from your own. We must recognise this gulf and frame our education accordingly. At bottom, and for obvious reasons, the native mind is grossly materialistic. The higher virtues and what we call "spirituality" are radically unintelligible to it, though it may learn to claim them and to talk their jargon. We must begin, therefore, with the first things, if we do not wish to get a dishonest parrot-like adherence to creeds which are not understood and have no power to influence life. I think there is more need for imagination and insight and foresight in a missionary among the black races than in most statesmen, for he has to study a mind and character most alien to our own and select from the vast storehouse of our civilisation the kind of nourishment suited to it.

"Remember that education is a thing which must take its colour from the needs that it is provided to satisfy. Your business is to inculcate in the native mind the elements of citizenship and Christian morality. It can only be done by degrees, but for heaven's sake begin with the truths that matter, and never mind the frillings for the moment. Get your foundations laid deep and solid. Preach the Atonement and the Fatherhood of God, and leave out your fancy dogmas. Teach the children to read and write, but do not aim at higher education, for that means black parsons and black schoolmasters, and for that class the market is overstocked, and they are outcasts from the society of those whom they would claim as intellectual equals. Above all things teach them trades and handicrafts and the simple laws of a decent life. It is not our business, as I keep telling my friends, to create a new heaven but to create a new earth. Get these strange, sullen, childish, dark-skinned people hammered into a peaceable and prosperous society, and you have laid the foundation of all the virtues. Teach them the elements of cleanliness and comfort and you will find them already grounded in honesty and loyalty; and you may soon get them to take their place in our complex system,—low down, of course,—but still indubitably within it. Don't try and make out of them theologians or schoolmasters or bagmen or electioneering humbugs. Leave the scum of civilisation for civilisation to deal with. You have still, thank Heaven! a simple community: keep it simple so long as you can, for it is on simple lines alone that it can make true progress.

"You may say that I offer you, merchants, planters, teachers, all of you, a gloomy programme. We are to civilise the land, you will say, by slow methods, and we shall be dead and buried long before the results come. Your complaint would be just if your only task were native administration. But it is not. You have the economic and political development of the land to think of, and you have your own future, for there is a white community growing up beside the black. And remember that the presence of the native races makes every man of you an administrator. If you face your duty, every white citizen will have the training of a proconsul, the same kind of problems to solve, the same qualities of character in demand. That is no small honour. What kind of race will your sons be if they grow up with the sense of civic duty alive in them, content to work slowly because hopefully and long-sightedly? I am one of the men who believe in the regeneration of the African continent. When the world has preached its lessons to her, she will also have something to say to the world. I do not think that the battles and the bloodshed, the young men who never came back, the lonely graves in the desert, the hopes crushed only to revive again—I do not think that these will have been in vain. Do you remember one of Pitt's perorations when that austere statesman gave rein to his fancy and delivered a prophecy whose justification you and I still await? I commend its rhetoric to you as a watchword. 'If we listen,' he said, 'to the voice of reason and duty, and pursue the line of conduct which they prescribe, some of us may live to see the reverse of that picture, from which we now turn our eyes with shame and regret. We may live to behold the nations of Africa engaged in the calm occupations of industry, in the pursuits of a just and legitimate commerce. We may behold the beams of science and philosophy breaking in upon this land, which at some happy period in still later times may blaze with full lustre, and, joining their influence to that of pure religion, may illuminate and invigorate the most distant extremities of that immense continent. Then may we hope that even Africa, though last of all the quarters of the globe, shall enjoy at length in the evening of her days those blessings which have descended so plentifully upon us in a much earlier period of the world. Then also will Europe, participating in her improvement and prosperity, receive an ample recompense for the tardy kindness—if kindness it can be called—of no longer hindering that continent from extricating herself out of the darkness, which in other more fortunate regions has been so much more speedily dispelled. 'Nosque ubi primus equis Oriens afflavit anhelis, Illic sera rubens accendit lumina Vesper!'"[4]

Late in the afternoon, as the yacht was once again slipping through violet waters, and tea was being served on deck, the Duchess found herself beside Mr Wakefield. "Francis is the oddest speaker of my acquaintance," she said. "It is such a mixture of straightforward prose and ambiguous poetry. And yet there is an art in it. You saw how he impressed these people. My brother might have spoken like an angel for hours without anything like the effect that Francis had with a few abrupt sentences. It is the man that does it. His figure, with his hands in pockets, has such a power about it, and such a past behind it, that people listen not so much to what his voice says as to his presence." Mr Wakefield looked back to where the forests and blue mountains of Entoro were growing faint in the evening haze. "On the second day of my visit," he said slowly, "I objected to the 'man of destiny.' I withdraw that objection now. The thing may be undemocratic, illiberal, and reactionary—I do not care a penny whistle if it is. It is the only power which can plant civilisation in the wilds and turn savages into orderly citizens. Our democracy is excellent in its way, but it can't do that sort of thing—you want the individual with his heart on fire to start the ball. You want faith and hope, and men have these things but not departments or nations. So much do I value the man of destiny now that I will describe him in the words of a writer I detest,—he is 'the Cyclopean architect, the road-maker of Humanity!'"

CHAPTER 8

AT dinner the following evening Carey announced that the subject for discussion that night was economic. A profound gloom fell on the company.

"I hate the word," said the Duchess. "When any one proposes some generous scheme the immediate answer is that it is 'uneconomic.' I believe that the whole thing is a false science, invented by the trading classes to conceal their own rapacity. They identify their penny-wise cunning with the laws of nature and claim a divine sanction for their misdeeds. Besides, I am sick of the kind of argument we have heard so much of for the past two years. To my mind even the few economic laws which are certain may very properly be overridden for the sake of higher interests. You tell me that Protection is good or bad economics, and I don't care a fig. I want to know if it is good or bad policy."

Lord Appin raised his eyebrows. "My dear Susan, do my ears deceive me? What you say is excellent Tory doctrine, which I have been industriously preaching for many years. Carey, living with you is turning all our heads. You have made Susan a Tory and Launceston a Dissenter."

"I am not going to ask you to talk Benthamite economics," said Carey, "though there is a great deal to be said for them. All I want you to do is to look at the eternal problem which you find in all States—riches and poverty, the use and control of the one and the cure of the other. It is an immense subject, and if we once get among facts and figures we shall be in a hopeless morass. At the same time there are general principles here as elsewhere, and I think it is possible to disentangle a few of them. To show fully how the recognition of the possibilities of empire will affect capital and labour would take a man's lifetime. But I think we can say roughly what the general line of the answer will be. I promise you, Susan, you shall not hear a word of orthodox jargon, for the excellent reason that none of us know any, except Lord Appin, and he doesn't believe in it."

Lord Appin protested vigorously. "As an ex-president of a learned society which concerns itself with nothing else, I claim complete economic orthodoxy. My objection to the science is that it tends to approximate in its methods to theology. Its votaries are apt to make laws of Sinai out of deductions from the commerce of a single epoch, forgetting to distinguish between what is sufficiently axiomatic to constitute a general law and what is only true under special and terminable conditions. Indeed, my chief complaint against the science is that it is too loose rather than too formal. My other complaint is that it mistakes its vocation. It starts from highly abstract data and builds up on them a structure of ingenious puzzles. It erects into a *Realphilosophie* what is purely formal, and, forgetting the abstraction of its starting-point, it imagines that it has provided a philosophy of life. A few elementary lessons in the art of definition would make the toil of economists of some use. As it is, they spend much of their time in the agreeable intellectual pastime of spinning cocoons. You may say, so does the metaphysician. But he is dealing with tremendous verities. And however fallacious, however over-subtle he may be, the magnitude of his task ennobles him. I cannot find the same elevation in tracking the vagaries of that quaint fiction the 'economic man.'"

As if to secure some cheerfulness for a dull discussion the party assembled after dinner in the Blue Drawing-room, which of all the rooms at Musuru was the most exquisite in its decorations. Its fluted white walls were set with panels of old turquoise-blue silk; the ceiling was modelled on that of a famous chamber at Versailles; the carpet was of rich white velvet pile; the furniture was all copied from a boudoir of Marie Antoinette. The books in the cabinets and on the tables were bound in vellum or blue morocco, and the few ornaments were of blue Sèvres ware or old ivory. The one picture, which hung over the chimney, was a Watteau of blue-robed nymphs dancing under a great expanse of spring sky. The lamps had shades of ivory silk, and in the soft light the pure colours swam in a delicate harmony as of a summer noon. The scene was so strange and perfect that most of the guests gave an involuntary gasp of admiration. Even Mr Wakefield snorted when he entered, and subjected the Watteau to the tribute of a long and critical stare.

"We are told," said Carey, "that the Empire is the dream of capitalism, and like every falsehood the saying contains the perversion of a truth. Large schemes over a large area require money and an elaborate organisation. Imperialism involves such schemes; therefore Imperialism demands wealth and organisation. That is our simple syllogism. Imperialism is not capitalism, but it is akin to it in method. The capitalist makes his fortune by recognising the value of combination and the wisdom of earning profits over the largest area possible. Imperialism depends likewise upon a form of combination. Both believe that Providence is on the side of the bigger social battalions.

"This, of course, is a truism. The difficulty arises when the imperialist State and the capitalist citizen come into conflict. Both have admittedly the same methods. Moreover, the great capitalist schemes must be semi-political, so the standpoint of pure individualism cannot be maintained. Our question therefore is, What is to be the relation of an imperial State to the rich citizen; and how far can the State imitate his activity on its own account? Or, to put it simply, admitting that combination and capital are necessary to any empire for imperial purposes, is the State in pursuit of such purposes to supervise or to supersede the individual?

"We are on the brink, you see, of the tremendous question of Socialism or Individualism, and you will be relieved to hear that I shall not embark on that wintry sea. I am afraid I cannot take the opposition of the two terms seriously. Like Protection and Free Trade, they are methods, not ideals: curative measures, not forms of diet. To declare for one or the other is as if anglers were passionately to take sides in the question of dry-fly against wet-fly. To say whether the Empire in the future will be socialist or individualist requires the gift not of reasoning but of prophecy, for to dogmatise on the character of its development you must foretell the circumstances which may control it. My own view is that we shall see the State become increasingly more concerned with matters which our forefathers left to private enterprise. Partly it will be the result of that new view of the State as something intimately and organically related to the private life of its citizens: partly it will be the result simply of our greater geographical area. Things which were once well within the scope of the individual now require an organisation so vast and complex that only the State can provide it, or, if the individual can compass it, he becomes a public menace. I can face with equanimity the day when our great shipping lines, our railways, our cable systems, even our mines, will be State-owned, but before that day can come the State must have learned more in the way of administration than it knows at present.

"At the same time, I cannot conceive that the day will ever dawn when the private capitalist can be wholly or even largely superseded. For many activities you will always want the quickening of the individual brain and will. Here I differ from my socialist friends, and I differ from them only because I am less of an idealist than they are. I do not think that men will ever spend themselves with the same fervour on behalf of a remote entity called the State as they will on their own private adventures. You may have the most admirable and conscientious officials, but they will be uninspired. They will administer, but rarely originate. In any case, any complete State-socialism is impossible to our Empire. I can picture it working well in a small neutralised State with no mysteries in her future. But what possible State organisation is capable of dealing with the whole life of a vast complex of States in all the latitudes of the globe?"

"The socialist would answer," said Hugh, "that if empire does not admit of his creed, then so much the worse for empire."

"He might," said Carey, "but I do not think he will, if he is given to thinking seriously about the question. I have never found his class a reactionary one. But if he does, then I say in turn, so much the worse for socialism. For of the two creeds there can be no question which is the stronger. The one is a method, a particular theory of administration; the other is an ideal, a gospel of a fuller national life. Few people, I think, will be prepared on behalf of a speculation as to the best mode of government to give up the task of government altogether—which is what the demand would be.

"However, I am not concerned to prophesy, and sufficient for the day is the evil thereof. I assume that the private capitalist will not be unknown in the future, that the State cannot wholly supersede him. Is it, then, to supervise him? Remember that the great fortunes of the future will not be made by old methods. Their makers will be no longer object-lessons in the wisdom of Benjamin Franklin's maxims. The millionaire of the future will be a statesman. He will administer affairs as complex and vast as the politics of a small nation. I am myself only a beginner, but politics in some form or other enter into every detail of my business. The great capitalist will have imagination and courage and foresight beyond most men.

"Now, there is to my mind a very great danger in the appearance of a class of men of the first order in ability and force of character, and with immense power at their command, and the whole outside the State. It is a government within a government, private citizens who in effect have governing powers. I merely point out the danger, for I have no remedy prepared. We must recognise that empire will extend the sphere of the great capitalist, and take measures accordingly. If I were sketching out a Utopia, it would, of course, be easy to fix a limit beyond which private fortunes should not go. We should allow our capitalist his energy but not his profits. He would be a tame revenue-earning machine for the State, making millions and receiving a few thousands as pocket-money. But I confess I can see no scheme which, as the world stands, would prevent the danger and yet not put an end to the fact of capitalism, and, since I believe that fact to be desirable on public grounds, I am not prepared for any heroic remedy.

"There is one thing to be said, however, which may give us hope. The capitalist of the future, we agreed, will not be the ordinary dull rich man. He will either be a great criminal or a considerable patriot. If he is the first I hope that the law may be strong enough to keep him in bounds, but if he is the latter he may be a great ally of the State. The millionaire who makes money solely to spend it on his pleasures is a cumberer of the ground. I do not care whether his pleasures are gross or refined, he is in any case a cumberer of the ground. But the man who with such a narrow soul will make a great fortune in the future will be rare indeed. He may make a million by rigging the market, but he will do little good at that serious exploitation which is closely akin to statecraft. It is only the latter which concerns us, for it is only if the latter falls into the hands of the fool or the knave that the political danger I dread will appear. Remember, I am talking of exploitation and of new production, not of the mere control of distribution, which is the object of the ordinary Transatlantic trust, for it is in the first kind of activity only that empire and capital come into close relation. The men who will succeed, I hope, will be those who find themselves capable of only spending a portion of their fortune on themselves and who have no desire to ruin their families by hoarding it for them. They will find their hobby not in rare furniture or on the Turf, but in doing, so far as the individual can, the work of the State."

Carey spoke these last words with a smile, looking towards Lord Appin. The shaft, however, failed of effect, for, as it chanced, Lord Appin's gaze was occupied with a beautiful cabinet, inlaid with agate and ivory. He looked up, caught Carey's eye, and looked again at the inestimable treasure. "No, Francis," he said sadly, "it is very clear that neither you nor I can live at that austere height. I hope you will spare the poor fellows some foible to keep them from the ennui of unvarying altruism."

"I am not very much concerned with the capitalist," said the Duchess. "I am much more anxious about labour. Mr Lowenstein, you once spoke at my Plaistow settlement on the subject. I wish you would say again what you told us then."

Mr Lowenstein was so frail in constitution that even the tonic air of Musuru had failed to give him complete health. His nervous activity made him the prey of headaches, and at the earlier discussions he had sat silent and miserable. For some reason, however, the trip to Entoro had done him good, and to-night he was in the best of spirits.

"What I have to say," he began, "can be put very shortly. And it has been put in far better words than I can command."

He opened a slim, well-worn book, that looked a very shabby intruder among the superb bindings around him.

"People say that Ruskin is not read now and that his day is over. I think Mrs Deloraine told me that he had done more than any other man to Corinthianise English prose. That may be true, but he was the first writer under whose charm I fell, and I cannot forget my early love for him. And he happens to say in one passage exactly what I wish to say to-night. It is in 'The Crown of Wild Olive,'[5] where he is speaking of the future of England.

These words seem to me to contain the truth about our social problem. England is too old a civilisation, and her natural productive forces have been exploited to the full. We have a vast industrial system which absorbs our energies, and since we have put all our eggs into the industrial basket, our prospects on the insular basis depends on its continuance at a certain high and artificial level. I say 'artificial,' for I think English industrialism must be admitted by every one to have long ago gone beyond the point where it is only one of many elements in the national life. Almost everything else has been sacrificed to it, and our peculiar position, historically and geographically, has given us the chance of achieving this abnormal development. But because it is abnormal it is all on a needle- point. We have no background such as other countries possess in their rural prosperity. We are urban and industrial or nothing. The ordinary large works are situated in some densely inhabited and highly rated neighbourhood. Their working expenses are enormous, and their margin of profit variable, since it depends upon so many undetermined conditions. Let there be a shortage in the foreign crop which furnishes their raw material, or a new tariff clapped on their manufactured article by some large consumer, or a new Factory Act, or a fresh rate, and the whole system gets out of gear. The work for the labourer is therefore generally speculative, and there is an equally speculative element on his side. He finds the housing problem insoluble, and he labours generally under conditions which break his health; and he is at the mercy of the organisation of his own trade, and may find himself called to sacrifice his own present comfort for the assumed ultimate advantage of his class.

"These and a dozen other elements of uncertainty, which spring from the extreme artificiality of our industrial system, tend to create the unemployed problem. Even the skilled workman finds himself frequently out of work, while the vast class of the unskilled—the unfortunates who are morally, mentally, or physically handicapped, or who through misfortune or lack of energy have remained at the foot of the ladder of labour—feel the insecurity more deeply. To my mind there is only one diagnosis of the evil. Industrialism has eaten us up, and, like all monopolies, has become a morbid growth, taking our life's blood and giving us little back. We are too preoccupied with it, and it is too preoccupied with itself. It is—how shall I say?—like a quantity of hot charcoal which, if spread through all the rooms of the house would have pleasantly warmed them, but if collected in one chamber will asphyxiate the inmates. And the result is the starving poor in our streets, and in every great city some quarter which is a sink of misery and crime.

"There are, of course, a hundred proposals. Some maintain that the State should turn itself into a kind of Universal Employer, and use the derelict classes on public works devised for no other purpose than their relief. I do not think such a course would do much good. The State, by its large outlay on unproductive and unnecessary works, would be lessening the wealth of the country, and thereby lowering industrial well-being and adding indirectly to that evil of unemployment which it purported to cure. Some again are prepared to nationalise means of production, and make all industry a State concern. No doubt that course would effect many startling changes, but it would overturn the foundations of our society, the good with the evil; and I do not think that the English people will be inclined to burn their house down in order to cure the damp in the cellar. Some people propose, vaguely but benevolently, a return to the land. The great proprietors would disappear, and their estates would be converted into a multitude of small holdings, on which the unskilled, who had failed to maintain themselves at simple trades, would be set down to the most difficult of all professions. Of all schemes this seems to me the most crazy. If you make the holdings small enough to admit of a great number of families being settled on the land, you will make it impossible for these families to make a living. It is the simplest calculation. In the present state of English agriculture we know exactly how much land and how much capital are required before there can be sufficient return to make an income. If, on the other hand, you create only a small number of largish farms, you do not touch the unemployed problem.

"There are many other suggestions which I need not repeat. But there is one feature common to them all. They all propose to settle the question on the basis of England, and England alone. Now I maintain that to attempt this is simply to reshuffle the cards without an atom of positive gain. The disease we are suffering from is congestion, a poverty of means to ends, a lack of breathing-space and opportunity. Millions are being morally starved because they have no hope in their lives, and their labour is without honour or ideals; and, may be, physically starved because they are not wanted in the present industrial market. What we have to realise is that these islands of ours are overexploited. You may arrange your beans in different ways, but you will never make more than. five; and if you want a square meal you must get more beans.

"Therefore I say with all the earnestness I possess, that we can never settle the labour question with its kindred problem of unemployment on an English basis. What would we think of a landowner whose fields were grossly overstocked and his animals starved, although he had a rich farm at the other side of the county which was wholly ungrazed. We must take into account all our assets and face the difficulties in a spirit of sober reason. Let us find out what margin of workmen are crowded out of regular employment, let us classify carefully, for each problem must be dealt with on its merits, and there is no short cut to a solution. But let us keep in mind all the data, for there is no hope for us if we refuse to admit more than one-third into our inquiry. Public works for the unemployed may be unnecessary and wasteful in England, but elsewhere in the Empire they may be both necessary and economical. 'Back to the land' may be a foolish cry in a country where the soil refuses to support its owners, but the same thing is not true of the whole globe. There are countries which need above all things men, that commodity of which we have enough and to spare. They will take our raw human material and shape it for us. And they will take our industries and plant them in places where the men employed can lead a free life. The day of the great factory with its operatives living in the acres of squalid houses around it is going, I believe, even in England. It is recognised that industries under such conditions sin alike against decency, patriotism, and true economy. Even in England to-day you have your factories in the country and your model industrial villages. What is done on a small scale within our island can be done on a great scale within the Empire. It is for wiser men than me to settle the details, but I am convinced that Buskin has found in the matter a truth which is hidden from Royal Commissions."

Mr Lowenstein spoke nervously and rapidly, and when he ceased he lay back in his chair as if much fatigued and closed his eyes. Lady Warcliff, who in spite of her energy and independence had always some prophet at whose feet she sat in her leisure, watched him with a solicitous face, and, since he showed no signs of continuing, took up his parable.

"As a woman interested in philanthropy," she began, "I heartily wish the thing had never been heard of. We are smothered with it nowadays. We want less charity, and more justice and intelligence. Some one has divided mankind into soft-hearted cruel people and hardhearted kind people. The first have had their day, and a pretty mess they have made of it. They have filled our hospitals and asylums, and given us our East Ends, and our unemployed demonstrations. Comfortable people like a little easy charity as the sauce to their enjoyment. They are too cowardly and supine to face the truth, so they hang over it the cloak of their egregious generosity. We shall never get one step farther till we recognise that the destitute must be divided sharply into two classes—those who may be saved and those who, being past hope, should cease to exist."

"Upon my word, Margaret, our sex comes very badly out of these discussions," the Duchess's voice had a startled note in it. "On board the yacht I heard Caroline airily advocating persecution, and now you want to cure our disorders by the euthanasia of social cripples. I am horrified that barbarism should find its only advocates among women."

"I was afraid I should shock you," said Lady Warcliff sweetly. "And yet— will you show me any other remedy? There are classes of the poor in every town who in all seriousness are beyond hope. It may be physical, or moral, or mental, but the weakness is there and cannot be overcome. We shut up criminals and lunatics, and yet we allow these people, who are as certainly a leprous spot in our society, to go on marrying and perpetuating their worthless stock and hampering the activity of the State. Sharp surgery is the only cure. I want to see these hordes of thriftless, degenerate, scrofulous pariahs treated as what they are, irredeemable outcasts from society, and compelled by the State to keep their noxious influence away from the saner parts. This, however, is beside the question. It is the people who are worth saving that I want to talk about.

"Like everybody who has been much among the poor, I have had many theories as to the cause and the cure of the evils I saw before me. But after I had tried many and found them wanting, I came round to the kind of creed which Mr Lowenstein has been sketching. It is this alone which makes me call myself an Imperialist. The common cant of empire is more obnoxious to me, I think, than any other cant. I have no liking for rhetoric or adventure, and most of my best friends belong to the school which is untouched by the glamour of foreign dominion. I want, like them, to cure our own evils before we proselytise up and down the earth, but it is just because of that desire that I am an Imperialist.

"Take the very poor—men and women who are capable of work and could be raised under decent conditions to a wholesome level of life. If you keep such people on charity you ruin their self-respect. Besides, there is not enough charity to go round. But what they want in their lives is not so much the bare means of existence as some kind of hope. They must have a horizon before them, not straight grey walls between which they will be shepherded till they die. They want to be given opportunity, where on their own feet they can fight with fair confidence, first for a living and then for the amenities of life. Now it is my conviction that as things stand to-day in England it is impossible to give them opportunity. We may slightly improve their condition, and save a few here and there from starvation, but it is all an attempt to cure an earthquake with a pill. If we are true reformers we must go to the root of the matter and change the conditions which make destitution possible.

"This is the creed of socialism, and so far we all agree with it. Our common position is, that we must create opportunity for all, not merely rescue hard cases. Where we part company is the method of this reform. One way is to lower the rich and raise the poor, until the whole State forms one vast lower middle-class in respect of income. By this means we should not increase the aggregate of opportunity, but we should make a fairer distribution. My objection to it— or rather the chief of my many objections—is, that it involves so complete a revolution not only in the material aspects of our society but in its whole thought and tradition, that it will be an uncommonly hard thing to achieve. Besides, I see little attraction in a society where, as Bagehot said, people would be forbidden to go barefoot, and everybody would have one boot apiece. I prefer the alternative, which is more logical, and to my mind infinitely more attractive, than a levelled-down middle-class State. My proposal is to add to the aggregate of opportunity. I want to follow the great law of supply and demand, and send men and women away from the place where they are not wanted to places where they will be welcomed.

"At the same time I do not call my scheme emigration. People are free to emigrate as they choose to any part of the world, and if this were the unfailing cure for poverty the poor would long ago have found it out for themselves. I advocate State-organised emigration within the Empire, because it is only under these conditions that you can have it scientifically organised and supervised. Emigration is the least easy art in the world. It needs careful selection, long preparation of land and people for each other, and it wants at the back of it all the authority of the State. I have seen many experiments made by private individuals and philanthropic agencies which have been successful, but for our problem the solution must be on a great scale, otherwise we shall not have faced the difficulties fairly. The State must be the great emigrator. It alone has the power to collect full information and decide whether this or that scheme is justifiable. It can make arrangements with the Colonies, and it can reduce the cost of transport to a minimum. An imperial executive, such as we talked of the other evening, will be equal to the task, for being representative of the whole empire it will be spared the long negotiations with Colonial Governments which we have to put up with at present. Besides, in its permanent Bureau of Intelligence it will have the machinery for framing its schemes on the surest and most scientific grounds.

"If you send the right man to the right place in the right way you will manufacture citizens out of material which at present is sinking into the slough of despair. You will give our empty lands population and reduce the congestion of our English slums. And you will bring hope, and a reasonable hope, into a kind of life which is starved for the lack of it. I do not say that the result can be achieved at once. But you will have opened up a path, and soon it will be well trodden. We Imperialists look forward to our people becoming more mobile, and seeking a home wherever life can be lived freely and sanely, instead of choking within the limits which were sufficient for the fathers but are too narrow for the sons. We agreed the other evening that our industries must move as occasion demands, and labour will naturally follow them. These are inevitable but unconscious processes due to the compulsion of facts. Meanwhile we can begin by a conscious attempt to redeem the tragedy of our civilisation not by any violent cataclysm but by using those means which are ready at hand. In Canning's phrase, we must call in the new world to redress the balance of the old."

"At last," said the Duchess, "we have got a proposal with which I can cordially agree. I thought when you began to talk about labour you were going to defend things like the importation of coolies into South Africa. You know how much I and many other good Imperialists were distressed by that."

"You are not going to escape, Susan," said Lady Lucy, smiling. "Lady Warcliff has been talking about English labour, and I have something to say about the other kinds which the Empire has to show. She pleads for greater elasticity for labour at home, but she has only touched on one part of a very large question. If we owe duties to English labour, we owe duties also to every man under our rule who works with his hands. You will find labour problems as difficult and as urgent as your English question in many parts of the Empire—in India, in the Far East, in the West Indies, in most parts of Africa. You have great tracts, like Southern India, which are so thronged with human beings that there is no room to live; and you have places like the Sudan and the Transvaal, and even this neighbourhood, where the land is far richer than the human population it supports. If we take up the task of government in a scientific spirit, it is surely our business to fit the people to the land. I agree with Lady Warcliff that nothing is so much wanted as mobility in labour. The old idea was that the labouring man was rooted by Providence in the soil where he was born. He might go away if he pleased, but the desire was thought to indicate frivolity. The notion that the State should encourage him to leave would have made the honest Benthamite blush. Happily that frame of mind is gone for ever. Where we see men suffocated for lack of space, and great spaces barren for lack of men, we are not to be kept from adopting the common-sense remedy by any *laissez-faire* croakings."

The Duchess saw danger ahead and made haste to meet it half-way.

"I have no fault to find with that, so far as it goes. If the Sudan can support ten millions and has got only three, then by all means import the natives of Southern India who, you say, are too many for their land to feed. Or let them come and cultivate the marshy coastlands near Mombasa, where the white man cannot live. All that is legitimate emigration, and no Liberal could object to it. What I am opposed to is the shifting of masses of men about the world, like chattels, at the will of private employers. You exploit their labour and pack them home again, and the main inducement to emigrate—the chance of a new home—is denied them."

"And yet," said Lady Lucy, "I do not see why we should subscribe to the mystical doctrine that emigration is a good thing if we carry it out to the full, but very bad if we stop halfway. I can imagine so many cases where the half would be more than the whole—where, indeed, the whole would be a positive blunder. There are districts in India where the people are landowners and farmers. What they need is a little capital to buy more land or stock, and so enable themselves to make a steady living. They have no desire to settle abroad for good, and they have no need to do so. But if they can give their labour for a few years at good wages to some country which wants it, why should they be prevented? Or you may have the case of a country such as this or South Africa, which is naturally a white man's country, and which we all hope some day to see filled with white settlers; but some urgent temporary work has to be done—a railway built or new mines opened—and we must import labour at once and in large quantities. Is there any reason why coolies should not be brought in on contract, paid well for their work, and shipped back again? They are not compelled to come, and they are paid for coming; their coming benefits both themselves and the land, but their remaining would in no way benefit the land. In such a case surely we can have restricted emigration without breaking any of the Commandments."

The Duchess looked round the company in despair. "What has come over my sex?" she asked. "According to Caroline the chief weapon of Imperialism is the rack or the thumbscrew; according to Margaret, the lethal chamber; and now, according to Lady Lucy, it is the chain and the sjambok we must really look to. I begin to be afraid that our enemies are right, and that we have got a taint of the later Roman Empire in our blood. As for this restricted emigration, I refuse to distinguish it from slavery. It is temporary slavery, to be sure, but the quality is the same."

"If you will really think what you mean by 'slavery,' Susan, you will change your mind. The word is like so many others—'despotism,' 'force,' 'filibustering,' 'perpetual tutelage,' which the heavy guns of our opponents fire daily,—it looks impressive in the air, but when it strikes it is found to be filled with sawdust. The word is formidable only when it is not examined. If you mean by it 'discipline,' then all types of organised action are slavery. A coolie who contracts to come here and work on a railway or mine, undertakes to do his work under such conditions as his employers prescribe. So long as these conditions are not such as to offend public morals, the men who organise it have an ample right to say what the particular work demands. The State says, further, that it does not wish these coolies to remain in the country. Is not the State the best judge of what the country requires? Is there anything immoral in a country shutting its doors against a special kind of emigrant? You say that it is wrong for a State to exploit the labour of these emigrants and yet to refuse them permanent citizenship. That, I confess, is a doctrine beyond my comprehension. You may as well say that I have no right to buy provisions from the Stores, when I prefer to order my wine elsewhere."

"I do not feel so strongly opposed to State action," said the Duchess. "After all, the State has certain rights, and its motives are disinterested, and its oversight will be rigorous. If the indentured labourers were only imported for public works, I should not complain. It is when they are brought in for the use of private firms that the taint of slavery appears."

Lady Lucy laughed. "Well, let us argue in the style of the Platonic dialogues. How, and by means of what qualities, are we to define State action? And shall we include municipal action in this category? And if State action is the action of the organised community for the good of the community, on what principle are we to exclude the action of public companies who control the main industries of the State? And again—"

"For goodness' sake stop, Lucy!" said the Duchess good-humouredly. "I never could bear the Socratic method. Its little pistol-shot arguments give me a headache. I daresay there is something in what you say. Slavery may be an inaccurate term to describe what I so much dislike, but in any case it involves a perpetual danger of slavery. If you tie up by contract the liberty of an individual for a term, you pave the way for restricting it without any contract for life. It is the thin end of the wedge."

"I shouldn't use that phrase, my dear," said Lord Appin solemnly. "It is the worst of our parliamentary *clichés*, and, besides, Hardcastle has made it comic for ever. I was privileged to hear his great speech in the Lords against the Deceased Wife's Sister's Bill. He declared that he did not object to the present measure, which was merely permissive. 'But,' said Hardcastle, 'it is the thin end of the wedge. Soon it will be compulsory, and it is my misfortune that my dear wife has left me without any taste for her family.'"

Lady Lucy, who at most times spoke little, had been so stirred by the Duchess's criticism that she had risen to her feet, and now addressed the company from beside Carey on the hearthrug.

"Susan does not mean what she says. She is only repeating the arguments of her party, like a pious brigand who mumbles a paternoster before robbing a coach. Her last phrase is typical of a frame of mind which is very common and very hopeless. You are not to embark upon a scheme, however clearly you define its limits, because of its possible maleficent extension. I cannot understand the creed. If we believed in it all energy and progress would cease. We should sit like Buddha, twirling our thumbs, afraid to move a muscle lest we blundered. Not that any one seriously holds this faith. They imagine they do, because they are confused and slack, and have never taken the pains to think out what words mean. That is one class of my opponents. The others frankly detest the Empire, and hide their bias under the cloak of humanitarian tenderness. They hate colonial indentured labour, as Macaulay's Puritans hated bear-baiting, not because it does harm to the labourer, but because it does good to the colony.

"The honest souls who dread the bugbear of slavery need not concern themselves. Slavery, which means that one man is at the mercy of another's caprices, will never raise its head again.

Even though it had done no ill to the slave, it was economically and morally ruinous for the master. No! what we have to do is to save men from the far more relentless tyranny of circumstance. The bondage of things, believe me, is more cruel than the bondage of men. I call a dock-labourer in Poplar, who sees no hope for himself or his children, a slave. I call men slaves who, whether they own their land or not, are living always on the brink of starvation. But I call him a free man who sells his labour under contract for a term of years that he may earn enough to make his livelihood secure. I grant you that liberty is beyond price; but, like Burke, I want to see a 'manly, moral, and regulated liberty.' How often must it be repeated that freedom is not the absence of restraints, but a willing acceptance of them, because their purpose is understood and approved."

Lady Lucy's quiet voice had risen to that pitch of fervour which betrays the natural orator. As she stopped, she looked with some little embarrassment at the Duchess, and with a sudden movement sank on the floor beside her chair and took a hand in hers.

"Please forgive me for scolding you, Susan dear! But you know you deserved it. You have still got the General Election in your ears, and somehow its odious phrases make a fury of me. I don't blame any one for talking nonsense at home, but one must leave it behind at Musuru."

"I am not convinced," said the Duchess. "Your principle may be right, but all your applications are wrong. And I am far from being sure about your principle. Without being a dogmatic individualist, I protest against the idea of the State incurring such vast responsibilities as providing employers with labour and moving populations about the world. I admit that the province of the State has been widened, but such an insane stretching of boundaries seems to me to court disaster."

"Your fears always make me nervous, Susan," said Carey, "for you have an uncanny instinct for being right. But I think I can persuade—"

He was not permitted, for the Duchess rose and held before him protesting hands. "No, Francis, you shall not lecture me. And I promise in return to talk no more platform stuff. Besides, I am to be left alone after to-morrow with you, and you will have every chance to convert me.... Dear, dear, how solemn we all look! A Social Science Congress is out of place in a turquoise boudoir. That little Watteau shepherdess looks ready to weep with boredom. If there were such things as card-tables in this room I might think of bridge."

CHAPTER 9

THE whole party, men and women, breakfasted at the same hour next morning, most of them with that look of mingled unrest and high spirits which marks the expectant traveller. All their clothes spoke of the road, though the various styles showed that that road was not the same for every one. Those who were to stay behind—the Duchess, Lord Appin, and Lord Launceston—had the bland air of ease and proprietorship which all steadfast things wear in a changing world. The clock-work regime of Musuru made bustle impossible. There was no running about of maids and valets, no ringing of bells and confused directions. Carey consulted a paper in his hand, and now and then gave an order to a noiseless servant. The vast size of the house prevented the guests from catching any unsettling intimations of departure.

"We are now," said the Duchess, to whom breakfast was a cheerful meal, "about to begin the inter-act in our comedy. I should like to know, before we scatter, what point we have reached in our discussions. We have talked about a great many different things, and on the whole I think we have been fair."

"When Susan calls any one fair," said Lord Appin, "she means that he is a little biased in her own favour."

"Of course," said the Duchess, "I have that complete candour which does not mind confessing a slight lack of it. We won't quarrel about words. We have examined home politics and found them largely at war about irrelevant issues. For myself, I think that we overstated the case, but I have no complaint against our positive conclusion—that Imperialism meant the treatment of all our problems on a wider basis. Then we took up certain questions in detail. Some, such as the kind of imperial constitution we must look forward to, and the kind of administration the Tropics will require, were imperial questions in the strictest sense—new conundrums which the fact of empire calls into being. Others, such as the proper way of remedying our social disorders, were ordinary home problems discussed from the imperialist standpoint. Am I right, Francis? You always said I had a logical mind."

Carey nodded, and the Duchess continued.

"I don't want to be unreasonable, but it seems to me that the subject wants a broader handling. I am old-fashioned enough to believe in principles. I want the principles, and not the details, of empire. Stop me if T am talking nonsense, please, for I never pretended to be a philosopher. But tell me, some one, if the orthodox way is not to get the general principles clear and leave the treatment of specific points to be deduced from them. Hugh, will you get me some cold partridge?"

"My complaint," said Mr Wakefield, "is just the opposite—I am in no great hurry for principles. A vague philosophy of empire seems to me of the slenderest value at the present moment. Wait till we have penetrated some distance into the new country before we begin to map it. It is surely our business to have a clear policy on the different imperial questions,—that is to say, on every phase of our political life,—and having got that, to consider the best way and means of forcing it upon the world. That is the omission which I complain of. We all know roughly what we mean by Imperialism. What I want to know is how to make the ideal a fact, to exchange Imperialism for Empire. We have discussed most of the great practical questions except that of the tariff—and I am content to leave that alone for the moment. But how are we to set to work to enforce our solution?"

"If you know what Imperialism is," said Lord Appin, "you know more than I do. I don't think your complaint can be admitted, Wakefield. As Carey declared a fortnight ago, we are here to get our minds clear. We are not in office with a solemn mandate to reconstruct the Empire. Our business is to create opinion. Our works, to adopt the old distinction, must be light-giving before they can be fruit-bearing."

"Then what better are we than other framers of barren Utopias?" asked Mr Wakefield, in the act of assaulting a ham.

"The distinction is easy. A Utopia is a scheme of things which is possible but not practicable. There is nothing in it inherently inconceivable, but it demands a change of conditions so complete as to be beyond reasonable hope. The empire we wish is not only possible, but practicable. We have all the elements of it before us. It only requires a slight adjustment of things as they are to make it a reality. If, then, it needs no magician's wand to change our dream into fact, but only a touch here and there, surely it is our first duty to see that the dream is clear and complete. Once that is accomplished, once something has been prepared which the mind of our people will accept as its creed, then with an easy conscience we can leave the rest to the hacks and journeymen of politics."

"There's something in what you say," Mr Wakefield admitted. "I don't ask for office-bearers, a committee, a list of members, and a telegraphic address. There is a foolish matter-of-factness as well as a wise. But I think we should turn our attention to methods as well as to ideals. All about us lies a stubborn and unregenerate world. Though we speak with the tongues of men and angels we shall not be listened to, unless we prepare for ourselves a hearing."

"Again, I say, that it is not our business. Imperialism is not a propaganda which needs to be canvassed like an election policy. It will find acceptation when it is acceptable—not before. Our trouble is that ours is still a cryptic faith, unformulated and incoherent. Our task is to bring its meaning to light, first for our own sakes and then for our people's. One man with a clear mind is more of a dynamic force than a dozen well-organised guilds for the dissemination of platitudes. When our symposium is at an end and we go back to the world, then by all means let us talk about methods. But do not let us confuse ourselves here by any obeisance to that intolerable fool, the 'practical man.'"

"That is all very well," said the Duchess, "but nobody has answered my question. I am content that we should discuss empire without any eye to the ways and means of speedy realisation. But I am not content that we should settle isolated details and leave our principles all vague and inconclusive."

"*L'ineptie*," Lady Flora quoted wickedly, "*consiste à vouloir conclure*."

The Duchess laughed. "A very apposite quotation, my dear, but I am not to be silenced by a tag from a French novelist. Francis, give me some comfort."

"I am quite ready to defend our course," said Carey. "A question so vast and so subtle as ours—one, too, which has a bearing on every interest of our mortal life—cannot be treated in a mechanical way. It would be easy for us to pass a string of dapper resolutions, but, if we did, we should leave things as we found them. Principles and axioms we have, but they will only emerge when we have re-thought the conditions of our new world. We must creep before we can walk, and feel our way humbly in the mysterious twilight of dawn. We shall make many mistakes in that half-light, for the objects are blurred and the morning haze is still on the hills: but at least we can learn something of the nature of the land, and we can tell where the east lies. All of us have slightly different standpoints, different principles, and different prejudices. When a man lays down a dogma he is bound to colour it in a large degree by his temperamental bias. The colouring is probably unconscious, but the result is that truths appear, not in their white light, but all shot across with rays from the thinker's personality. There is a vast deal of irrelevant stuff in them, which is dear to some minds and antipathetic to others. Now, the best way, in my opinion, to get rid of this embarrassing surplus is to let the various temperaments conflict, for out of such conflict emerges the ultimate agreement. Ideals expressed crudely and summarily in conversation may be far from the perfection of a dogma patiently elaborated in the study. But they will have the merit of life, and the strife of living things always bears fruit in the end. Our object, as I said before, is to get our minds clear, not to frame a political catechism. And if this is so, then the minds must speak in their own accents, for it is only when we have understood wherein we differ from each other that we can realise wherein we agree. There is a method which philosophers call dialectic—the attainment of harmony by the reaction upon each other of opposing theories—and the plan we are following is in its way a homely kind of dialectic. Clearly we could not begin by laying down principles, for they would have been intelligible only to the man who laid them down. But at the start we found we were agreed, not on our axioms, but on our attitude. Imperialism, we decided, was the realisation of new conditions for all our problems, an enlarged basis, and fuller data. We did not attempt to find an answer to any of the great political questions: we only indicated the lines on which the answer must be sought. Imperialism, so ran our conclusion, is a spiritual change. We next looked at some of the simpler results which flow from the acceptance of the fact of empire,—especially the need for a new machinery of State,—and we applied the conception to our eternal labour problem, not to solve it, but to see how far it lit the path to a solution. But the kernel of our inquiry still awaits us, though we have cracked the shell. We have all by this time got a rough idea of what is the general meaning of the imperial attitude. But we must understand more fully the nature of the spiritual change we have talked of. I suggest, therefore, that we look at some of the great compartments of life and see how our conception will apply. It is a political conception, remember, but since politics in their new meaning are so intimately inwoven with life, we may learn something of its meaning by examining its bearing on art and conduct. And then, having got some understanding of the concrete significance of our ideal, we can hazard a fuller definition. So you shall have your principles, Susan, but at the end instead of at the beginning."

"And in the meantime," said the Duchess, "we are to be assisted to understand what you call 'the concrete significance'—odious phrase!—of Imperialism by going off into the real wilderness for three weeks. I daresay we shall get the atmosphere of empire into our souls, but I shall be surprised if some of us don't get fever into our bones. I do hope you have been careful, Francis. I don't want Musuru to end as a nursing home."

"There is just a chance of fever for those who go to Ruwenzori, but I think it may be avoided, and in any case it would be slight. The other expeditions are as healthy as a cruise in the North Sea. Shall I tell you the plans?"

Carey had privately arranged with each member of the party as to how the next weeks should be spent, but no one had been permitted to divulge the arrangement. Hence, while all knew their destinations they had no inkling of who their companions might be, and their host's announcement was awaited with much interest. "First of all the Duchess stays on at Musuru with me; and Lord Appin and Lord Launceston keep us company. Lady Warcliff is going to Aden by the Austrian Lloyd to meet Sir Arthur on his way home from India. Mrs Deloraine was anxious to explore the East Coast, and Mr Wakefield wanted to have a look at the South African colonies, so they will join one of my yachts to-morrow at Mombasa. Mrs Wilbraham, Mrs Yorke, and Mr Lowenstein are going too, and I think they should be able to get as far as Durban, and spend three or four days ashore. I am a little doubtful about the next expedition, which is Astbury's idea. He and Graham and Marjory and Lady Lucy propose to go off to Ruwenzori, and make an attempt to ascend Kiyanja. It is well worth doing, for there is no stranger or lovelier mountain scenery on earth, but it is a long job, and the country before you reach the Mubuku valley is a little wearing. However, I have collected for them a good caravan, they can cross the lake in the yacht to the best starting-point, and two Chamonix guides, who live here in the settlement, will accompany them. They took me up the second time the ascent was made, and know every step of the road. Last of all comes the hunting-party,— Lady Flora, Lady Amysfort, Hugh, and Sir Edward. Teddy still yearns for a good eland head, so they are going off to the north to look for one—first, the Uasin-Gishu flats, and then up towards Rudolf. Remember you have only three weeks, and you won't be allowed to outstay your leave, for my men have orders to bring you back at all costs to Musuru twenty-two days hence. *Bon voyage* to you all, and good hunting to you, Teddy, and for Heaven's sake, Hugh, give up the habit of stalking lions with a pop-gun."

"I wish," said the Duchess, "that I were not an old woman. Or, since that is a foolish thing to say, I wish that, being old, I did not feel so young. I suppose some one must remain behind to write to sorrowing relatives. You must be very kind to me, Francis, for I foresee I am going to be in a bad temper."

CHAPTER 10

THREE weeks later Lady Flora and Hugh were riding with slack reins over the great downs which sweep from Musuru to the north. Their caravan was visible some miles in the rear, a small dot in the interminable expanse of green. The riders were facing south, and far away appeared the dark line which told of the forests which surrounded the house. It was a windless afternoon, but at that height the air had the freshness of a mountain-top. The world slept in the still and golden weather—only the sound of their horses' hoofs, and now and then the cry of a bird, broke in upon the warm, scented silence. The bent, green with springtide in the near distance, mellowed in the farther spaces to a pale gold, which stood out with entrancing clearness against the crystalline blue of the sky. It was a plateau on which they rode, for to the west the tops of little hills showed up on the horizon, foreshortened like the masts of ships at sea. This sight, and the diamond air and the westering sun, gave the riders the sensation of moving in some cloud-built world raised far above the levels of man.

The three weeks had worked changes in their appearance. In spite of veils Lady Flora had become sunburnt, and she had exchanged her prim English seat for the easy pose of the backwoods. Hugh, tanned like an Indian, wore clothes so stained and ragged that he looked like some swagman who had stolen a good horse. He caught the girl's amused eye and laughed.

"I know I'm pretty bad, but I'm not so bad as Teddy. I wish his wife could see him at this moment. And I wish the whole round earth could behold Lady Amysfort. Who could have guessed that the wilds would have wrought such a change?"

"You don't know Caroline as well as I do, or you would wonder more. I was afraid she would be bored, or have a headache or something, for she is so accustomed to being served and worshipped that I did not think she would see any fun in roughing it. I suppose Mr Carey knew her better. But when I saw her making pancakes the first night, I knew it would be all right. Before we started, she was the last woman I would have chosen to travel with, and now she is the first. And that is a pretty high recommendation, I think."

"Like Charles Lamb's praise—' What a lass to go a-gipsying through the world with!' I think so too. Well, it's all over now, Lady Flora. Have you enjoyed yourself?"

"Shall I ever forget it—those magical weeks? We are not going back to anything half as good as we are leaving behind. I know now what Mr Astbury meant by Nirwana, for I have been living in it. Do you remember when we camped in the little ravine above Asinyo? When you and Sir Edward were away hunting all day, Charlotte and I used to climb up to the top of the rocks among the whortleberries, and watch the shadows running over the plain, and get blown on by the cool winds from the Back of Beyond. I never knew one could be so happy alone. And then the evenings, with the big fire and the natives' chatter, and Sir Edward's stories and Caroline's singing! Do you remember one night we argued for hours about what could be done to make Ascot more amusing? And then we suddenly remembered where we were, and burst out laughing. What fun it was, too, to lie awake in bed, quite warm and comfortable, and see the stars twinkling through the door of one's tent, and hear the wolves howling to each other! I hate coming back—even to Musuru.

"And in all that huge, heavenly country," the girl went on, "there was not one white man. I shall soon be as fanatical about settlement as Lady Warcliff. Only I am going to preach a different creed. Think of the numbers of young men of our class who have sufficient money to live on and nothing to do. They somehow fall out of the professions, and hang about at a loose end. But there is excellent stuff in them if they found the kind of life to suit them. They would have made good eldest sons, though they are very unsatisfactory younger ones. But out here they could all be eldest sons. They would have a Christian life, plenty of shooting, plenty of hard work of the kind they could really do well; and then they could marry and found a new aristocracy. I don't suppose Mr Carey wants the new countries to be without their gentry. What a delightful society it would be! I can picture country-houses—simple places, not palaces like Musuru,—and pretty gardens, and packs of hounds, and—oh, all that makes England nice, without any of the things that bore us. There would be no Season, because there would be no towns, and everybody would remain young, because there would be nothing to make them grow old."

"Would you be one of the citizens of your Utopia?" Hugh asked.

"I think I should. At least my Better Self would. At this moment I look on the complicated world with disgust. My tastes are half pagan and half early Christian. I want to have all the things that really matter in life, and nothing else. I want to be able to look out on everything with clear eyes and without any sentimentality or second-hand emotion. Do you know, if I spent many weeks like the last three I should become very like a man. I have caught Sir Edward's slang, and I have almost fallen into his way of regarding things. What was that odd poem he was always quoting, something about the 'wind in his teeth'?"

"'May I stand in the mist and the clear and the chill,'"

Hugh repeated—

"'In the cycle of wars,
In the brown of the moss and the grey of the hill,
With my eyes to the stars!
Gift this guerdon and grant this grace,
That I bid good-e'en,
The sword in my hand and my foot to the race,
The wind in my teeth and the rain in my face!'
'Be it so,' said the Queen."

"Well, I am all for 'the wind in my teeth and the rain in my face,' though it would be very bad for my complexion. Where does Sir Edward get his verses?"

"Heaven knows! Partly he invents them, and partly he misremembers things he has read. They are the strangest mixture. And he hasn't an idea who wrote what. He will put down some hideous doggerel to Shakespeare, and credit Whyte-Melville with the best things of Browning. He argued with me for a long time the other day about 'The desire of the moth for the star.' He only knew the last verse, and maintained that it had been written by an Australian poet of his acquaintance called Buck Jones.... How long do you think this new mood of yours will last? I am coming to shoot at Wirlesdon in November. Shall I find it gone?"

"I don't know," said the girl dolefully. "Of course I shall go back and become a conventional young woman again. And yet I shall never be able to forget the other side. I shall always be longing for this plateau, and the sun, and the smell of the camp-fire. And when I see myself in a mirror at balls, my Better Self will say to my Ordinary Self, 'Now you are like a thousand people in a crowd; but once, little goose, you were a woman that mattered!' ... But, indeed, we can never get away from Musuru so long as Mr Carey lives. All that is delightful in the place is in him. I could not help thinking while we were on trek that the wilderness was his real setting, and not the splendours of Musuru. He broods over the country like a fate."

"I have had the same feeling in all our travels," said Hugh. "Carey has the wilds so much in his soul, and he lives so entirely among elemental things, that he has the same aura as this land. When I think of him it is never at Musuru or in London, but as I first saw him in Rhodesia forcing his great shoulders through the bush with a dusty caravan behind him. No divine teacher would ever bid him sell all his goods and give to the poor, for it would be no sacrifice. He sits as loose among his great possessions as if he were a pilgrim with only a begging-bowl to his credit."

"You once praised detachment," said Lady Flora, "and I didn't quite agree. I think it often means selfishness or a cold heart or a weak digestion. But Mr Carey's detachment is the most wonderful thing on earth. He has such a fire in his own soul that he does not need to warm his hands at any of the blazes which we poor worldly mortals shiver around."

"You know how every now and again he breaks out into some proverb. I remember once in London walking down Piccadilly, when suddenly Carey came up and put his arm in mine. He walked with me for a hundred yards without speaking, and then he said in that abstracted way of his, 'Every man should be lonely at heart,' and went off. He, at any rate, has the true spiritual austerity. Do you remember the story of the Italian poet's mistress, sitting at some fete in beautiful clothes, when a scaffolding broke and she was crushed to death? And then they found that beneath her silken robes she had worn sackcloth. The world pictures Carey with his power and his wealth, and notes only the purple and fine linen, but few can penetrate to that inner austerity which looks upon such things as degrees of the infinitely small. He is, if you like, a practical mystic—an iron hand to change the fate of nations, and all the while a soul lit by its own immortal dreams. As you said, Lady Flora, while he lives we, who are his friends, can never sink altogether into the commonplace. And when he dies we can write over him that most tremendous of all epitaphs—' Blessed are the pure in heart, for they shall see God.'"

The darkness was gathering fast, and the travellers were almost on the edge of the first belt of forest, beyond which lay Musuru. A clatter of hoofs behind them made them turn their heads sharply, and they found themselves overtaken by Lady Amysfort and Sir Edward.

"We hurried on," said that gentleman, who in the twilight seemed longer and leaner than ever, "because we couldn't stand the pace of those confounded mules. So we left Akhub to bring in the caravan. We are not more than a mile from Musuru, so you'd better stick that hat of yours straight, Hugh. You look as if you had escaped from some Wild West show. Do you mind if I push on by myself? I am very keen to know what has won the Leger?"

The dinner-table that evening was a very different sight from that presented on the first night of the visit. Then every one was fresh from home, a little" strange and shy, inclined to be in awe equally of their neighbours and their host. A month of close comradeship in the wilds had made smooth the rough places, and the whole company had become excellent friends. The men were all tanned to a uniform brown, which in Sir Edward's case had deepened into a Mephistophelian duskiness, and all had the clear eyes and alert figures which tell of perfect health. Even Mr Lowenstein had so greatly benefited by the voyage that he showed no trace of weakness. The women had changed the pink and white of civilisation for wholesome sunburn. As for the Ruwenzori party, they had escaped fever but had left their complexions on the high snows, and Graham and Astbury showed faces so wonderfully tattered that by contrast Hugh looked modish and refined.

"Francis," said the Duchess, "may I beg a favour? Don't let the name of empire be mentioned to-night. I want to hear all about these young people's doings. Besides, they will soon be much too sleepy to talk. Flora says she rode thirty miles to-day."

"First you must tell us what has been happening at home, Aunt Susan. I haven't had time to read my letters. I know what won the St Leger, for Sir Edward has told me the news eighteen times, but I don't know anything else."

"What could happen at home in September? My letters are mostly from Scotland, where your uncle is still saying hard things about the fishing. All the history manufactured lately has been made here. You cannot imagine the profound peace of Musuru when you are all away. Bob read, and Lord Launceston wrote, and Francis was either shut up in his den working or roving about the estate. I dozed a good deal of the day, but we all woke up in the evening, and talked, no politics, only simple friendly gossip. We made Bob read Scott aloud after dinner, and we got through the 'Heart of Midlothian.' Never in my life have I spent a more restful time, and now I feel like some quiet old abbess whose convent has been invaded by Goths. You must atone for the jar to my nerves by giving me a faithful tale of your adventures. You may begin, Margaret!"

"Alas, nothing happened to me," said Lady Warcliff, with that air of mingled petulance and candour which was the chief of her charms. "Aden was a simple inferno with heat and dust. I saw Arthur, and tried to get him to come on here with me, but the call of the partridges was stronger than my eloquence. He hurried home, and I came back and stopped for two nights to explore Mombasa. My story is a very dull one. How did you enjoy the East Coast?" she asked, turning to Mrs Deloraine.

"It was all I had hoped for. We put into little decayed wayside ports, with a background of palms and green-shuttered white houses. All were hot and some smelt abominably, but there is nothing quite like them elsewhere. You feel around them still the romance of that greatest of the Crusades, the Portuguese Age of Adventure. You can picture the days when those fierce dark sea-captains, with half their men sick and their own faces haggard with the long voyage round the Cape, put into their harbours and said prayers of thanksgivings before the humble mission shrines. Those were the great days, when Albuquerque was conquering the Indies and in treaty with the Sultan for the Holy Sepulchre. And you can read in them, too, the visible record of the degeneration of a race. Once, in spite of heat and fever, they were the abodes of men. Hard-handed seigneurs lived in the *prazos*, and the soldiers who swaggered on the quays were no carpet-knights. But now you have a breed of dwarfish people, with black blood showing in their eyes and finger-nails, and the soldiers, in flapping trousers and tinsel medals, might have walked out of a comic opera. They have long ago forgotten Europe and the white man's pride, and Albuquerque is only a myth to swear by. The fathers have eaten sour grapes and the teeth of the children are set on edge. There is something about the weather, and the colour of the sea, and the colour of the vegetation, which speaks of decadence and apathy. But some places have found a life of their own, which has no reminiscence of Europe in it. I found out Inhambane, Mr Astbury, with your river and boatmen and everything. There's no decadence there—only a wholesome, sleepy barbarism."

"I did not land," said Mr Wakefield stolidly, "till we reached Natal. I refused to land, for I am depressed by the imperial failures of other peoples. Personally I attribute Portugal's fiasco to that dead-weight of Roman Catholicism which she carried with her. But I was much cheered by Natal. Some of the Ministers got up a dinner for me, and I made a speech in which I hope I gave the colony some useful advice."

"He made a speech," said Mrs Wilbraham tragically, "and the name of Natal was never mentioned in it. Nothing but Canada, Canada."

"How could I deliver a panegyric on a place in which I had only lived for two days? I told them about the country I do know and left them to draw the moral. If I had begun to patronise them with advice on their domestic affairs they would all have been in arms. When we get the Premier of Natal over to Toronto you may bet that he'll talk about Natal and nothing else. The secret of keeping the peace in the colonies is for each man to expatiate on his own hen-roost. Colonials have known that for a long time, but English statesmen are just beginning to learn it."

"In another minute," said Mrs Yorke, "we shall be talking politics. What is your story, Flora?"

"Sir Edward got his big eland and thinks it a record, but he hasn't looked up Rowland Ward yet. There isn't really much to tell about our doings. We wandered along from day to day in perfect weather through a great green country. Ask Caroline."

"I can't add anything," said Lady Amysfort. "It was a time of perfect rest. I thought of nothing in the daytime except the beauty of the place and the flowers and the wild beasts, and how good it was to look forward to dinner and the evening round the fire. After dinner we talked about everything in the world and rediscovered all the most profound platitudes. And one went to bed thinking how nice waking would be. It was a very happy time, but like all happy times it had no landmarks."

The Duchess turned dejectedly to Lady Lucy. "It is what I always find. People who do interesting things have not a word to say about them. Surely you have something to tell me about the Mountains of the Moon?"

"Oh yes. We climbed Kiyanja, and Marjory nearly ended her mortal career by sliding down a snow-slope. It is impossible to give you any conception of the upper Mubuku valley by mere description. You have to see it to believe in it. Imagine a giant Alpine flora—groundsels like shrubs, heather in trees, azaleas and Alpine roses making a flame-coloured forest, and creepers of every tint blazing between the trunks. And at the end you come out on a glacier, and far up in a rocky cup there is a spring. It took me some time to realise that this was the real source of the Nile—the place which Alexander the Great saw in his dreams, and Speke and Baker thought they had found in Lake Victoria. All around us was a snowfield which might have been on the aiguilles above Chamonix. I have often felt the lack of the true geographical imagination, for I could not focus the place in my thoughts. The little trickle I drank of, instead of running down to feed some tame Swiss torrent, was the head waters of the greatest and most mysterious river in the world.... We camped beside it, and bitterly cold we found it, and then before dawn next morning we started for the summit. I thought the snow very difficult, and it was a blessing to get on hard rock. In one couloir Marjory fell and pulled Mr Astbury out of his steps. They were well held, but it took us an hour to get them up, for we had to dig gigantic caverns before we got a step that was really safe."

"Had you any view?"

"For five minutes on the top we saw the kingdoms of the earth spread out beneath us. Then the mist came down, and we had a weary descent before we reached our high camp. Marjory and I were utterly tired and soaked to the bone. Do you remember that evening, Mr Astbury, with the rain pelting on our tents, after we had drunk soup and brandy and got into dry clothes? You said that these occasions got rid of every difference of education and temperament and sex, and made us all elemental human creatures, and I quite agreed with you. It was worth while travelling a long way to hear our critical Marjory gloating over food like a glutton and talking wild mountaineering slang with the guides."

"She's an uncommonly fine climber," said Mr Astbury with conviction. "There was a bit on the highest rocks, as bad as anything on the Grepon, and she took it like a chamois. I don't praise you, Lady Lucy, for there's nothing you can't do. Besides, you are an old mountaineer. But it gives me enormous pleasure to have made another convert."

"Perhaps I should not care for ordinary climbing," said Miss Haystoun, who looked very beautiful with the flush of sunburn in place of her wonted pallor. "But Ruwenzori can be like nothing in the world. The sharp contrast between the rich moist glens and the cool snow is an intoxication in itself. Besides, why should I not be a lover of mountains? We have all in our breasts odds and ends of strange souls. If we were clean-cut, four-square beings we should not be worth talking to."

Lord Appin nodded approval. "When I was a very young man at Oxford," he said, "I evolved what I flattered myself was a new system of philosophy. I called it Romanticism. It was a very crude system, strong on the aesthetic and ethical sides, but lamentably weak in logic and metaphysics. Its central doctrine, if it could be said to have one, was that truth, virtue, happiness, all the ideals, were attained by the clash of opposites. Holiness was possible only as the result of the struggle of the soul with an alien world; happiness as the outcome of pain endured and difficulties surmounted. The beauty of art was the conquest of human genius over intractable matter. And romance—an abstraction of my own which I interwove with the whole system—was the perpetual contrast between the human spirit and its environment—nobility side by side with baseness in one soul, or the courage of man transcending impossible disasters, or beauty flowering in a mean place. It was a very young man's confession of faith, and yet there was the glimmering of a truth at the back of it. It was my instinctive protest against the undue simplification of life. We are all a strange compound, and we shall never reach our full stature by starving certain parts of our nature of their due. What you call romance, Marjory, is another form of the old conflict between the real and the ideal, the world into which we are born and the world which we would recreate for ourselves. It involves conflict between ideals, but not the neglect and starvation of any. Of course this truth is at the bottom of our new conception of empire. Imperialism"

But at this point the Duchess rose. "You are slipping into politics, Bob," she said. "Never mind Imperialism to-night, but by all means let us talk about romance. Letty has a fascinating story she might tell us if you asked her very nicely...."

Soon the company were settled comfortably around the fire in the inner hall. Mrs Yorke, after a little pressure, had sent to her room for a despatch-box, from which she took a small manuscript book.

"I don't know why I should bore you with family history," she said, "but I was once rash enough to tell Susan this story, and she liked it, and said it was an allegory and true of us all I have no theories about it, except that it seems to fit in very well with what Lord Appin has been saying. So if it amuses you, you shall have it.

"There was a certain relative of my husband's whom I shall call Sir Charles Weston. It is not his real name, and Lord Appin will probably see through the disguise, as Susan did, but I owe it to my self-respect not to be more explicit. He was an eminent lawyer—at least he made a large fortune in the law courts—and, above all things, he was an earnest Liberal. His life was published not so very long ago in two volumes, and I remember that his biographers said that he was almost the last of the old stalwart God-fearing statesmen. They said that he lived only for the great causes of peace, economy, and reform. He left among his papers some notes, called 'Reflections on certain modern tendencies,' which are not very cheerful reading. He assumes the role of a minor prophet, and cries 'Ichabod' to the future of Israel.

"I only met him once, shortly after my marriage. He had disapproved of it strongly; indeed there was hardly a vice which he did not trace to the 'Americanising' of England. He said that the people of the United States had fallen like Lucifer from their high estate, and the latest American he had any respect for was Jefferson. Once he made Henry very angry by telling him that all American women seemed to be serving behind an intellectual counter. However, he disapproved so much of Henry on every ground that one blunder more or less did not make much difference. I had to be taken to see him, and the prospect made me very nervous. But he turned out quite kind, and he had nice, courtly, old-fashioned manners, which I thought sweet. He was a great philanthropist, but rather a dictator, I fancy, for he had no idea of giving the poor any choice in the way they should be helped. His face was like an old woman's—amiable, vacant, a little foolish, though he had moments of mental activity when a kind of power would come into it. His talk was one mosaic of moral and political platitudes; and I should have said that he had never possessed the imagination of a cow.

"Well, he died, full of years and honour, and to our amazement he left all his papers to Henry. We sorted them out, and the Liberation Society, or something of the kind, wanted to have his life written, so we handed over the bulk of them. But one little diary we kept to ourselves. There was a big diary in about thirty volumes which plays a great part in the biography. But the little diary which we found in an old safe did not appear in that work.

"I shall never forget the day we found it. Henry picked it up and said, 'Another diary,' opened it at random, and began to read: 'Rhoda came to-night as I sat alone in the Purple Chamber. There was no lamp, and her pale beauty shone in the dusk like the silver of moonlight. I thought how in this little dancing-girl one caught something of the mystery'—and then Henry could read no more, but sat down and gasped. When he found his breath he could only keep repeating, 'The old scamp!'

"We tried another page, and found an account of some battle that Sir Charles talked of having fought, and then a long tale of a mid-winter march on the Danube. Henry, when he heard this, observed that to his certain knowledge his relative had never been out of England. Last of all, we came on a reference to Theodora, his wife. 'My great-aunt,' said Henry, 'was christened Elizabeth Anne. There are three possible explanations of this affair. Either he was a most uncommon old sinner, or a most accomplished liar, or as mad as a March hare. I incline to the last.'

"But he was wrong, for in a little while we hit upon the right explanation. I think I was the first to see it, but after we had read the diary through, doubt was impossible. We saw that behind the bland Sir Charles there had stood another figure, Heaven knows what revenant from the splendid past. There were two souls in his body, one timid, pragmatical, humane, slow, and stupid—the soul of all democratic lawyers from the beginning of time; the other the soul of a king, merciless, passionate, and incomparably able. So all the time he lived a double life. In the daytime he went through the ordinary routine. He was a great advocate of the reform of the criminal law, he was president of the London Missionary Society, and in the House of Commons he was famous for his attacks upon Tory extravagance, and especially upon militarism. He emptied the House, for he was the prince of bores. Disraeli said that he made a solitude and called it a Peace debate.

"But late at night and in the early mornings and at odd moments the other soul had its chance. And then he was an Emperor of Byzantium, ruling half the world with an iron hand. The diary showed his accession to power, for to begin with he was only John Chrysaor, the General of the Army of the East. Bit by bit he became the strong man in the empire. He won the Church to his side, and when he fought a great battle on the eastern marches which turned back the tide of Mohammedan invasion, he became the popular hero. The Emperor died, leaving an effeminate son as his successor; but John hurried back to New Rome, cleared out the mob of eunuchs and parasites, and seized the throne with universal goodwill. Then began a reign of iron, as appeared from the little diary. The Emperor John fought the Church and won, he subdued a Dacian insurrection, he built palaces and churches, he ransacked East and West for art treasures, and he had great dreams of restoring the unity of the empire and carrying his court to Rome.

"I am not going to retell this wild story, but once, after I had been ill, I amused myself with taking the two diaries and comparing the entries. In the little book no year was given, but it seemed to correspond to a certain epoch in the long one, and the days and months followed as regularly as in the other. So I chose parallel passages of the same date, to show the gulf between the two souls.

"The first is dated June 10th. In the large diary he wrote—

"'I have been in the House all afternoon. Indian frontier policy was discussed, and Disraeli made a flippant and hectoring reply to the profound arguments of Mr G. Many applauded, and, being unable to find a chance to speak, I came away greatly saddened. Liberalism for the moment is eclipsed and shadowed by a vulgar worship of reaction. Do these vain people who prate about the prestige of Britain ever reflect, I wonder, on the shallow foundations of their creed? We have taken upon ourselves responsibilities which carry with them no increase in moral stature—nay, which minister to the lowest and most depraved elements in our nature. We claim a right to rule certain dark-skinned peoples, thereby offending against the oldest and most indisputable of human rights—the right to liberty. It tickles our sense of authority, and degrades alike our reason and our conscience. And it always brings war. These stay-at-home roysterers are very ready to unsheath the sword. Well for their peace of mind that they cannot realise the horrors of which they are, before God, the cause. The older I grow the deeper becomes my conviction that in these days of enlightenment no war can be justified. Every war—I do not care what its pretext—must be a blunder in statesmanship and a sin against the Most High.'

"On the same day he wrote in the little diary—

"'It is the evening of the greatest day in my life. The blood is crusted over my eyes, my left arm is crippled, and I am caked in dust. A quarter of my men are slain, but the enemy have been ground between the millstones. I staked everything on a great throw and I have won. I sent my cavalry into a death-trap well aware that few would return, but the ruse succeeded, and the Emirs found their own shambles before the sun set.... To-morrow at dawn five thousand captives, with the Cross branded on their shoulders, shall be sent to New Rome as the first fruits of my victory. The plunder follows, and I can see the weak eyes of my Imperial Master glitter when he sees the spoils of Damascus in his treasury.... I have taken the first step in the great march to a Throne and nothing but death can stop my pilgrimage. Nay, death is an ally: he will not betray one who has offered him such princely bribes....'

"The strange thing," Mrs Yorke continued, "is that the entries in the two books always correspond. If any subject has been occupying his mind in the one diary it reappears in some form or other in the second. For instance, he made a great speech at a meeting at Exeter Hall to protest against Gordon's proposal to take Zebehr Pasha, the ex-slave-dealer, as his colleague. It is printed in full in the Life, and the editors remark that 'the passionate conscience of England spoke through its chosen mouthpiece.' In the entry in the little diary we read—

"'To-day the fruits of my Dacian wars were sold in the market. Fifty maids were kept for the Palace, and five hundred of the lustiest young men were enrolled in the Praetorians. New Rome will be full of stalwart barbarians, and the Circus enriched by promising recruits. Would that each year could see an infusion of such virile stock among our languid citizens!'

"On September 25th he was adding to Fairholme, his place in Surrey, and was very much worried about the cost. Says the big diary—

"'I can postpone the addition no longer, but I seriously grudge the outlay. I have taken the best advice I could find and have made considerable reductions in the estimates, but the expense still seems to me undue. The ground-floor of the new wing will be occupied by a library and a billiard-room, the floor above by six bedrooms, each of which—my wife insists—must have its own bathroom. Elizabeth is anxious that the housemaids shall have better quarters, so the top-floor will be utilised...'

and so on with many tiresome details. "Now for the little book—

"'To-day the building of my summer Palace begins. The walls will rise level with the cliffs, and the portico will be open to the sea. For months ships have brought Parian marble and cedar logs to the little wharf below, and this morning the first hammer rang on the foundations. The great library is on the side facing the hills, so that I may have the open air even when the wind blows. There the hundred thousand volumes which Philotimus has gathered for me will be housed in cedar cabinets, and there I may find peace to wrestle with the problems of the state. It has been my order that the work should proceed by night and day, and the torch-lit dusk will be a sign to Theodora of my love, for it is for her sake alone that I burden my soul with trifles.'

"Which," said Mrs Yorke, "brings us to Theodora. The Emperor John had a wide choice of princesses, but he imitated Justinian in falling in love with a slave-girl who was also a popular actress. He married her, and judging by the diary, she seems to have led him a pretty dance. She had other lovers, and there is a really horrid passage in the book where he describes the revenge he took on the man he found in the Empress's boudoir. The two most piquant contrasts in the diaries concern the two women whom he thought he loved. On January 17th we read in the big diary—

"'I have just returned from the churchyard where all that is mortal of my dear wife was this afternoon laid to rest. Even in my private diary I cannot write the thoughts which are now surging in on my mind. The sense of loss has crippled my power of reflection and drugged my memory. For forty years she was my comrade and friend, the sharer of every hope and every sorrow. Elizabeth was one of those rare women whose price is indeed above rubies. In her husband's work and in the calm atmosphere of the home her sweet, pure domesticity found perfect content. No passion ever ruffled the calm surface of her soul. As I think of her, I realise how unstable a foundation for wedded happiness is the volcanic love which modern poets prate of. Mutual respect, a vivid interest in the personality of each other, a gentle and constant affection, are the only guarantees of that private tranquillity which enables a man to face the rough fortunes of the outer world. Passion! The word should be expunged from our language, for when it is not begotten of folly and weak emotion it is first cousin to morbidity and vice.'

"Under the same date in the little book there is a rhapsody on Theodora's beauty which is not unlike the Song of Solomon. And there is a long passionate appeal to her to give him her heart as he had given her his. I will not read these passages, for the style of Byzantium was—well, Byzantine. And then the statesman appears, for the Emperor John was, like Napoleon, *un être politique*. He tells his love of the power which shall be hers, and the honours and treasures that he will cast at her feet.

"'These dogs of the Senate and the Church have again besought me to break with you. They say that the sacrosanctity of the throne will be gone if it is shared with a dancing-girl. Who are they to dictate the choice of an Emperor of Rome! I swear to you, angel, by the Most High God that I will create for you a new earth. Cities and temples shall be ground into dust to make a path for these delicate feet. Your white hand shall fling open the door of a new Empire. Together we will sweep across the west, and when we have crushed the barbarians and shaken down the dotards of Italy, our palace shall be the Capitol, and you and I, little one, side by side, shall rule the world from the secular throne of Augustus.'"

"And what happened in the end?" Marjory asked.

"Alas, the diary stops long before Rome was conquered. He had an illness some years before his death, and after that he never resumed it. But how I wish that I had known that all the while, when he was talking platitudes at Henry, one-half of him was revelling in such a dream!"

"And the moral of that is?" asked the Duchess.

"Surely, Susan," said Lord Appin, "that we are such very composite creatures that, as Marjory said, we should be very shy of dogmatising on each other's natures. That, I suppose, is the worst platitude I have ever uttered, but then, all morals are platitudes, and you asked me for one."

"Well, I think they were both very unpleasant characters—especially the Emperor John. Sir Charles was at least respectable."

"Really, Aunt Susan," said Lady Flora, "we have all got to the stage of talking like Alice in Wonderland. Don't you think it is time to go to bed?"

CHAPTER 11

THE evenings had grown milder, and after dinner it was possible to sit in one of the airier drawing-rooms which opened on the stoep. So soft was the weather that the great windows were left half open, and through them blew scented wafts from the gardens.

Mrs Deloraine's beautiful head was silhouetted by a little lamp against an ebony screen. She arranged some papers on a table beside her and began to speak in her curiously gentle voice.

"I have been given my orders by Francis, and I can't disobey them. But I hope you will be a very charitable audience. I am not a controversialist, and, though I have written a little it is very hasty and imperfect, and I shall have to supplement it as best I can. I want to speak about the bearing of our creed upon the aesthetic side of life, and my only claim to speak on the subject is that I was warned that I should be expected to deal with it, and I have been trying to think it over on our Ruwenzori trip. Mountains give one a hill-top prospect, but they do not help one to put ideas into a clear system. So if what I say is very full of loose ends, you must remember the mountains and forgive me.

"I know no pocket definition of Art. But as I understand it, it is the quest of beauty under certain conditions. All honest work, all right conduct, all true speech, have beauty in them, and the worker and the speaker are in one sense artists. But in its usual acceptation it means a conscious quest, where beauty is the goal sought for its own sake, and not the attendant of an alien ideal. And this beauty must be presented in terms of our common life. Poetry must be written in some tongue familiar to mankind; painting works through the homely medium of paint and canvas, and makes its appeal to eyes accustomed to the rough world; music is contained in notes within the range of the human ear. In a deeper sense, too, Art is rooted in life. For its material must not be sought in some rarefied world, or even in certain carefully defined provinces of that world which we know. Our poetry must not come from the stars or the Far Islands, but from the men and women we see daily, and the warm breathing life which we call 'real' because we cannot escape from it. To Art nothing can be unclean or common, provided it has the warrant of reality. If we limit ourselves by any of the many conventions which have stifled growth, and say that Art can deal only with the fortunes of gentlefolk, or, at the other extreme, of peasants; that Art belongs to civilisation and is urban at heart, or that it is natural and untamed and can be found only in the wilds; that it must deal with things fair and comely or only with the ugliness and tragedy of life,—then we sin against its catholicity and truth.

"But all this is only to define the material and to leave out the spirit. The realist is so absorbed in the variety and multiplicity of the world, that he imagines that in a dull chronicle of details he has fulfilled the purpose of the artist. But the essence of Art is that it is creative. It brings into the wilderness the shaping spirit of imagination, and by selection, by a deeper instinct, it shows us harmony in chaos, nobility in the squalid, and a fugitive poetry in the commonplace. The temporal, in the hand of Art, takes on the guise of the eternal. The ordinary man sees in a passing face comeliness, or want, or vice, or misery, but when fixed on the canvas of a master the original is forgotten, and the whole tale of mortal passion is enshrined in that face for the seeing eye. Art is the revolt against the bondage of the superficial, the accidental, and the trite. It means always a spiritual adventure and the conquest of new worlds for the mind—worlds none the less new because they are the re-creation of the old. Every one has known what it is to visit a place many times and find it dreary and uninspiring, till one day comes an hour of illumination, and the common fields and woods are touched with a light that never leaves them. Art brings this fairyland gleam to life, and we realise that it is no importation from without but life itself laid bare in its profoundest meaning.

"I am one of those who hold the orthodox view about Art. Its purpose to my mind is not merely to inform, or merely to delight, but to illumine. I believe that there are fixed laws of beauty, canons for the artist which are as eternal as beauty itself. But we need not delay now to discuss these ultimate questions of aesthetics. The truth I wish to enforce is, that while the canons of Art may be limited and stationary the subject-matter to which they apply is endless and ever growing. Its boundaries are extended with each addition to the world's knowledge. To my mind the worst crime against the laws of Art is the attempt to limit their sphere of application.

"For mark what happens. We are left with a weary catalogue of things which Art may play with. And because a wall has been built round them, they are divorced from the rest of life, and become in themselves a phantasmal world. Their roots are no longer in reality, and therefore there can be no growth. The artist becomes a manipulator of mechanical toys, very subtle, exquisitely clever, and utterly futile—a purveyor of second-hand emotions and academic tragedies. The Muses become either genteel spinsters or stupid housemaids. For you cannot subdue the winds of the world to orderly breezes which never ruffle or chill, and when Art becomes domestic it dies.

"I seem to find in our Art to-day something of this vice, not so much in creed as in practice. We have not the wits to see that life is a violent, far-ranging thing, delighting in large contrasts and nobly tolerant. We are too fond of little prettinesses, too complex, too preoccupied with the small intricate things to have leisure for the great simple things which are the root of the matter. So we spend our time spinning cocoons, excellent as cocoons go, but, if I may borrow Lady Flora's pet phrase about people, they 'don't matter.' And the result is that Art misses that direct emotional appeal which is the final test of its truth. Great Art affects us with something of the emotion of life. The high rubs shoulders with the low, and the face of the laugher changes suddenly into the face of the seer and prophet. Cleopatra passes from banter with a peasant to the loftiest of human soliloquies. But in our dim half-world such heights are beyond us. We have too little of the real, for we are apt to limit arbitrarily the material of our art, and the ideal eludes us because it belongs to a nobler philosophy than ours. I am afraid we are in danger of decadence, and our only hope is in finding a new world.

"If I were a great poet I should write an epic on new worlds. A veil seems to lift when life is becoming dingy and narrow, and, behold! the gleam of dawn on untravelled seas. Men suddenly look up from their daily round and become aware of a great hope. It may be the revelation of a new Messiah or a new social creed, or in the literal sense a new world. Now, what we especially need is the last, for our Art wants above all things something of that spirit which you may call Ionian or Elizabethan or romantic, as you please. It is an enlarged basis of life that we require, rather than a new interpretation of our present routine. We must be shaken out of our content and our cynicism, and shown that the earth is full of wonderful and beautiful things, and that the wisdom of our grandfathers has not exhausted it. I believe in my heart that such a revelation awaits us. Mankind stands at the end of one long epoch, and has made itself master of the material globe. Science has opened her door half-way to us, we have circumnavigated and explored the whole earth, but still we are only at the beginning. For there still remains the task of taking possession—of reshaping all our creeds to correspond with our new heritage, and remodelling our heritage on an ideal plan. I am only concerned with the meaning of this illumination for Art, and two truths seem to be vital. The first is that we must absorb this enlarged material basis and make it part of our spiritual life. Otherwise it remains only a mysterious background, such as we find in the Roman decadence, while all the time we go on living among our stale conventions. To us, as to the poets of the Silver Age, the outer empire will be only matter for a metaphor or a jest, unless we draw it within the circle of our lives. The second is that we must carry into our new sphere the inherited traditions of our culture, and not jettison them as useless ballast. Art, remember, looks towards the future, but her foundations are always in the past. Otherwise we shall become outlaws from her kingdom, and all the freshness of a new earth will not avail since we have lost the canons of interpretation. This, I think, is the weakness of so much colonial poetry. The novelty of the matter is believed to atone for the absence of the great tradition in the manner. But the rococo phrases of Fleet Street will never reproduce the mystery of the wilderness. What is lost, however, in Art which is colonial, and therefore provincial, may be recovered in Art which is imperial."

"I think I understand what you mean," said Lady Warcliff, "but I am far from certain that I agree with you. I should have thought that the essence of empire is the indefiniteness of its horizon and the unexplored chances of its future, whereas the essence of Art is that it works within clear limits. Surely, for 'great verse' we are taught to look to a 'little clan.' Material greatness is generally assumed to be hostile to spiritual perfection."

Mrs Deloraine was always embarrassed by Lady Warcliff's precision. "I know that opinion," she said a little nervously, "but I most profoundly disagree with it. Of course, Art works within limits and abhors loose outlines. This has been said a hundred times, as in Goethe's famous line— 'In der Beschränkung zeigt sich erst der Meister.'

But these limits are the eternal laws of Art's being and not the accidents of circumstance. Power and space will kill Art unless they are absorbed by the spirit of the artist. But that is not to say that when properly used they may not be Art's best allies. Just as asceticism is only possible for those who have some inner core of grossness in their nature, so those who would make Art a nun are those who are also capable of making her a courtesan. It is a creed whose spirituality is not more but less than ours. If we limit Art to simple men and a little nation, we assume that her spiritual power is so slight that she will be overwhelmed and coarsened by a richer material environment. What warrant have we for so low a view of the fire in her heart? I grant you that in a great empire she walks in dangerous paths, but then the goal is more splendid, and it would be the part of cowardice to shirk the journey.

"I do not think that in this company at any rate I need linger on this point. My business is to try to show wherein the creed which we call Imperialism offers Art that new world which she needs. I remember that when I was a young girl the very name of Empire was a hateful thing to me. All the old orderly life which I loved seemed to be threatened by these barbarians who talked in a strange jargon, half mercantile, half Jingo. Their Palace of Art seemed to be constructed on the lines of a New York sky-scraper, and their music was the thumping of a brass band. And yet even then I seemed to hear behind the shouting a new note which haunted me in spite of my prejudice. As I grew older I came to live less in the past, and looked more to the realities of the world around me. Art came to be less a thing of dainty memories and delicate echoes, and more and more something solemn and tragic, and yet instinct with immortal humour, the voice of God speaking through the clamour of His creations. And then I felt the need of a wider horizon, a hope which should not be the perquisite of the few but the treasure of the humble. And suddenly I saw that I had been blind and deaf to a new world of which simple folk had long ago entered into possession.

"Imperialism brings into life, and therefore into Art, which is life's interpretation, a vision of a wider world. It shows us all the hard walled-in highroads which we had thought eternal, opening out on an upland which still retains the light of morning. That is the first of its gifts. Stale conventions, preciosity, all vapouring and trifling prettiness, must perish in that high air. Democracy, we agreed some time ago, cleared the way for superiority. So, too, this Imperialism of ours will clear the way for great Art by withering all that is petty and unreal. There is a profound maxim of S. Augustine's, 'Ubi magnitudo, ibi veritas,'—a maxim which, like all truths, is equally true in its converse. Greatness and truth in Art must walk hand in hand. And this vision brings with it a new hope, and without hope there is no enduring quality in any mortal work. Art demands in its creator an abounding optimism and vitality. He must see beyond all the tangles and deserts of the way to the ultimate city on its hill-top, and he must go singing on his pilgrimage.

"This new world, again, is not only a world of cities but of wilds. We have grown deplorably urban in our civilisation. We still talk of nature, but it is a garden-nature, and its interest for us is only in its bearing upon our petty life. We are always on the watch for the 'pathetic fallacy,' and we read into the inanimate world some trivial human moral. But nature, equally with man, is the cipher of the Divine, and we shall never fathom it until we learn that it has a key of its own.

"I mean," said Mrs Deloraine, looking up from her notes, "that we want a new poetry of nature, nature in its simplicity and vastness and savagery. Our modern civilisation, with its suburban country, gives us no scope for getting at the heart of the great forces which endure when we and all our work have perished. We take them as a pious opinion, something to make phrases about, but what chance does our normal life hold of any true communion? An ampler and newer earth will bring us back to the beginning of things. We shall feel the spray on our faces from antediluvian seas, and our lips will be salt with their brine. Our great poet when he arises will not be a Wordsworth, for he will be too bowed down with the wonder of it all to have any desire to read into it a system of philosophy. He will look on the world, I fancy, as Homer must have looked on that youthful world of his, rejoicing in its marvels, and seeing in them the working of some ageless plan, and yet facing it all with that frank human hope which tells him that neither space nor time can conquer the spirit.

"But there is no hope without mystery. The horizon must not be too clear if the adventurer is to have the true joy of his enterprise. Something magical and beautiful must lurk behind the twilight haze. Art cannot rise to the heights, except in the consciousness of a destiny too infinite to be expressed in formulas. We have tried our best to materialise life. We have stifled it with prudential maxims, we have turned policy into a profit-and-loss account, and we have striven to analyse and docket the aspirations of the human heart. And we have failed, grossly and finally. Science, once the ally of the economists, has ranged herself on the side of the poets. It is because Imperialism gives us a world whose boundaries no man can define that it ministers especially to the needs of Art. You remember the chorus in the *Bacchae*:— 'Knowledge, we are not foes!

I seek thee diligently;
But the world with a great wind blows,
Shining, and not from thee;
Blowing to beautiful things,
On, amid dark and light,
Till Life, through the trammellings
Of Laws that are not the Right,
Breaks clean and pure, and sings
Glorying to God on the height![6]

"But this creed of ours has a vertical as well as a horizontal extension. It not only carries the few into a wider world, but it carries all classes in the State. In the true sense it is democratic, for its ends can only be attained by the union of all citizens. It cries out for a new sense of civic duty, a richer and more enduring ideal of civic well-being. Politics will cease to be the hobby of the few and become the duty and the privilege of all. So, too, the Art which is to come to fruit in such a State must be, as all great Art has been, a democratic thing. Art has never truly flourished when it was the perquisite of a class or a sect. The minor poet who creates a little garden of his own, and declares that no vulgar wind from the outer world shall ever shake his rose-trees, stands confessed by his declaration as eternally second-rate. If a man has not the wit to be a citizen he has still less the wit to be an artist. In an empire inspired throughout with a corporate ideal we shall recapture for our Art something of the immortal simplicity of the Greek spirit, which did not disdain the market-place or the schools or the battlefield. Our Muse must put off her modish silks and gems, which so quickly tarnish, and go out like a beggar-maid to the highways of the world. But in the end she will find far nobler jewels, for in her eyes there will be starlight and on her brow the glory of morning.

"But, as I have already said, we must carry into the new world all that is best in our past. For Art at bottom is conservative. The laws of her kingdom are immutable, though her subjects change and her boundaries expand. The categories remain the same though their content may alter. This morning I went fishing in a meadow on the edge of the downs. Angling has long been a classic sport, and Izaak Walton ages ago gave it a certain literary atmosphere. When I think of a trout-stream I think of the Lea or the Dove—English meadows, with clear, slow-flowing water, little fishing- houses on the bank, old country inns to lodge at, milkmaids and gipsy choruses, and Corydon's song among the willows. Or I think of some Scotch burn falling in golden pools, overhung with rowanberries, with the scent of thyme and heather around, and all the magic of long tradition. But my fishing to-day was a revelation. Only the big trout and the clear water and the limpid air belonged to my old picture. I cast my flies over strange flowers, and the birds which I stirred were not larks or curlews. My gillie was a Masai hunter, who carried a gun in case of meeting wild animals. And when I stopped to rest and looked round, I did not see English woodlands or a Scotch glen, but the immense mystical panorama of Equatoria. I realised how, even in a little thing like a sport, it was only the essentials that mattered, and that it might be carried to any clime, provided the spirit remained unchanged. It seemed to me a kind of parable for Art. She may trim her sails and set her helm for new seas, but the ship and the compass are the same as of old. Abana and Pharpar are running rivers like Jordan. And though the waters are strange, and wilder forests clothe unfamiliar hills, she will still hear the pipes of Pan among the trees, and in some secret glade have sight of Venus and the sister nymphs— 'Panaque, Silvanumque senem, Nymphasque sorores.'"[7]

Mrs Deloraine paused and looked deprecatingly at the company. "I am afraid that what I have had to say has been very confused and schwärmerisch. Perhaps I can put it better in verse, for I am more accustomed to write in that form than in prose. I have here a kind of dialogue between Youth and the Spirit of Art, in which the same idea appears as I have been trying to expound. May I read it, if it does not bore you?"

Being assured of the attention of her audience, Mrs Deloraine read the following poem:— **Youth**.

Angel of love and light and truth,
In whose deep eyes the stars are set,
And in whose calm unchanging youth,
The mysteries of the world have met,

What means thy forward-beckoning hand,
The steadfast brow, the enraptur'd gaze,
They point me to a lonely land—
I cannot pierce the twilight haze.
With thee of old I walked at noon
In gardens where the airs were kind,
And from thy lips I read the rune
Of joy in every wave and wind.
We roamed blue hills of far romance,
We worshipped at the ancient shrines:
For us the oreads joined their dance
At even in the moonlit pines.
What darkling spell has rent thy skies
And turned thy heart to steel and fire,
And drawn across thy starry eyes
The curtains of a wild desire!

The Spirit Of Art.
I change not. I am old as Time
And younger than the dews of morn.
Those lips will sing the world's high prime
Which blessed the toils when life was born.
I am the priestess of the flame
Which on the eternal altar springs;
Beauty and truth and joy and fame
Sleep in the shelter of my wings.
I wear the mask of age and clime,
But he who of my love is fain
Must learn my heart which knows not time,
And seek my path which fears not pain,—
Till, bruised and worn with wandering
In the dark wilds my feet have trod,
He hears the songs the Immortals sing
At even in the glades of God.

Youth.
Angel, that heart I seek to know,
I fain would make thy word my stay,
Upon thy path I yearn to go
If thy clear eyes will light the way.
But ancient loves my memory hold,
And I am weak and thou art strong;
I fear the blasts of outland cold,—
Say if the way be dark and long.

The Spirit Of Art.

On mountain lawns, in meads of spring,
With idle boys bedeck thy hair,
Or in deep greenwood loitering
Tell to thy heart the world is fair.
That joy I give, but frail and poor
Is such a boon, for youth must die;
A little day the flowers endure,
And clouds o'erride the April sky.
Upon the windy ways of life,
In dark abyss of toil and wrong,
Through storm and sun, through death and strife, I seek the nobler spheral song.
No dulcet lute with golden strings
Can hymn the world that is to be.
Out of the jarring soul of things
I weave the eternal harmony.—
In forest deeps, in wastes of sand,
Where the cold snows outdare the skies:
Where wanderers roam uncharted lands,
And the last camp-fire flares and dies:
In sweating mart, in camp and court,
Where hopes forlorn have vanquished ease:
Where ships, intent on desperate port,
Strain through the quiet of lonely seas:
Where'er o'erborne by sense and sin,
With bruised head and aching hand,
Guarding the holy fire within,
Man dares to steel his heart and stand—
Breasting the serried spears of fate,
Broken and spent, yet joyous still,
Matching against the blind world's hate
The stark battalions of his will:—
Whoso hath ears, to him shall fall,
When stars are hid and hopes are dim,
To hear the heavenly voices call,
And, faint and far, the cosmic hymn—
That hymn of peace when wars are done,
Of joy which breaks through tears of pain,
Of dawns beyond the westering sun,
Of skies clear shining after rain.
No sinless Edens know the song,

No Arcady of youth and light,
But, born amid the glooms of wrong,
It floats upon the glimmering height,
Where they who faced the dust and scars,
And shrank not from the fires of hate,
Can walk among the kindred stars,
Master of Time and lords of Fate.
And haply then will youth, reborn,
Restore the world thou fain wouldst hold;
The dawn of an auguster morn
Will flush thy skies with fairy gold.
The flute of Pan in wild-wood glade
Will pipe its ancient sweet refrain;
Still, still for thee through April shade
Will Venus and her sister train
Lead the old dance of spring and youth.
But thine the wiser, clearer eyes,
Which having sought the shrine of truth
And faced the unending sacrifice,
Can see the myriad ways of man,
The ecstasy, the fire, the rod,
As shadows of the timeless plan
That broods within the mind of God.
Kin to the dust, yet throned on high,
Thy pride thy bonds, thy bonds release;
Thou see'st the Eternal passing by,
And in His Will behold'st thy peace.

Mr Wakefield had listened to Mrs Deloraine's theories of art with an interested but puzzled expression. He was so wholly under the spell of her charm that he was prepared to take every word she uttered for gospel, and his sense of the ridiculous, which made him explosive in the presence of the transcendental, was rapidly perishing from disuse. A strenuous career at the Bar, and a middle age spent mainly in fiscal controversy, had not fitted him to appreciate a discourse on aesthetic. But he was cheerful and congratulatory about the poem.

"I know what you mean by a background of mystery," he said. "I wish I could take you up with me to the great lakes and forests of our northern country, and show you some of our voyageurs. You might make a lot out of them. I think you are perfectly right in saying that what poetry wants is a fresh subject, and not something that has been hammered at by every poet since King David. I can no more read Tennyson than I can drink stagnant water."

Mrs Deloraine looked a little aghast at this version of her conclusions. Sir Edward, whose eyes had a far-away look, said abruptly from a dark corner— "Do you know that what you have been saying is what I have been trying to think out for a long time? It is what distinguishes our own people from any other breed of pioneer. We won't admit any hard-and-fast line between the known and the unknown, and so our horizon is always a little misty. The Frenchman wants to draw a clear line and say that all on one side is civilisation, and all on the other side is barbarism, and he doesn't care a cent what becomes of it. He wants a cosy self-contained little kingdom, because at heart he fears the wilds, while we love them. Our people won't admit any final march where they must stop short and pitch their tents. They must always be pushing on and possessing some new country. And therefore there is no limit to their hopes, for any evening may bring them to the Land of Promise. There's a lot in that if you think it over. I don't know much about art, but I am sure Mrs Deloraine and I mean the same thing."

Mr Lowenstein intervened as if to rescue the unfortunate lady from Philistine approval.

"You have said many beautiful and convincing things, for which I am very grateful. Our difficulty as Imperialists has always been that, though the common people may hear us gladly, the elect will shrug their shoulders and turn away. We are in danger of making Imperialism purely what Mr Wakefield calls 'a business proposition,' and therefore of identifying it with an arid, mercantile view of life. The people who love beauty—the artists, the scholars, the poets —will behave towards it like a well-dressed woman towards a street accident—cast a glance of pity or dislike, and then pass by on the other side. I almost think that our most urgent duty is to insist upon the spiritual renaissance at the back of everything. For, properly regarded, our creed is a religion, and we must hold it with the fervour of a convert."

Lord Launceston abandoned his seat by the window and came forward into the firelight to get himself a cigarette.

"I think I agree with most of your conclusions," he said, looking down at Mrs Deloraine; "but you will not think me dull if I put the thing more prosaically. We seek to show that empire is not antagonistic to a high spiritual development. I think we can go further and prove that it may be a positive aid. But when we have said that, we must be careful of going further. For Imperialism is in its essence a political thing. It is concerned with man as a political animal, man in the social aspect, and not directly with the spiritual life of the citizen. It provides a fuller basis for art and morality, and, I think I may add, religion, but in itself it is none of these things. It deals—it must deal—mainly with the formal side of life. I grant you willingly that the tendency is for the *vie intime* of any man to be more closely knit to the communal life. But there must always remain something which no state, however noble in its character, can give—that inner peace and satisfaction of the soul. Many of us, I think, tend to exalt Imperialism to too high a plane, and seek in a political ideal that which belongs only to what, in the widest sense of the word, we call religion. This seems to me a very real danger. For if we make claims for our creed which it cannot fulfil, sooner or later we shall discredit it. No alchemy can turn the stones of our dream-city into bread for the hungry."

Mrs Deloraine cried out in warm approval. "I am so glad to hear you say that, for it is what I should have liked to add if I had thought my subject allowed of it. I feel that the overstatement of our creed is one of the gravest perils which it has to face. We must maintain that it has its spiritual aspect, but we dare not claim that in itself it will satisfy the eternal cravings of the spirit. We may make a new earth, a prosperous and happy and civilised earth, but if our citizens can look no further they will be worse off than at the beginning. The poor man even now, broken by want and disease, who can declare in his last hours that his Redeemer liveth, has reached a spiritual height to which no ideal citizenship of itself can ever rise. I do not wish to preach about those viewless things on which we all must make our peace with our own souls, but I ask that we recognise their profundity, and do not attempt to allot them to a creed which has no answer to make to them."

"That is the most sensible thing I have heard you say, Barbara." The Duchess had slept peacefully through the earlier discussion, and had awakened in time to be shocked by Mr Lowenstein. "Don't you see that if you confound religion with politics you are falling into the very blunder which you were kind enough to say was the favourite pastime of my party? You will vulgarise the one and sentimentalise the other. I am old-fashioned enough to think it impious, and, what is more to the purpose, it is extremely silly. There is a kind of disease in men's minds which compels them to break down all the common-sense boundary-fences and to turn every nostrum into a complete philosophy of life. Why can't they be content with the Here and leave the Hereafter to its proper exponents? Tories like Caroline are always telling me that politics have no principles and are wholly opportunist, but if they were faithful to their creed they would never try to stretch the bounds of politics so wide that they include provinces like religion where opportunism is unthinkable."

The Duchess turned a friendly eye upon Mr Wakefield, in whom she believed she would find a supporter. Mr Wakefield, however, was too much a devotee of Mrs Deloraine to be willing to argue with his wonted brusqueness on a side where he was uncertain of her sympathies. He took refuge in a distinction.

"Of course you are right, generally speaking, but then Imperialism is not quite an ordinary political creed. We have already defined it as an attitude of mind, and that implies some sort of philosophy of life. I think Mrs Deloraine has made the distinction clear. It gives us a better basis for art and religion, but it does not take the place of one or the other. I think that is true, although, as I have often said, I am mortally afraid of getting too high-falutin on the subject. I detest mysticism and want to keep close to fact, but at the same time that is no reason why I should make our creed narrower than it really is. There are many who will prefer the dessert to the joint, and by all means let them have it if it is in the bill of fare. The instinct of empire is towards comprehension, not exclusion."

"Mr Wakefield has suggested the true parallel," said Lord Appin, who had listened to Mrs Deloraine with grave approval. "We do not profess to teach a religion, but, if we are not theologians, we are in a sense ecclesiastics. The state, remember, has now taken the place of the mediaeval church. Once we had popes and bishops supervising the lives of their flock and making themselves sponsors for their spiritual well-being. But their pride crumbled, because they fell into that very error against which Lord Launceston has been warning us, and sought to imprison the longings of the human spirit within the narrow walls of creed and ritual. Religion has triumphantly proved itself stronger than ecclesiasticism, and to-day we see a revolt—perhaps an unwise revolt—against all that savours of formality. And yet man cannot advance except through organised action, and if his Church is destroyed under one guise he will revive it under another. The Church in the Middle Ages had three great attributes. In the first place it was a brotherhood, a body of men linked together by a common faith. Again, it was inspired by an ideal which was professedly spiritual, a creed where success or failure was defined by other than material standards. Lastly, it was surrounded by an alien and hostile world, so that its members were drawn close to each other, and filled with a zeal which, according to our view of history, we label missionary or intolerant. That old church can never be re-established, for we have travelled too far from the sanctions which gave it strength. But we can no more do without a church than without a religion. Only we have learned nowadays that the true and lasting work for which such an organisation is adapted is rather political than doctrinal, and that the Seal of the Fisherman is better affixed to state decrees than to edicts against conscience. I maintain that our view of empire gives that empire something of the character of a church. We are a brotherhood banded together in a common quest. Our union, if less mystic than that which Augustine preached, has yet in it something not wholly human, not merely the sum of individual effort. In the midst of all our failures the work advances, for the plan is greater than the builders. Above all, we must achieve our desires in face of a stubborn and alien world. All around us are the frontiers of barbarism—I use the word as the Greeks used it. It is this environment which will perfect our brotherhood and give us something of the old crusading fervour. And if we have this clear purpose, not untouched with emotion, our empire will be another, and more truly Catholic, church. Then—to use Plato's phrase—the quest of truth will not lack the warmth of desire."

The party had hitherto been sitting in darkness, broken only by the glow from the hearth and Mrs Deloraine's lamp. Now the lights were turned on and there was a general shifting of seats. Lady Flora, who had sat with exemplary patience through the long discussion, discovered that only a walk on the terrace would be sufficient reward, and carried off Hugh and Mr Wakefield in her train. Soon wild laughter and the barking of small terriers showed that some mischief was afoot.

"What I feel about all that has been said to-night," said Mrs Yorke wearily, "and about everything that you all have said since you came here, is that Imperialism promises to be a very exhausting faith. It demands a superb vitality like Flora's or Sir Edward's. We are all to live at high pressure. We must try all our easy-going beliefs by a new touchstone, we must forget all our comfortable cliches, and we must never weary in well-doing. For the young, I grant you, it is an inspiring creed, but for a woman drawing towards middle life it is—well, exacting."

"So is any creed worth the name," said Carey. "They are all counsels of perfection, requiring us to strain every nerve for their fulfilment. Of course we tire and slacken, but our energy revives if we have got the true fire in our hearts. As for growing old, I do not believe in the thing. If our vitality sinks in one direction it increases in another. You are a much more active man now, Appin, than when in your youth you slumbered peacefully on the right hand of the Woolsack. We can no longer climb mountains like Astbury, or go lion-hunting like Teddy, but we make up for it by getting rid of the preoccupations which distract the young. Wise men never grow up; indeed, they grow younger, for they lose the appalling worldly wisdom of youth. Wakefield, for example ... "

But at this moment Lady Flora came in breathlessly from the verandah.

"Oh, Aunt Susan, do you know what those extraordinary men are doing? They have made a kind of toboggan and are glissading down the steep part of the lawn into the Dutch garden. I daren't try it, for I know I should ruin my gown."

CHAPTER 12

LADY FLORA woke early, before daybreak, and found it impossible to go to sleep again. The strange foreglow of dawn looked so attractive that she dressed and descended a silent staircase to the inner hall, where already the houseboys were beginning their labours. The verandahs were still in dusk, but when she had crossed the terrace and reached the lawns on the edge of the hill she came into a patch of pale sunlight and found that the skies were clear and that the sun was rising over the crest of the downs. The place intoxicated her, so quiet it was, so cool and fresh and dewy. She drank great draughts of the delicious air, and wondered why she had never discovered the charm of early rising before. At this hour most people were still wrapt in dull slumber with a doleful getting-up before them when the natural hour should have passed and the world become noisy and common. In this airy clime one's thoughts must perforce be clear and beautiful. Even a flower-pot looked an exquisite thing with the dew on it and the gold of sunrise on the dew. It occurred to her that it might be well if life were to be so rearranged that all the things which mattered were done before breakfast. Or it might be enough, she reflected, if one could attain to this morning frame of mind and keep it unsullied at all hours. Some creed might give this, or some great passion. And as the girl wandered through the ineffable colours of the awakening day she thought very deeply.

Hugh, coming back from an early gallop on the moor, found her sitting on a sunny corner of a parapet absorbed in thought. His horse shied at the apparition, and the rider, who had been half in a dream himself, promptly came off and disappeared in a bed of lilies. The horse began to graze peaceably, and Hugh, emerging dishevelled and surprised, found that the Muse of Contemplation had changed into a laughing girl.

"'The lark now leaves his watery nest,'" she quoted. "When you have shaken your 'dewy wing,' Mr Somerville, you might get one of the garden boys to take back the horse to the stable and come for a walk with me. I've been up since before daybreak, and I don't a bit want to go back yet."

Hugh commandeered the services of the nearest gardener, and with Lady Flora wandered back across the lawn.

"What brought you out of doors at this time?" he asked.

"Restlessness and this glorious morning. And, once out, I made up my mind that I must find a creed. I had nearly got one when you came tumbling off your horse among the lilies. Do you remember the contract we made our second day here? You were to explain to me all the things I could not understand. Well, I haven't bothered you much, for I found I was cleverer than I thought, and I followed most of the discussions quite easily. But last night Barbara stumped me completely. It wasn't so much what she said, for I understood her meaning more or less, but she and all the others seemed to find so much more in it than I could see. I am not an artist of any kind, or ever likely to be, but I agree with her argument about the new field for art which empire gives. And of course it makes life pleasanter all round to have big horizons and a great deal to do. But in spite of all that Lord Launceston said, I think we are making more out of the creed than reason allows. Though we deny it in words, yet we behave as if this were a new religion instead of merely a better groundwork for one. We can't turn politics into something which satisfies all our longings and fills all our life."

Hugh looked gravely at his companion. "You have your aunt's appalling clearness of mind. I agree with every word you say. What next?"

"Well, I want to know how I am to find the *trait d'union*? For I have become an Imperialist, you know. I have got an interest so absorbing that I do not think I can ever be bored again. I suppose there are things I can do to help, for you said that in our new state no one would be left out of citizenship. But Barbara and Mr Carey and Lord Launceston—but especially Barbara—make me feel as if Imperialism shaded off into all manner of beautiful and far-off things, and I can't see it. I have my own private dreams, but they are my own, and I can't fit them in with politics. I wish I could, for I am sure the happiest people have only one creed which covers everything in their lives."

Hugh began to laugh, but stopped short at the sight of the girl's serious eyes.

"Please forgive me. I didn't mean to be rude, but I was never so surprised before. What you want is a synthetic philosophy, and that you should want it and know that you want it staggers me. You are a very remarkable young woman."

"I will not be treated like a child," said Lady Flora indignantly, "and I will not have philosophy talked to me. I agree with Mr Wakefield that metaphysics are a bore, and only useful in staving off a difficult question. I have no more a desire for a synthetic philosophy than for the moon. But you might give me a Christian answer."

"I have given it you. You must find a philosophy, and it will take years in the finding. Don't you see, Lady Flora, that your question goes to the very root of all things? We want a key to life, an ideal which will leave out nothing and completely satisfy the hunger in our hearts. When you were a child and invented fairylands you brought into them everything you loved—cats and dogs and toys and people—and so with the bigger fairyland we make when we grow up. Everything shades sooner or later into metaphysics, and the humblest difficulty—if we press it home—

brings us within hailing distance of the Infinite. Well, I have no philosophy to teach you. Lord Appin to-night is going to give us what he calls 'some elementary notes on the speculative basis' of Imperialism, and I hope you will be very kind and keep Mr Wakefield quiet in a corner. But no ready-made philosophy will be of any use to you. If you and I were great geniuses we might sit down and think it all out from the beginning, but we have neither the time nor the patience for that. But the synthesis, remember, must either be made honestly by ourselves or come to us as a slow distillation from experience. Years, you know, bring the philosophic mind, and a certain unity creeps into life without our knowing it. Mrs Deloraine is absorbed in art, and she is also in love with a new political creed, and the two merge in a common ideal. So with Carey. His interest in empire is so consuming that everything in his life is brought into line with it. It is not the result of a conscious philosophy, for the thing is psychological rather than logical. The nexus is the human character."

"Yes," said Lady Flora, "that sounds as if it might be true. So you advise me not to trouble about the high-falutin side, but to leave that to my old age. And yet—I don't know. A morning like this makes one feel as if it were the only side that mattered. And after all, unless we can keep the morning freshness we must fail, for to create our new world we must have uncommon vitality."

"We must have vitality, but each must get it as best he can. We all of us, if we are to keep up our heads in the world, must have some secret fountain of youth within us. But an arbitrary unification of life will only choke the springs. Wakefield said a thing to me at the beginning of our visit, and I am daily growing more convinced of its truth. He said that all Imperialists would add their own poetry to the facts, but that it was only on the facts themselves that we could expect agreement, and if we tried to dogmatise on the poetry we should quarrel at once. So by all means let us try to be prosaic, for I don't think any of us will sink too deeply into prose."

"Mr Wakefield said that? What a wise old Philistine he is! He has asked me to go and stay with him next year in Canada. He says that people will call me either 'Lady Brune' or 'Flora,' and that I shall be an enormous success. And we are going out to camp in the northern woods, and fish the lakes, and voyage in canoes, and have the time of our lives ... Oh, by the by, Mr Somerville, you know you promised me a motto for my journal of our trek. It must be Greek, to look learned, and it must be about camping. Have you found one?"

Hugh rummaged in the pockets of his coat. "Yes—the very thing you want. It's Greek—latish to be sure, and it comes out of the Anthology. The sportsman who wrote it was called Antiphilus of Byzantium, and flourished in the reign of the Emperor Nero. I have done a sort of translation, rather rough and free. Here it is:—

"Give me a mat on the deck
When the awnings sound to the blows of the spray,
And the hearthstones crack with the flames a-back,
And the pot goes bubbling away.
Give me a boy to cook my broth,
For table a ship's plank laid with a cloth
(But never a fork or knife);
And after a game with a rusty pack,
The bo'sun's whistle to call us back—
That's the fortune fit for a king,
For oh! I love common life!"[8]

After dinner, by a general impulse the party sought the library, where Lord Appin ensconced himself in the central arm-chair.

"I don't want any lamp," he said, "for I have nothing to read. My business, as I threatened long ago, is to try to put to you the fundamental question in Imperialism. If we cannot make good our defence on it, then we have surrendered the key of the position.

"But first of all, there are a few preliminaries to be got over, and I am afraid I must take you through some elementary philosophy. I apologise to you, Launceston, for what must seem very trite and obvious; but unless one condescends to platitudes now and then, there must be gaps in the argument. Let me relieve Mr Wakefield's mind by saying that I am not going to talk Hegelianism or any other creed. What I have to say is admitted by all philosophers, and belongs to the world's common stock of speculation.

"I remember that once in my public career I was twitted with being a philosopher in politics. My critic urged that philosophy unfitted a man for making the clear distinctions which are the working hypotheses of life. Good is good, he said, to the average man, and bad is bad, and on the distinction depends the moral life. Progress and reform are real and ascertained benefits, and on this assumption the State is governed. But the philosopher, he went on, will tell you that black is black only because in some sense it is also white; that vice is only virtue regarded from another plane of thought; that there is no truth in this or that isolated dogma, but only in something which he calls a system; that progress is illusory, since reaction may be one of the forms through which the Infinite is moving towards realisation. All differences are smoothed away by him in some trumpery unification, and yet it is on the reality of these differences that human aspirations and human happiness depend. Therefore, my critic argued, the philosopher must be kept out of politics like a bull out of a china shop, for if he have a persuasive tongue he will end by corrupting the manhood of the nation. I remember that he became quite witty on the subject. 'Let us remove,' he cried, 'such philosophers from public life. There are places already appointed for their reception. Lunatic asylum is a vulgar word, so let us change their name to contemplative retreats. There let them live, happy and well cared for, hobnobbing with the Infinite, and leave the management of human affairs to unsophisticated human nature!'

"My friend would have been surprised could he have known how cordially I agreed with him. The philosopher has no business in politics, unless he can bring himself to the mode of thinking which that province requires. The pastime of bursting old, but valuable, bottles by putting new wine into them will not commend itself to the sane man. Then what is the mode of thinking which is proper to the political life?

"I do not propose to trace the history of thought from its first psychological embryo. Let us take the stage where it is manifest to all the world, the stage which is indicated when we speak of a man's having common- sense, or a practical mind, or a great intelligence. I do not wish to use German words, so let us call it the sphere of the Understanding. Now the essence of this mode of thought is that it insists upon clear divisions, upon the distinctions rather than upon any fundamental unity in things. A vast datum is presented to it by experience, and its business is to classify and arrange that datum. The distinctions which the Mind makes it regards as hard and fast—it must, for it has to act upon them. It acknowledges principles of union within such data, but the union is mechanical and external, like the classification of devices in heraldry. It refuses to theorise, to go one step further in its synthesis than practical needs require. Let us take some of the ordinary political counters. Law, for example, is not and does not profess to be complete justice. It is a working solution under which certain things are called right and certain things are labelled wrong, and have appropriate penalties attached. The good lawyer is he who can make the most of the mechanical unity within such a system; not he who pushes the analysis too far, and gets into metaphysics. But legal dogmas, such as they are, must be treated as final; the half-way house of thought must be regarded as the ultimate goal. Or take Liberty, that old will-o'-the-wisp of man. The Understanding, looking to the common needs of the State, declares that on one point the individual shall be untrammelled, and on another restricted. It does not examine the conception which is provided for it; it only takes steps to give it a practical meaning. So too with other general conceptions, such as education, national character, or the welfare of the people. The Understanding does not consider the welfare of humanity at large, but of humanity in a particular area—the nation or the race. It demands always the practical test, for it is purely utilitarian. It is not cosmopolitan; it is British, or French, or Siamese.

"The chief features, then, of this half-way house of thought are that the world is classified with sharp distinctions between the classes, that the distinguishing principle—race, liberty, law, anything you please—is something given to the mind and not examined by the mind, and lastly, that such distinctions are considered and acted upon as final. It is emphatically the sphere of the practical man. It does not confuse the common issues of life with any of the uncertainties of speculation. Its guiding principle is the law of the Sufficient Reason; it explains everything by something else. The world it creates for itself is orderly, logical, and free from any atmospheric haze. Such is the true world of politics, for it is the Understanding which makes states rich and well governed, and their citizens prosperous and contented. I have said that it is a world of compromise, but remember that most of the people who live in it see no compromise about the matter. It is for them a world of final and unalterable truths. I need not labour the point, for Lady Amysfort on the second day of our visit gave us an admirable exposition of this half-way house of the Understanding on its political side, and Mr Wakefield, if I may say so, is a living instance of it."

Mr Wakefield, hearing his name mentioned, awoke from a short nap, and prepared to give Lord Appin his critical and hostile attention.

"I shall not be accused of underestimating this most admirable attitude if I say that if it were universal the world would come to an end. Happily it is not universal, for there will always be many who, while insisting upon its merits, bring to it in practice a principle from another and a further stage of thought. Mr Wakefield, for example, would not be an Imperialist if he were content to dwell wholly in its confines. Its merits, let me repeat, are that it insists upon clear working distinctions, and that with its practical bias it looks always to facts, since its datum is Experience. Yes! But with Experience we admit at once one of the dynamic forces of revolution. I will not bring in any metaphysical doctrine of the Absolute Process of Thought. I will take this one recreating and reforming element in the sphere of the Understanding itself, that Experience which is its foundation. Sooner or later, as facts change, the change impresses itself even upon their formal interpretation. There will always be some who, living in the greater world of what, in contradistinction, we may call Reason, will be conscious from the start of the limitations of the Understanding; they will see its laws as compromises, its solutions as working hypotheses. Such men will be the mid wives of change, and their maieutic skill will be aided by the slow compulsion of Experience. There is a name for this compelling force which has been in common use since Plato—Dialectic.

It is the sceptical dissolvent, the *inquiètude poussante*, which acts upon the dogmatism of the Understanding. Hegel has an instance from theology which I daresay Lord Launceston remembers. But please keep in mind that, though I use this illustration, I am not giving you Hegelianism, but one of the accepted platitudes of philosophy. We first of all, Hegel says, conceive of God as a remote but beneficent force. We see seed-time and harvest return, children born and growing gently to maturity, and God following a laissez-faire policy, and suffering nature to run smoothly in compartments. Then suddenly comes in Dialectic in the thunderstorm which ruins the crops, the plague which devastates the family, in the awful terror of the Unseen, and the mystery of an inscrutable Fate. We are shaken out of our ease, and know that the Lord is a jealous God, and that nature is careless of our pigmy life. And then, at the last, comes the reconciliation in the domain of Reason, when we learn that God is made one with man. With this final stage of the infinite Reason we have no concern to-night. Politics is a mundane and a dusty game at best, and does not call for the highest function of thought. Sometimes, it is true, the humblest among us have seasons of revelation when a new dawn flushes our prosaic sky, and we have a glimpse of a City without foundations, and aspire for a moment to...

'...the shining table-lands To which our God Himself is moon and sun."

A great seer or mystic will kindle a nation to pursue for a little an ideal, of which the Understanding knows nothing, and that patchwork, which we call our world, seems in very truth the garment of God. But these sublime imaginings are not for practical men such as Mr Wakefield and—*magno intervallo*— myself. In politics Dialectic acting upon the Understanding does not lead us, as Hegel's illustration suggests, to the deeper unity of the Reason, but only to a reformed Understanding in harmony with changed conditions. The right mode of political thinking, I repeat, is this sphere, where the manifold world of experience is broken up into a clear system, where distinctions are regarded as final, and where the practical end is never lost to view. But for those who would lead their generation the Understanding must be tinged by Dialectic, compromises must be seen as such, and the coercive force of change which resides in experience must be aided and abetted. The result, as I have said, will be only another world of the Understanding, but the datum will have been revised. So in a roundabout way, and from a different side, we get back to the definition of Imperialism which we reached quite early in our stay here. We claim as our attitude this dialectical Understanding, or, in other words, while we needlessly destroy no one of the distinctions which compose our traditional creed, we desire to rethink them in the light of a new world."

"It is an extraordinary thing," said the Duchess, "how much wisdom there is in ordinary political labels. I should have said that Caroline and you, Bob, though you both call yourselves Conservatives, were at the opposite poles of opinion, and yet, when you come to a frank confession, you reach almost the same conclusion. I am not at all certain that I don't agree with you. Only, what I feel about your definition of Imperialism is that it does not distinguish it from any other sound political creed. You define it by the attitude of mind which it implies—clearness, practicality, an adequate recognition of the conditions of policy. But the Liberal might say the same thing of his faith, and the Conservative, and the Socialist. There is no serious politician alive who would not subscribe to the formula."

"Most true, Susan, but I have not nearly done with my definition. The attitude I have described belongs to all sane and practical creeds—creeds, that is to say, which incline neither to reaction nor to revolution. No faith which claims to be in tune with the spirit of its age would dare to disavow it. No; the difference is between those who hold the belief merely as a pious opinion and those who are prepared to act strenuously upon it. The difference, that is to say, lies in the rigour of our examination of our data. We Imperialists, whatever our political labels at home, are confronted with two alternatives. A huge empire has grown up around us, full of problems on which we can gain little light from our precedent history. We cannot deny the existence of that empire and those problems: so far we are all agreed. But we may regard it as an encumbrance, a menace to our older traditions; or we may see in it a hope of a richer and better public life, where greater responsibilities are counterbalanced by nobler rewards. To be an Imperialist demands two things—the eye to discern the new conditions and the will to accept them."

"Do you argue, then," said Hugh, "that the opposition we have to face is due not to intellectual blindness, but to moral lethargy?"

"Not to moral lethargy in the best cases, but to a quite honest and logical fidelity to a doctrine which I believe to be false. Our opponents may be divided into two classes. One class admits that these new conditions may be valuable, and that Imperialism is a beautiful dream; but they add that it is impossible. It is beyond the power of humanity, they argue, to construct such a state. Now, I am far from advocating impracticable ideals. It is a perfectly good answer to any proposal to say that it is impossible. But we must be careful how we admit the defence *propter infirmitatem*. If it were a question of building out of the void a Utopia where war should be unknown and property held in common, I should declare it impossible, because it would demand a revolution in human nature and human methods so complete as to be inconceivable. But when we are given the foundations to build on and the materials are ready to our hand, and the only further requirements are intelligence and vitality in the builders, then to say that the work is too hard to attempt is a confession of moral lethargy. It is not political wisdom, but political cowardice.

"The other class have a more formidable defence. They altogether deny the value of the new conditions and the new ideal. They complain that a vast material extension has no organic relation to national well-being. Britain, they say, owns one-fourth of the territory of the globe, rules one-fourth of the population, and conducts one-third of the trade; but she is no greater on that account than if she possessed not a rood outside the British Islands. In a word, they deny that principle which I have always maintained to lie at the very root of Imperialism—the need of a quantitative basis for qualitative development.

"Let me try to state their case as fairly as I can. No state, they say, owes its greatness in any real sense to its material equipment. Russia may govern from the Baltic to the Behring Sea and yet be an inferior power to Germany. Themistocles will always defeat Xerxes, and rich Carthage must yield in the end to poverty-stricken Rome. The claim of Britain to a great place in the world is due to the liberties which she has evolved in her long history; to a constitution which has been a model for all free nations; to her propaganda on behalf of humanity and liberalism; to the vitality of her sons who have led the way in exploration and invention and adventure. It is true that great wealth and great possessions have been the result, but they are the accidents, not the springs, of her greatness. Her true magnificence is seen in the way in which she has built up nations overseas with no thought of her own advantage. Britain, confined to her islands, with every colony elevated into an independent state, is richer in all that constitutes national wealth than if she owned a quarter of the globe in fee-simple, and administered it as a tributary province. By remaining loyal to her faith in liberty she provides the conditions in which her people can grow to their full stature far more effectively than if she compelled the other nations of the world to become her servants to this end. So far I, for one, am ready to admit that the argument is indisputable.

"But, they continue, this modern talk of empire introduces another ideal, and a grossly material one. It brings in mere size as in itself of value. It seeks to extend the borders of Britain so that a quarter of the world shall be one state. The assumption on which it acts is that a complex organisation, which taxes all the powers of its organisers, is likely to produce a higher civic development than a simpler polity. The whole creed, they argue, is simply a shelving of the question. Granted that many things are ruinously wrong in our public life, surely the right way to remedy them is to get at the root of the mischief, to reform the heart, to transform the spirit, and not merely to say there is a big empire which will cure these ills if we allow it. They add—and I know I am repeating what has already been better said—that an immense material environment will cripple the soul. We shall think in continents instead of in truths. Our prosperity and its responsibilities will choke us till we become leaden-eyed galley-slaves killed by a too generous fortune.

"I can distinguish two separate points of attack. The first is that Imperialism tends to seek material cures for spiritual diseases. That is to say, our opponents deny that qualitative development can depend upon a quantitative basis. The second is that a vast material environment is not only no remedy for moral ills, but a direct menace to moral well-being. Let us take these arguments separately.

"The first, to my mind, is true up to a point. It adopts an illustration from biology, and holds that organic disease in a living body is not removed by growth in size or by any stimulants which promote such growth. Well, I am in entire agreement. But to adduce this illustration as an answer to my contention is to be guilty of a glaring *ignoratio elenchi*. I have used the word 'development,' not health. And my argument is that just as you cannot find the mind and spirit of a man in a body which has been starved and stunted till it is no better than an infant's, so you cannot find true spiritual progress unless you provide adequate material conditions. But I do not care for this pictorial reasoning, so let us put the matter differently. What do we mean by spiritual development? Surely, the broadening and deepening of the mind till it regards the world in its true perspective, and the strengthening of the character so that the will is a tempered and unerring weapon in the charge of a man's soul. And this end is to be achieved only by the exercise of the mind upon the largest possible manifold of experience, and by the conflict of character with the alien forces of the world. I am talking, remember, not of the saint and recluse, but of the citizen. What is true of individual development is no less true of the state's. A nation becomes great in the most sublimated sense of the word by its ability to present its citizens with a sphere of action wherein their civic responsibilities may be fulfilled. A microcosm, however perfect, will never be a true arena for civic virtue.

"But, it may be argued, no one denies that the state must have an ample sphere of action; the objection to your doctrine is that you declare that the sphere of action involves a spacial extension, whereas we say that it may be intensive. There is sufficient work for the citizen in settling his home problems without embarking on foreign adventures. My answer is that for a state such as ours the two things are synonymous. I do not for a moment deny that for a new colony intensive activity may be the path of wisdom. But in all old and highly developed lands there comes a time when, without spacial extension, all that is possible is a barren rearrangement, a shuffling of the cards. Just as we cannot describe a mere analysis and readjustment of a few dogmas as mental progress, so I call any preoccupation with what after all must be the formal aspect of our own affairs—their emendation without the introduction of fresh elements,—I call that national stagnation. And this brings me to my second answer to the first argument of our opponents. I am prepared to maintain that spacial extension may cure a disease, when that disease is itself the result of undue confinement. If a man is fainting from foul air, he will revive under the winds of heaven. A palm may be perishing in a flower-pot, when it would thrive in the forest. Mrs Deloraine has suggested that certain of the vices in our modern art are due to the narrowing of its borders. Take, again, our labour problem. You may talk about the reorganisation of industry, you may accept any socialist nostrum, you may abolish capitalism, and yet you will be no better off, if, as I believe, the radical fault is that we are over-industrialised. The cure for our economic ills, if cure there be, is to bring fresh capital into the business. One of the misfortunes of our age is that in one sense it is too ideal, too prone to neglect the material conditions without which no great end can be achieved in this world or any other. It is a flimsy idealism at the best, for the great idealists never forgot that, if it was well to trust in God, it was no less right to keep their powder dry."

"We are too ideal," continued Lord Appin, meeting the approving glance of Mr Wakefield, "and at the same time we are not ideal enough. If we were, we should not hear the second argument which our opponents use. Material greatness, they say, is an enemy to moral well-being. It debases our standards, inflames our pride, and stirs our passions. To this I have only one answer to make. If our national life be of so poor a quality that it is smothered by possessions, then the battle need never be joined at all. The 'small nation' fallacy is like the 'sheltered life' humbug in education. A people must keep itself clear from the world lest its garments be spotted, just as a boy should not be sent to a public school in case his moral sense be dimmed. If our soul is to be lost because we go down into the arena of life, then the odds are that it was not worth saving from the first. If we will escape the danger of decadence, we will also forego the hope of progress; and remember, the nation which stands still is doomed. If we do not go forward, we shall most certainly go back.

"But at the same time it is well that this objection should be stated, because it contains a warning against the sins to which great empires are prone,—what the French call the disease of 'grandeur.' I believe most firmly that in the deepest sense Providence is on the side of the bigger battalions. I cannot see why size should not have its ideal as well as littleness. All the world inclines to reserve its affection for small things—a small country, a small people—because I assume there is a stronger sense of proprietorship attaching to what is limited in bulk. Yet I can conceive of as deep a patriotism in an empire as in a city, and a love of great mountains and plains as real as any affection for a garden. But size has its own disease, and we may easily fall into the vice of looking upon it as something worthy in itself, however alien it may remain to our culture. Whether we call the disease 'Jingoism' or 'grandeur' or 'self-complacency,' its root is the same. It means that we regard our empire as a mere possession, as the vulgar rich regard their bank accounts—a matter to boast of, and not an added duty. All the braggart glorification we sometimes hear means a shallow and frivolous understanding of what empire involves. No serious man dare boast of the millions of square miles which his people rule, when he remembers that each mile has its own problem, and that on him and his fellows lies the burden of solution.

"Jingoism, then, is not a crude Imperialism; it is Imperialism's stark opposite. It belongs to the school of thought which thinks of the Empire as England, with a train of dependencies and colonies to enhance her insular prestige; but it has no kinship with the ideal of an empire moving with one impulse towards a richer destiny. The true Imperialist will be very little inclined to a cheap complacency. He is kindled at times to ardour by the magnitude of his inheritance, and he has always, if he keeps the faith, optimism and hope to cheer him. But he is equally weighed down with the burden of his duties and the complexity of the task before him, if he would translate his dream into fact. A dependency to him is not a possession but a trust. The glory of England is not the mileage of her territory but the state into which she is welding it.

"And therefore I say that Imperialism, sanely considered, is the best guardian of peace. Its aim is not conquest but consolidation and development, and its task within its own borders is so great that it has little inducement to meddle with its neighbours. I am no believer in cosmopolitanism. I have always thought that a man must cleave to his own people, and that the purpose of God is best attained by the strife of race with race and ideal with ideal. War will remain as the last resort when two race ideals, passionately held, meet in conflict. But the war which comes from a vague lust of possession I abhor, and the remedy for it is a preoccupation with nobler tasks. England has completed her great era of expansion. Her work for ages was to find new outlets for the vigour of her sons, and to occupy the waste or derelict places of the earth. Now, the land being won, it is her task to develop the wilds, to unite the scattered settlements, and to bring the whole within the influence of her tradition and faith. This labour we call empire-building, and above all things it is a labour of peace."

"I thought that you were going to talk metaphysics," said Mr Wakefield in an aggrieved voice. "Instead, you have talked ordinary common-sense, with which I can pick no quarrel. I object to having my patent infringed."

Lord Appin had got himself a cigar and was smoking steadily.

"In the last resort," he said blandly, "the two things are not distinguishable. I feared I had been a little too high-coloured in my argument to earn your approval, for Mrs Deloraine has affected us all with a tendency to emotion. Still, I think, the main position is sound."

"Sound!" cried Mr Wakefield. "There is no answer to it. But I am glad that I am not obliged to make the defence too often, for I am not an adept at this kind of discussion. In the colonies we go on simpler lines. One opponent says that he wants a republic, another declares that England is played out, while a third idiot—and he is the commonest—is too anxious to get his township started to care what happens to the Empire. His only question is, 'And what am I to get out of it?' I meet these reprobates with business arguments—figures, you know, and a little sentiment. In the colonies, happily, they do not get down to fundamentals."

"Nor in England," said Hugh. "The people who go back to first principles, as a rule make the journey only to find some defence for a prejudice which nothing will induce them to forego. There are no conversions in that rarefied air."

"Well, let us leave it at that," Lord Appin said cheerfully. "We, too, have recourse to fundamentals merely to justify to ourselves the faith which comes to us from other sources. I have a great belief in common-sense, which, after all, is the method proper to the sphere of the Understanding. Only, as some of us have inquisitive minds, it is as well now and then to go a little farther for the sake of a more reasonable satisfaction. Heaven forbid that I should ever try to transfer for good the case for Imperialism to the cloudy plateau of philosophy. Philosophy is not a necessary of life, it is not even a special pleasure; but, remember, if it once lays hold of the mind, it is the only thing which can solve the doubts it creates.... There, Wakefield, I hope I have climbed off" my perch with sufficient humility to please you. And now, having blasphemed my idols, I shall restore my self-respect by beating you at billiards.

CHAPTER 13

"WE shall get back," said the Duchess next night at dinner, "just in time for the autumn session. I am told I must give a political party, and I want you all to come. Bob always does, and our people stare at him as if he were a strange new beast. It does them good to find out that he has not a cloven hoof, and I am sure it is the best thing in the world for him to be civil to people who annoy him. Will you come, Sir Edward?"

That gentleman had been unaccountably glum during the meal, so that Mrs Yorke had given up in despair the effort of making conversation.

"I'm afraid I can't," he said moodily. "I shan't be in England till after Christmas, for I promised Carey to go up to Kashmir and have a look at his place there. But it would be worth while going back if I thought I would meet that fellow Bronson, and tell him what I thought of him with a dog-whip. Of all the damned scoundrels!—I beg your pardon, Duchess, but it's a fact. Have you seen the home papers? You know there's a row in West Africa, a very ticklish affair for us, for we hold a big country with a handful of troops and no base within hundreds of miles. Well, because we have killed a score or two of natives in the way of duty, the fellow has been spitting venom about our men, calling them murderers, and accusing them of every unmentionable atrocity. I don't mind his slinging accusations into the air; it's the favourite game of these vermin, and eases them without doing anybody much harm. But when it comes to calling old Mitchinson a blackguard, who, as everybody knows, is the straightest and kindest fellow on earth, then, I think, it's about time for somebody to interfere. If half a dozen Englishmen in lonely stations are massacred and have their eyes gouged out, in the language of that rabble it's the effort of a brave people rightly struggling to be free. But if in self-defence we teach some of the sportsmen the ways of the Maxim, then it's a cold-blooded brutal murder. I would give all I possess to show some of these gentry the pretty habits of the full-blooded savage."

"My dear Teddy," said Lord Appin, "your language is a little unparliamentary. No, I forgot. You would consider that a compliment, so I shall say unnecessarily abusive. I don't object to Mr Bronson, who is merely an honest well-meaning ass. He feels in his way as deeply about the affair as you do, and means as well by his country. As Bismarck said, 'Every nation must have its national fools.' The sentimentalist is a much worse fellow, for he has no earnestness to justify his folly. Let me quote from my favourite newspaper a few remarks about that fight in Northern Nigeria you were talking about.

"'On Sunday—the day of rest and gladness throughout the Christian world— three hundred brave, black British citizens were murdered in West Africa. Their offence was that they had taken up arms for their native land. Remember that these men were not a foreign foe, but subjects of our King, sharers with ourselves in the benefits which are assumed to follow our flag. What account have we to render of our stewardship towards them? Before we came into their country they were living their simple lives happily and innocently—in darkness, it may be, but yet in peace. We come among them, outrage their traditions, violate their sanctities, coerce them in an unfamiliar bondage. Can we wonder that a high-spirited people rebels? And we meet their revolt with the savage measures which weakness and panic dictate. West Africa is, indeed, a signal and ominous lesson in imperial futility and crime, but it is a lesson, we hope and believe, which is now scarcely needed. Already the grandiose dreams of empire are foundering in the bud.'"

"There!" said Sir Edward triumphantly. "There you have the stuff I mean. Launceston, you defended the Nonconformist conscience when we were crossing the Lake. Have you anything to say in defence of that?"

"I make the same distinction as Lord Appin." Lord Launceston, who had scarcely smiled during the reading of the extract, spoke with a grave deliberation which hushed the talk. "Two men may differ profoundly and yet be equally entitled to the name of patriot. Take the case of conscription. I may desire to see every citizen trained to arms, and my neighbour may hold all war immoral and military training no better than a preparation for crime. I desire the thing because I wish my country well, and he opposes me because he also wishes it well. We differ because we are patriots: if he, with his convictions, were less of a patriot, he might agree with me. There are many people who must be troubled by the incidents of a native war—quite honestly and reasonably troubled. They believe that their country is degrading herself, and, because they love their country, they are bound to protest. We differ intellectually, but morally we are at one with them. I do not object to the killing of men in a right cause, just as I do not object to capital punishment, because I have no extreme respect for human life. Nor do I object to flogging when it may be expedient, because I do not believe in the dignity of the human person. But I recognise that many good men do not share my scepticism, and that for them to condone these things would be a betrayal of their moral standards. I want to see every genuine fanatic fought tooth and nail if need be, but respected as a foe who by a turn of fortune's wheel may become an ally. Fanaticism means steel and fire, and we are nothing without them. Every true Imperialist, it seems to me, must be at heart a kind of fanatic. We can do something with the cranks, but we can do nothing with the *flâneur*. They differ from us only in opinion, not in purpose, and any day a new light or a wider experience may range them on our side."

Sir Edward grunted. "Then if we are to respect them so much, how are we to fight them? You can't fight without a little animosity, and it looks as if that excellent quality were to be swamped with unwilling admiration."

"We fight them because we believe them to be utterly and mischievously wrong. We are in as deadly earnest as they are, and we are as certain of our faith. When fanaticism comes in our way we must convert it or destroy it. But when that is done we can build its tomb and give it a friendly epitaph."

"Do you mean to say that the fellows who are screaming about Mitchinson are only mistaken patriots?"

"Some are undoubtedly," said Lord Launceston. "But not over many, because the true fanatic is rarely a fool, and this attack is so curiously foolish. No, I fear it springs in the main from a quality for which I have no defence to make—a shallow and calculating sentimentality."

Lady Flora protested. "Please, Lord Launceston, don't join in the conventional abuse of sentiment. I like it, for it means that people are simple-minded and cheerful."

"I don't mean your kind of sentiment, my dear child. We shall all pray for its continuance. The sentiment I mean is the decadence of everything simple and cheerful. It comes from a mind and heart whose powers have gone rotten."

Lady Warcliff nodded her agreement. "I like that distinction I used before between the hard-hearted kind people and the soft-hearted cruel people. The sentimentalist is the egotist who cloaks his selfishness by claiming a monopoly of the purer emotions. There is no province of life which he does not pollute. In love he is the philanderer, in politics the Jingo or the humanitarian, in art the purveyor of all that is weak and fatuous and second-rate. He is incapable of greatness: he is incapable of even common truth. He goes through life without ever seeing the world in its reality, for between him and it hangs the veil of the second-hand emotionalism. He is the kind of being who calls physical cowardice moral courage, who will shed tears over the poor and bully his own servants, whose mouth is full of noble words and his heart of little fears and vanities. There is nothing to lay hold of in him, only rottenness, like a decaying tree. He has so debauched his soul that he is incapable of any clean strong passion, and therefore I say, God pity the man or woman who trusts in him. For, like all weak unwholesome things, he is capable of the last extreme of cruelty."

"Poor sentimentalist!" sighed the Duchess. "Really, Margaret, you are too unkind, for we have all a bit of him in our nature, and your censure is horribly personal. Let us walk round the terrace while the men smoke, and then we may be in a better frame of mind for Lord Launceston."

Half an hour later in the inner hall the company reassembled. Lady Flora had begged for lights. "I feel so eerie in the dark," she said, "and besides, I like to watch people's faces. Mr Wakefield, will you sit beside me and translate the fragments of the dead languages which no one seems able to do without?"

Lord Launceston began with a great air of diffidence.

"I have been given an appalling task by our host—nothing less than to sum up the kind of conclusions we have been hovering round since we came here. It was no use my protesting and quoting Fichte's reply to Madame de Staël, '*Ces choses ne ses laissent pas dire succinctement.*' He replied that if we had any clear ideas at all, there were always words to fit them. I suppose he is right, and though our body of results is not very great, yet there are one or two points established. Like all living faiths, Imperialism must grow insensibly into men's hearts. Almost the last thing it finds is its principles, but long before that it has revealed itself in a new way of looking at the world, a new hope, vague, indeterminate, and yet so priceless that those who catch the gleam are ready to leave everything and follow it.

"Our first conclusion, therefore, was that Imperialism was not Liberalism or Conservatism or any other traditional creed. It was a new attitude of mind which admitted certain new conditions into the problem of statesmanship. On the interpretation of these conditions there will be a great difference of opinion. We shall have liberals and conservatives, socialists and individualists, free-traders and protectionists, but all these differences will exist *within* Imperialism. The sign-manual of our creed is the belief that our problems must be settled on the basis of the Empire, that it is our business to look at all the facts instead of at only a few of them. "This is, of course, the merest formal statement, and gets us very little farther. On these terms we could enlist, I believe, ninety-nine out of every hundred Englishmen in a lip-service to the creed. What we desire to create is the Imperialist with the intelligence to estimate his data correctly, and the will to act upon his conclusions. That is to say, we ask for a more highly-developed type of citizen. Lord Appin has already explained to you the practical standpoint of such a citizen, and the philosophical justification for it. We do not need theorists or sentimentalists or anarchists: we want the practical intelligence which is acute in foresight and sober in ideal, and which is joined to an unhesitating instinct for deeds. He has also explained the kind of philosophical preconception which is involved in any examination of our new data, and which must be taken as the sine qua non of Imperialism. He defined it roughly, if I remember, as the recognition of the value of material greatness for spiritual development, the belief that since ideals can only be realised under conditions of space and time, it is right and proper to attend to these conditions. So our Imperialist—liberal, conservative, individualist, socialist—we may take to be the man who accepts the Empire as the basis of all our problems, who believes that spacial expansion is not inconsistent with civic well-being but may be a valuable ally, and who carries to his task a mind which understands the limitations of political activity, and at the same time is quick to apprehend and resolute to act. Many Imperialists, no doubt, will fall short of this high standard, but we define a party by its ideal.

"In the early part of our discussions much was said about the relations of Imperialism to current politics at home. We do not seek to create any new party, but to have all parties accept our doctrine as the ultimate basis of their activity. But at the same time there are certain types of mind which are of more value to us than others, and certain types which are almost wholly useless. I have something to say on this subject which I can best introduce by a quotation from Lady Flora. I overheard her the other day arguing with Astbury about that hoary question—the proper definition of Whig and Tory. And this was her conclusion. A Whig is a man who is prepared to go to the stake for his beliefs, but who will not send his opponents there. A Tory is one who will not only burn himself, but is quite prepared in the last resort to burn those who differ from him. I take that as a parable, and I am prepared to defend the Tory attitude as the one which in the future must triumph. We are many hundred years removed from burning, but the point of view remains the same. One man is very much in earnest about his creed, but he will not coerce his fellows into agreement. He must justify himself to his own conscience, but he will not take it upon himself to compel other consciences to follow suit. *Laissez-faire* is his motto and individualism his religion. A second man has the same private depth of conviction, but his conscience has a communal tinge in it. He cannot conceive that that which deeply concerns himself does not also concern the State. I do not mean that he is the crude propagandist. That is a type that is common enough and worthless enough to-day. Every human being itches to make converts, whether it be to theosophy or to dry-fly fishing. I mean the serious conviction that no man lives to himself alone, and that we must settle our problems not only for ourselves but for the State. A political creed cannot be a private possession. If it is true it is true for the whole race, and the type of mind which I speak of is prepared to coerce the world into accepting it. One man says, 'I think this or that, and I hope to find enough like-minded people to give the view the support of a majority.' Another says, 'This is my opinion, and since it is God's truth, the world shall accept it." And it is the latter who must conquer. The earth is not yet the heritage of the meek, and the Kingdom of Heaven will yield only to violence. That is what I mean when I say that the natural ally of the Imperialist is the fanatic. We demand first of all wisdom, but we believe that wisdom is a voice in the desert, unless there is a power of conviction behind her to compel the market-place to acknowledge her godhead.

"We have spoken of English conditions from the party point of view, and we have found that we can disregard conventional party distinctions. I would rather consider them under a more organic division. We have still the great threefold classification—the lower classes, the middle, and the upper, or, as I should prefer to put it, the classes which have wants, the classes which are satisfied, and the classes which have ambitions. Some men are so near the margin of life that their horizon is bounded by material wants—food, housing, security. Others live on a plane where their desires are either less self-regarding, or if self-regarding are less material, and such desires I call ambitions. Between these extremes lie the great contented classes, the bourgeois in mind. They may have no positive satisfaction in life, but they desire in their dumb way the maintenance of things as they are. They may clamour for this or that reform, but they are not reformers at heart, for their minds are asleep. I need scarcely say that this distinction of classes does not correspond with the conventional one. Some of our own class are in my lower, and a vast number in my middle class, while many of the lower class as usually defined, and not a few of the middle, would belong to what on my definition is the aristocracy of ambition."

"How true!" said Mrs Wilbraham. "If we had a spiritual Debrett prepared by a committee of archangels what havoc it would make in Society!"

"I do not wish to disparage my middle class," Lord Launceston continued. "It plays a useful part and it has many virtues. As some one has said, it is the 'force of social persistence.' It has also, I believe, been likened to a backbone."

"A most dangerous metaphor," said the Duchess. "What warrant has a backbone to make so much noise? I always thought that it was the duty of that valuable part of the human frame to remain decently covered up with flesh. An aggressive backbone is a contradiction in terms. And yet there is no doubt that we are governed by our middle, our stupidly satisfied class."

"Yes. That is our danger, as it has been the danger of all great civilisations. It does not think, because it has no need to. The burdens of citizenship mean nothing to it, because they are not felt. The lives of its members are beyond the reach of ordinary want, they are secure from attack, they have no reason to pester themselves about the problems of statecraft. Their attitude to the poor is one of slightly contemptuous patronage. Since their standards are material they have little sympathy for those who cannot command material success. Towards the class with ambitions they feel an innate hostility, save in so far as that class contains their social superiors. I have no doubt such people are kind friends, excellent husbands, and wise fathers, but in no sense of the word are they citizens. And yet by a paradox of fate they govern. It is their votes that must be sought before any policy can be realised. It is this dull residuum who must be cajoled or persuaded before one step forward is possible. They are the support of traditionalism in all departments of life, not from conviction, like the true Tory, but from apathy.

"To such people we make no appeal. Imperialism, like all constructive policies, asks for science, for ideas, for *Geist*, above all for courage. But it may act upon this inert mass like fire upon ore, and sublimate it into something of value. The sense of citizenship comes not from governing but from administering, and till problems are translated into homely terms, and the demands of the State hammer at the doors of those self-satisfied homes, there will be no salvation for their inmates. In the meantime our appeal must be to the first and the third of my classes. The third is obvious enough. The aristocracy of ambition in whatever social rank they may be found are our natural propagandists. We appeal to all who can think clearly and feel cleanly and act wholeheartedly—the 'patrician spirits that refine Their flesh to fire and issue like a flame On brave endeavours.'

But we appeal no less eagerly to the rising democracy, the men who are still preoccupied with the elementary wants of life. These men know that they can only make their power felt by superior energy, by loyalty to their ideals, by a relentless fidelity to facts. Like us they demand that the rubbish be cleared away, like us they clamour for a recognition of the needs of things as they are. They may show signs of hysteria and impatience, but never of stagnation. Their attitude of mind is one with ours, and we have sufficient faith to believe that the same attitude will in time produce the same creed.

"There is another side of the popular cry which to my mind is most hopeful. Your labour leader to-day wishes to bring the humblest citizen into the life of the State. That is to say, he would extend the opportunity of administrative experience by means of subordinate councils, and with such an extension must come a growth of the feeling of corporate responsibility. The lower classes, if he had his will, should not govern without administering. Now our appeal is to practical statesmen, those who know the difficulties of administration and who have acquired from experience a wider view of public interests than the merely selfish. At present, I grant you, there is too much inclination in this class to identify the interests of the State with those of one section, but I am optimistic enough to believe that a wider experience carries within itself the cure.

"The first moral condition, then, which Imperialism demands is a quickened civic conscience and a tireless intelligence. The second, for want of a better phrase, I will call a wider patriotism. The affection which with many is limited at present to their birthplace must be extended to the Empire. I do not mean that we should forego old attachments. Just as no man will ever love his fatherland in the same way as he loves the village or parish where he was born, so to the Englishman, the Canadian, and the New Zealander, England and Canada and New Zealand will always have more intimate claims than any wider geographical area. But Imperial patriotism will stand to national, as national patriotism to-day stands to local affection. A man is not less of a patriot because the 'lone sheiling and the misty island' are nearer his heart than the whole realm of Britain. And a man may be a good Imperialist although his country of origin has a larger share in his interests than the Empire. There is a gradation in patriotism, and one grade differs from another in kind. If we have at one end the sentiment for what is small and unique—the village, the glen, the cottage—at the other we may have a sentiment as genuine for what is omnipotent and universal.

"This wider patriotism, as I understand it, seems to me to harmonise with the nature of our race. Our land no more than Hellas has a paltry local unity. The English genius has never regarded its civilisation as tied down to the place of its birth. Its task has been to absorb the unfamiliar and to lay bare the unknown, admitting no *terra incognita* into its scheme of things. There is always the home country, the centre of memories, but the working loyalties of life go to those lands it has created. As every man loves the work of his own hands, so any race must love what comes from its own toil and adventure. Such a love is no thin cosmopolitanism, but the jealous affection for its own household, and once the unity of the Empire is realised, patriotism must embrace it as naturally as family affection embraces each new inmate of the home.

"These are platitudes which are scarcely worth repeating, were they not so often forgotten. We need not greatly concern ourselves with the by-products of empire. If the motive force is there—the new attitude of mind and all that is implied in it—we may safely trust to natural laws to produce the secondary results we desire. Our first business, then, is to have the Empire accepted, not as a pious opinion or a phrase of rhetoric, but as a living faith. It must become an unconscious presupposition in all our politics, otherwise it will not influence our conduct of affairs. Remember that a truth is only potent in English life when it has become a truism. Our duty, as we all agree, is first of all to create opinion,—to guide the alert, and to compel the inert into a certain attitude of mind.

"So far, I think, I carry Mr Wakefield with me. But after that, he will ask, what next? After that, I am afraid, he and I must agree to differ. It is not a fundamental difference, for it is only on methods, but the methods seem to me so vital a matter that I fear it is a real difference. Let me repeat some of the conclusions we have reached in our discussion. We saw that while legislative federation was out of the question as things stand to-day, some executive union was not only urgently needed, but up to a point practicable. Mr Wakefield himself, outlined a scheme which promised to create gradually and without any wild change a true Imperial executive. We saw that the present theory of our Empire was one of alliance, but that it must be made a working alliance. We have a dozen great common problems, and they are all administrative—the control of subject races, the development of the tropics, labour, defence, emigration, commercial union. Our survey of these has been very slight, but we have found reason, I think, to believe that in all there is a hope of a successful settlement on an Imperial basis. But questions which concern all must be answered by the co-operation of all. At present our method is either to leave them unanswered or to answer them ourselves after a make-believe of consultation. This is bad enough, but in my opinion it is less dangerous than the other proposal which Mr Wakefield upholds. That seeks to effect a union on a matter of immense importance to each unit, while retaining the old loose alliance system unchanged. I am not dealing now with any economic doctrine. I am perfectly content to see our traditional faith revised if necessary, but that revision must come from a body empowered to undertake the task. To plunge the empire into a wrangle on what is after all a detail, without providing the machinery within which alone that detail has any meaning, is to my mind a gross blunder in statesmanship."

"As if," said Lord Appin dreamily, "a man were to embark on a violent discussion about the career of his eldest son before he had proposed to the lady of his affections."

"Carey," said Mr Wakefield, "I thought that subject had been forbidden. If it hasn't, I ought to be allowed to state my case. In two words it is this. I say that before you can have an executive union you must create a desire for it. The most vital of our common problems is that of our commerce. If we once show the different peoples in the empire that on this point they can have a union to their mutual advantage, why, union will follow as a matter of course."

Lord Launceston laughed. "My dear Wakefield, if that is all your case then I have no quarrel with you. That is very different from the 'high priori' line of most of your school. Many of them are Imperialists only by accident. They are insular at heart, and they stand like Ruth 'in tears amid the alien corn' because they lament the decline of England, not the disintegration of the empire. If the creed of a common commercial policy is only an argument for an imperial executive, then you have my best wishes in your crusade. But remember there are many other common needs, and that to attempt to meet any one without the common machinery will mean failure, utter and final, and good-bye for many a day to all hope of union. These discussions have left me with two convictions intensified. One is that in the end our creed must prevail. The other is that we are dealing with fragile things and must go very warily. We are not welding lifeless matter together, but coaxing into one growth a number of separate forms of life. And since we are handling life our touch must be delicate and sympathetic, for one hint of coercion may snap the vital link. I am one of those people who rejoice in colonial nationalism. I would not have it one jot weaker than it is to-day. When I hear of Australia clamouring for a navy of her own, and Canada asking for the treaty-making power, I am honestly delighted. They may be asking for the wrong things, but the fact that they should want them is right—right—right. I want to see every one of our daughter-peoples grow into triumphant and self-conscious nationhood, for it is all contributory to the well-being of the Empire. There is no value in the union of weak things: we want the unity of strength, the unity where every part has a vigorous self-subsistent life out of which it contributes to the common stock of imperial vitality.

"In our discussion we have insisted—rightly, I think—less upon the material splendour which our ideal involves than upon its spiritual greatness. Empire is a dream—on the brink of realisation, it is true, but still a dream. Too often these Imperial visions have a Byzantine colouring. They dwell on size and numbers and wealth, but not enough upon the new life which is bound up in them. All my days the epic of our future has sung itself in my ears, but as I grow into late middle age I think less of the pomp and pageantry and more of the grave austerity at the heart of it. I can foresee an empire where each part shall live to the full its own life and develop an autochthonous culture. But behind it all there will be the great catholic tradition in thought and feeling, in art and conduct, of which no one part, but the empire itself, is the appointed guardian. In that confraternity of peoples the new lands will redress the balance of the old, and will gain in return an inheritance of transmitted wisdom. Men will not starve in crowded islands when there are virgin spaces waiting for them, and young nations will not be adventurers in far lands, but children of a great household carrying the fire from the ancestral hearth. Our art will be quickened by a breath from a simpler and cleaner world, and the fibre of our sons will be strung to vigour by the glimpse of more spacious horizons. And our English race will vindicate to mankind that doctrine which is the noblest of its traditions—that liberty is possible only under the dominion of order and law, and that unity is not incompatible with the amplest freedom. We of the old countries shall give and receive. Our Trojan manhood, our Trojan Lares and Penates will be there, but so too will Latium and the ancient Ausonian rites. Do you remember how at the close of the AEneid Juno asks from Jupiter that Italy may remain herself in spite of foreign conquest?

'*Sit Latium, sint Albani per saecula reges,*
Sit Bomana potens Itala virtute propago."

And the King of the Gods replies :—

'*Sermonem Ausonii patrium moresque tenebunt,*
Utque est nomen erit; commixti corpore tantum
Subsident Teucri. Morem ritusque sacrorum
Adjiciam faciamque omnes uno ore Latinos.
Hinc genus Ausonio mixtum quod sanguine surget
Supra homines, supra ire deos pietate videbis,
Nee gens ulla tuos aeque celebrabit honores.'[2]

There was silence for a little as Lord Launceston's quiet voice ceased. Then Carey from the fireplace spoke.

"It is a religion," he said, "to me, and I think to others. If you quarrel with the word, I can only say that what any man desires with his whole heart, what wakens all that is best in him and curbs all that is worst, is a religion, whatever else the term may mean. No man can be religious who is not a fighter, who does not know the odds which the world sets against him, who has not suffered and struggled and tried the temper of the human spirit against the iron rigour of nature. Religion is not a comfortable thing of easy prayers and ready thanksgivings, but something as fierce and stubborn and consuming as life itself. How else is it to wither the hosts of the enemy? I want my allies to be fanatics. If my religion is not to include my politics, then I am content to have none, for to me the one as much as the other is an attempt to subdue the material world of our common sight into harmony with an unseen world of the spirit."

The stillness which still reigned in the room showed the Duchess that an atmosphere had been created too emotional for her comfort. But in spite of herself she had been impressed, and the cool tones of her voice had an unwonted feeling in them as she once more brought back the discussion to what she considered a reasonable level.

"It is a great creed, no doubt, and I am not going to criticise. Some of it frightens me a little, but then I am old-fashioned and easily frightened. The merit of it all seems to me to be that it allows for such ample differences among its disciples. You can add to and subtract from it without altering its character. I suppose, Bob, that you would say that that is because it is a living thing, with all the generous waste and superabundance of life."

Lord Appin rose and walked to the window, where he stood for a little before he replied.

"Yes; it is alive, and in saying that we have used the final word of commendation. There is room within its shadow for all the policies which can inspire the hearts of wise men to a keener public duty. There is room for Carey's mysticism, and Wakefield's practical good sense, and Susan's Liberal principles, and Lady Amysfort's Toryism—room, too, for the hard scientific faith of young men like Astbury and Hugh; room even for Sir Edward's anarchic individualism. It is still a far-away ideal, and there is a long task before us till it has become a fact. Few of us here will live to witness the realisation, but we shall see the outworks passed, and Flora's grandchildren perhaps may see the winning of the fort. I have always been suspicious of political fervour. To me there is something ill-bred and irrational about a heart worn on the sleeve of the shabby garments we use in public life. But I hold the man in contempt who is afraid to stake all on his ideal, and on this one ultimate ideal I have never wavered. I am on the verge of old age, and I can claim the privilege of a life of candour and fair criticism and permit myself once in a while to become an enthusiast. So in all hope and in all humility I would paraphrase the words of another converted cynic and adopt them as my confession of faith: 'I shall see it, but not now: I shall behold it, but not nigh.'"

CHAPTER 14

THE party wandered out to the verandah where a young moon was beginning to climb the vast arch of sky. So thin was its horn that it did not diminish the brilliance of the stars. The great trough beneath the house was lit by a stellar glow, which caught a few out-jutting headlands in the sea of shadows, and outlined without revealing the abysses around them. The air was very quiet, cool without a hint of frost or wind; and only the tinkle of falling water broke in upon the stillness. The light from the drawing-room filled half the verandah, but the edge near the parapet was dark, and to one standing there the great house, looming up against the sky, was like a pharos in the wastes of night.

The Duchess with Lord Launceston and Mr Carey walked slowly towards the edge of the escarpment, their eyes caught by the magic of the scene.

"This old earth," said Carey at last, lifting his head from his breast,—"that is what we have business with. How to shape her into something more worthy of our best, and how in the process to learn from her her mysterious wisdom! That is our problem. We have been too long away from her in barren cloudlands. Our new precept is that the kingdom of God is around us and within us."

Lord Launceston laughed as they stopped to lean over the balustrade. "You have been anticipated," he said, and he repeated:—

"This way have men come out of brutishness
To spell the letters of the sky and read
A reflex upon earth else meaningless.
With thee, o fount of the Untimed! to lead;
Drink they of thee, thee eyeing, they unaged
Shall on through brave wars waged.
More gardens will they win than any lost;
The vile plucked out of them, the unlovely slain.
Not forfeiting the beast with which they are crossed,
To stature of the gods will they attain.
They shall uplift their Earth to meet her Lord,
Themselves the attuning chord!"[10]

"To-morrow," said the Duchess, "we all go home. I should not like Musuru to last for ever, but it rather spoils one's satisfaction in any other place. To-morrow we shall be crawling through the bush in the Mombasa train, and beginning to realise what a length of sea and land separates this house from those in which we live our ordinary lives. That is an allegory as well as a fact. We have behaved rather nicely, I think, Francis. Every one has been good-humoured and well-mannered, and we have kept more or less in the paths of sanity in spite of Barbara and you. I know I have tried to do my duty and coax people out of blank verse, and I have learned a great deal in the process, and am half inclined to the blank verse myself. Now, I suppose I must go on explaining to dull people that the Empire is something more than corrugated iron and an unpleasant accent, and that that something more is not bloodshed to the strains of a brass band. It will be very difficult for all of us to get back to the right political groove. When we go home the dear idiots who govern us, including George, will probably be at each others' throats about whether the school children are to be taught the Church Catechism or the Sermon on the Mount. Of course we shall have to take sides, for it is the rule of the game: and yet how often I want to cry 'A plague on both your Houses!' Is it possible that I am sickening for the disease of 'grandeur'?"

"No," said Carey, "it only means that you are dropping some of your blue spectacles. You will find them and wear them again, but it does the eyes good to lose them for a little."

"At any rate we are going back to some kind of work, and that is cheering. What happens to you, Francis? Remember you are coming to us for Christmas."

"I am always busy, and next week I have to go to the States. Then I join Wakefield in Canada, but I shall be home for Christmas. There is only one thing that depresses me in life,—the amount to be done and the little time left to do it in. After all, the great deeds are not for the middle-aged. Our business is to inspire the young, with whom the hope of the world rests."

"And yet we middle-aged have been galvanised into a surprising activity. Lord Launceston is coming back to politics, and I believe that Bob has some wild scheme of colonial travel. Most discussions only leave one with a sense of the futility of all things, but ours has made us optimists. I suppose that is due to the nature of our subject. If you talk much about something prosaic and practical, you remove it many degrees from reality. But if it is something which still lives only in the air, you may make it shape itself into body and form. What may have been only a mirage, becomes an authentic country, far away, to be sure, but quite as real as the ground we walk on. Let us go and find the young people in whom Francis says our hope lies. Hugh is probably composing sonnets to Flora's eyebrows, and Mr Astbury sitting at Marjory's feet, while Alastair and Sir Edward console each other for going back by abusing civilisation. How in the world am I to shepherd them all home?"

...

At the other end of the terrace those whilom antagonists, Lord Appin and Mr Wakefield, were walking arm in arm, their cigars glowing in the darkness.

"I shall take your advice," the elder man was saying. "After all, what business have I to theorise about Empire when I have only studied a little corner of it? I know English opinion; I now want to know the way the different classes in the colonies feel about the whole thing. You cannot get that from newspapers, not even from the men who come to see you in England. You must go and live in the place if you want to realise the true atmosphere of their thought. I fancied that you and I should differ violently, Wakefield, but I find we are nearer than we dreamed of. You emphasise parts of the question with which I am unfamiliar, and perhaps I should focus the details differently. But on the essentials I believe we are at one. If you may be taken to represent colonial opinion, I confess myself surprised at its idealism and statesmanship."

"Excellent!" said Mr Wakefield. "And now I shall return the compliment. I came here prejudiced against what I called academic Imperialism and very particularly prejudiced against you. With some of the things said here I have disagreed. Some I thought wrong, some too fantastic for practical politics. Parts of the discussion I am not sure that I understood, parts did not interest me, and if I had had my will I should have arranged the whole conference on a more businesslike system. But yet I have learned so much that I go away a wiser, as well as a much humbler, man. On the whole, I have been astounded—yes, astounded—by our common-sense."

NOTES

[←1]

De Rerum Natura, ii. 1-6. "Pleasant it is, when the winds are tossing the waters of the mighty sea, to behold from the land another's mighty toil—not that there is sweet delight in another's affliction, but that it is pleasant to see griefs from which thou thyself art free. Pleasant also is it to witness the great conflicts of war joined through the plains, thyself with no share in the peril."

[←2]

Juvenal, viii. S3: "Count it the last disgrace to prefer life to honour, and for living's sake to destroy all that makes life worthy."

[←3]

AEneid, xii. 1S9-191. "I will not bid Italian serve Teucrian nor for myself seek I kingdoms. Let the two races, unconquered, and with equal rights, join in eternal friendship."

[←4]

Virgil: *Georgics*, i. 250, 251. And while on us the fresh East breathes from far, For them the red West lights her evening star!

[←5]

§ 159. 'Are her dominions in the world so narrow,' he asks, 'that she can find no place to spin cotton in but Yorkshire? We may organise emigration into an infinite power. We may assemble troops of the more adventurous and ambitious of our youths, we may send them on truest foreign service, founding new seats of authority and centres of thought in uncultivated and unconquered lands; retaining the full affection to our native country no less in our colonists than in our armies, teaching them to maintain allegiance to their fatherland in labour no less than in battle; aiding them with free land in the prosecution of discovery, and the victory over adverse natural powers; establishing seats of every manufacture in the climates and places best fitted for it, and bringing ourselves into due alliance and harmony of skill with the dexterities of every race and the wisdom of every tradition and every tongue.'

[←6]

Bacchae, 1007-1010 (Mr Gilbert Murray's translation).

[←7]

Vergil, *Georgics* 2.490. And Pan, and old Silvanus, and the sister Nymphs

[←8]

Anth. Pal. ix. 546.

[←9]

AEneid, xii. S26, S27; S34–840. "Let Latium stand, to all ages let there be Alban kings! let the Roman stock be potent in Italian valour.... Her ancient speech and ways shall Ausonia keep, and as her name is, it shall be; mingled into her blood shall the Trojan sink. Law and holy rites will I add, and I will make Latins of all with a single tongue. Thence thou wilt see a race arise tempered of Ausonian blood, transcending men, yea, and gods in duty, and no other folk will so nobly pay thee thy meed of worship." I take these words as the best and simplest statement of our faith. That idea has been the master-passion of my life, and I ask no higher task than to contribute my mite of effort to so divine an end."

[←10]

George Meredith, 'Hymn to Colour,' 13, 14.

Printed in Dunstable, United Kingdom

68963229R00102